PORTRAIT OF DEBBIE

A Deborah Rosenfeld Narrative

Richard Thrift

p 184
258

ISBN: 9798701973112

Cover image: Oil painting by Randi Hvatum
Library of Congress Control Number: 2018675309
Printed in the United States of America

To Leslie Armsby

The past is never dead. It's not even past.

WILLIAM FAULKNER

……..Deborah Rosenfeld strides across a plaza, a camera slung over her shoulder, as if she were traversing some quiet field alone in spite of the crowd of people thronging about her. Long shapely legs carry a lean body, slim-wasted and naturally full at hip, clad only in light khaki trousers, softly clinging, and a white scoop neck t-shirt (and wearing a pair of scuffed up brogans). A shock of light auburn hair falls backwards in thick waves over the forward thrust of her shoulders like she is leaning into a wind. The simple, unconscious tilt of a perfectly rounded chin giving her an aura of purposefulness - no, of wanderlust yet. Is the image, however fatuous, I carry of myself like a very personal snapshot. Since there are no photographs of me, published or otherwise, none that I have been made aware of at least (okay, passport, but who can recognize themselves even in a passport snapshot). I am the photographer. I shoot others, preferring to keep those of myself loosely imagined, to be viewed with tongue in cheek humor. It is not that I am in hiding. I simply avoid being conspicuous, innately so. And for years already, I have been successful at it. In spite of the fact that my name is well known to any number of professionals in my field, and to some extent the public. My name that in my heart I share with another, my alter ego as it were, that I, to a certain measure of acclaim, have made my own (that wasn't completely my own name until I was bestowed it, by a streak of good fortune, by way of a great sorrow, one summer day years ago now).

I was running late from my afternoon jaunt to Haifa to pick up needed photographic equipment and the fast-falling Mediterranean dusk caught up with me just past Afula, plummeting as it does like a heavy black curtain - as I slowly descended, "Sir Rubble II's" headlight beams tunneling through it, into the Jezreel Valley beneath a dome of emerging stars. I was going to be too late for dinner on Neve Rom, the kibbutz that housed the archaeological team excavating the nearby Tel Ronish site that for the past couple of years I had been associated with on the dig, thanks to my old friend Stefan, as the Israel Antiquities Authority's designated (though but a stringer, I might add) photographer on the site. But before I'd left Haifa I'd had a late, hefty lunch at one of my favorite Arab eateries.

(Incidentally, "Sir Rubble II", that I would shorten to Rubble in conversation, was the name I'd dubbed this much used - and abused - "vintage" Land Rover that several summers before when on another excavation I had more or less rescued out of a junk yard for both my personal mode of transportation - for the occasional Shabbat getaway - and for, when needed, the dig's all- purpose donkey: the original "Sir Rubble" being the 16-year-old Debbie's white painted VW bug that Deborah posing as me had died in. Daily, or whenever on the road in it, I expect it, as a given, to leave me in the lurch, much as did the crate Jack Nicholson's character drove in Antononi's "The Passenger" in his attempt to cross that North African desert - I have more often than not visualized myself giving Rubble here that finial existential kick, like Nicholson's character did his before walking off. But somehow Rubble has managed to lumber along, if often it has sounded like about to belly up somewhere between gears, with about as much pickup to boot - that evening being no exception - yet it has always, by sheer magic the only explanation, kept trucking on, though definitely against my dire expectations.)

And speaking of dire expectations, whatever curve ball could come flying out of Deborah's past continued to haunt me at odd moments - some long-ago relation having come across my name on the net; some Rosenfeld family genealogist, even, asking for a DNA sample. But it never had really occurred to me that I might ever come face-to face with a member of my long ago erstwhile family, that is "Debbie's family", even if they couldn't possibly have an inkling that it could be me alive still. And of all places here in Israel (and on an archeological dig in the Galilee

3

at that). And with the one person in that once-upon-a-time family whom I'd forever held close in my heart - if as but an ancient memory - one whom I had not seen nor heard from (though early on during my former life I'd hear tidbits about him) since I was eight years old.

1

It was as if a meteor had crashed into my life, burrowing into the depths of me while raising a dust that threatened to cloud the furthest reaches of my horizon. If I allowed it.

Stefan had introduced him to us in the meeting room Neve Rom had made available to the dig's team, as Reuben, this old friend from the distant past only recently gotten back in touch with, a novelist from the States who'd just flown in from London that morning. Before Stefan had gotten down to the business at hand - to read the "riot act", as Siri, one of the Scandinavian volunteers had laughingly put it in passing, upon my emerging from stashing the new equipment in my room. (Since Stefan, he of a Biblical length beard, was the least likely person to read a riot act, not that Stefan couldn't come down ferociously upon any behavior that threatened the progress, or the overall safety, of both us and the summer program.)

While Stefan delineated some minor and one major "infraction" (essentially the team had grown lax in thoroughly washing each day's artifact finds that was done afternoons en groupe, before quitting time; plus buckets at the site were not being stacked nor tools properly stored; and we were to be paid a visit the next morning by several archaeologists from the IAA), my concentration remained riveted upon this Reuben seated next to him. To the point where the rest of the room had sort of blurred out under the harsh glare of a ceiling fluorescent fixture; much like the sounds in my ears were akin to that when pressing a conch shell to them. (What had he written? I read novels, but had never heard of him, if he and the one I was thinking of were one and the same. It couldn't be, could it?)

From the moment I'd caught sight of him, upon my belated entrance, I felt there was something familiar about him if I could just put my finger on it, that was simultaneously disturbing and intriguing. Though I didn't recognize him at first sight, I knew I had seen him before - just "knew it"; his was no ordinary presence. I gathered, by the way he sat there somewhat on display, that he would be a tad shorter than me - but then I stand 5 feet ten inches in my bare feet. And was in his mid to late 30s, by the looks of him, though if it were he he'd have to be in his early 40s already. His hair, a russet brown, was not so much long as thick, almost curly, falling in bunched waves over his ears and down the back of his neck. And the lower half of his face was covered with a rusty colored beard he kept fairly well trimmed. Physically, he looked like he took care of himself, and for one with a studious, well contemplative, demeanor he did have something of an outdoors complexion, slightly ruddy. He'd glanced up at me when I'd entered (what with some of the humorous greetings I'd gotten, some calling me "Deborah", or "Debs", others "Devorah", its Hebrew pronunciation, mostly from the young Israelis that - like as if they to a one hadn't expected me to have made it back, given that I was driving Rubble). For just an instant our eyes had locked, his a soft, curiously gazing blue. I told myself not to read too much into it, it wasn't an unnatural reaction when two strangers see each other for the first time. But had he, if perhaps unconsciously, recognized something familiar about me too?

This curious phenomenon I was wrestling with, when Stefan said his name was "Reuben". At that moment is when the floor felt about to fall from beneath me. And what had possibly been on the tip of my tongue all along burst through my walls of denial - so improbable it seemed upfront. They both had the same given name (I was tempted to say, "So what, it is a million to one chance, merely a coincidence, he could be anybody, this neatly if not quite fastidiously dressed - in a white cotton shirt, khaki colored jeans wearing leather moccasins - guy sitting directly opposite from me."), he and that cousin of mine, also a Reuben, who had been the recipient of utter adoration from my eight year old self - my six and seven year old self as well, the self of my former life as a child. Shortly after which the connection had been abruptly severed by circumstances I understand now that had been beyond our control, my being "sold into Egypt", as I prefer to humorously think of it, by my sister, Joy, following the premature deaths of our father and mother that precipitated the draconian cut.

This was the stuff of fantastical daydreams - when not bordering on the bitter irony belying the "tragic" in those O. Henry stories I had to read in high school. And I remained far from certain that this could actually be him. I mean, how could it be, and here of all places, and in this drab, perfunctory room for all purposes? The person I remembered, I came but up to his elbow; and when he'd talk to me, he'd squat on his haunches and look up into my face (but then I suppose I was already tall for my age.) He had been clean shaven, his hair a conventional cut, parted and plastered down, a teenager still. (what had he been at that time - sixteen - the summer we first met). He did write poetry, I remember, it was Joy who'd mentioned it later on (Joy who I'd sense had been jealous of the attention he paid me, if perhaps at my demand), and later on too our mutual cousin, Kerry, told me that he lived in Israel, on a kibbutz, had studied at Tel Aviv University, but at the last time I'd asked, he was either traveling in Europe or maybe living and working in England her mother had had from his mother, my mother's much older sister. Me, I remember my wishing I might have been old enough to have joined him somehow, given the measured restrictions my guardians had laid upon me. (I had been ever so lucky to have had that all too brief an interlude with Deborah.) For the sake of argument, I tell myself, let's say it is him. (The prospect truly frightened me, to the core of my being, like as if I were to be thrown out of a plane without a parachute - it is scary enough to make that jump with a parachute, the things I have done for a photograph, and would do again, I know.) Even if he likewise had had a moment of "recognition", of some kind, some intuitive itch as I had had (that no amount of scratching will relieve), if it were him, when our eyes had so momentarily met, my face was hardly a facsimile of the six year girl he'd known, perhaps had humored, whom he had taught to play chess and who had checkmated him three games in a row, who had demanded he tote her about piggyback, who would write him once back home in her childish scrawl about her "academic accomplishments" (in the 1st grade, or was it 2nd already), her telling him that she loved him, that she was going to marry him, and that he better wait for her until she grew up. But what if he'd seen a copy of that supposedly "graduation" photo-graph, perhaps shared by my guardians with members of my birth family in the wake of my death as Debbie? There would be a cursory re-semblance to my 16 year old self, if that much. A resemblance with one long dead the result of an automobile accident out of which I like the phoenix had risen from the ashes no less.

Then, just as the meeting was about to break up, he announced that he'd be staying on for a few days and would like to pitch in wherever it was thought he could help out on the dig, having never worked before on an archaeological exca-vation. (He spoke well, articulately, with a rush of enthusiasm; I noticed he had an accent, kind of British but not quite.) And this gave me my cue. Better sense told me to hang back and sim-ply observe him from a safe distance, don't put myself in harm's way so to speak. So far no one had stepped forward to take him up on his offer, that I was certain had Stefan's blessing, perhaps they figured that Stefan would simply assign him, like to haul buckets full of "dirt" for sifting, grunt work for the bottom rung of the pecking order, so that he couldn't do any harm - perhaps they were simply too shy, he being an older man, one seemingly reticent by nature that could be mistaken for his being "standoffish".

There are times when I simply follow an in-stinct, however much against "reason" it might be. With my hair tossed back I simply strode over to where he stood, conspicuously alone like, amid the buzz of conversations around him. Telling myself once in motion that it might not be him after all, that it all might just be a co-incidence. There was no way I could ever reveal to him who I had once been, if it turned out to be really him - he who would no longer be the him of memory any more than I as my present self would be to him. He was simply going to be this old friend of Stefan's, much as I too was an old friend of Stefan's. And he really was shorter than me, by an inch or more, not that that mattered.

"I'm Deborah Rosenfeld," I said, offering my hand. "I'm the site photographer. Welcome to Tel Ronish."

"Reuben Headey. Thank you."

I hoped my palm didn't break out into an ice cold sweat as he took it into his. It was he! The same last name was. That flicker of curiosity I'd detected in his eyes now exhibited itself in his smile, a none-the-less sort of bashful smile, not the customary boastful smile I had had from most men. It was no less a self-confident smile, unconsciously so, without guile.

His had been a strong, warm hand that had briefly held mine in it, almost calloused. Apparently he wasn't immune to physical labor.

"I could certainly use your help," I continued, without a second to waste, lest I lose my courage, turn into a vegetable, the proverbial pumpkin, or something. "If you can put up with my often contradictory directions - contradictory to you if not to me. I need someone to set up things for me before I shoot, while I shoot - light reflectors, light shields, the odd ladder or two. Not that I won't help. It'll just give me more time for shooting, it is always a race against light, which never stands still, not for me any way. But you'll get the hang of it, if I haven't driven you over the edge beforehand. You game?"

"I'm game, Deborah," he laughed. "Or do you prefer Devorah?"

"Deborah's fine."

"So when do we start?" He asked. "In the morning bright and early?"

My cocky Deborah grin must have done it, broken the ice or whatever. He appeared suddenly relaxed, possibly relieved. Like one could almost feel a certain tenseness fall from his shoulders. It had certainly saved the day for me. Sometimes I couldn't believe myself, like my chutzpah knew no bounds. Though I had to remember to be careful, not to trip over my feet. Hubris was a dangerous indulgence.

"At the break of day, we all do," I told him, as we were unable to work much beyond the noon hour- maybe stretch it to oneish - due to the rising heat that often reaches above 100 degrees Fahrenheit, we had to raise the tarpaulins over the work areas that shield us from the sun, if not the air, before we could start to work, and he could ride out with me, if he dared to risk life and limb in Rubble (my vintage Land Rover, I explained, having caught the odd expression that had crossed his face). Tel Ronish was not on the kibbutz, but close enough - sometimes breakfast, even lunch, was brought out to us, if so arranged, but usually we returned to the kibbutz for meals, eating with the chaverim in the Chadar Ochel, the kibbutz dining hall. (I assumed he'd already experienced the culinary fare on Neve Rom - not the worst I will admit - his having eaten dinner with Stefan.) I quickly told him the time and place to meet me, suggested various articles of clothing he'd be advised to wear (perhaps Stefan could find him some suitable shoes), and not to forget some head cover as that sun by mid-morning was not something to mess with, because we weren't always under those tarpaulin covers - a large handkerchief if nothing else. With that I wished him a good night, that I was off to check out the new equipment I'd picked up in Haifa, it had been a long day for me and I planned to turn in early.

"Then I will see you in the morning," he offered. "I'm looking forward to it."

"Had I lost my mind, what the fuck was I doing?" I kept repeating it to myself, almost out loud, as I made my way along the lighted path to my room. If this was really, truly him - and it certainly seemed to be, of all people. Wouldn't it have been truly wiser, to have kept a distance and observed him from afar, feel him out from the safety of detachment? But I knew we would have inevitably gravitated towards each other in any case, being in such proximity as we were, knew it in my gut, since that first momentary glance. What for? Where was it going to lead to? All I knew at that moment was that from now on I was going to have to play it by ear. Because hand in hand with an abiding sense of curiosity, a certain thrill to be honest, was this existential "terror".

2

Dawn in full had broken for some minutes already over the mountains of Gilead, that range of hills east of the Jordan, with a fiery red streak low still on the horizon, while the sky overhead was growing lighter by the minute, as I pulled up Rubble at the foot of the truncated mound that was Tel Ronish.

"We are here," I said to the still a bit groggy Reuben beside me. Though he had been summarily alert on the drive out, staring at the landscape, he had said little. Both of us had kept our thoughts to ourselves. But he did say that he'd had a hot cup of scalding coffee at the Chader Ochal, having been dragged to it in a stupor by the guy he was sharing a room with, Avi, one of the Israeli student archaeologists, just out of the army - which had been how he'd managed to meet up with me on time, if by a hair's breadth, he'd laughed, somewhat apologetically. Someone too, had supplied him with an old army desert hat and a pair of kibbutz brogans, like my own. His feet will stink of sweat but better than then the debilitating pain of stepping on rocks wearing soft soles - or climbing ladders for that matter. That hat gave him a rakish look, humorously so.

"Wait," I said as he fumbled with the passenger side door to open it. "We have a little time before the others arrive. I have fresh bread, a couple of avocados, and a thermos of tea. It could be a good three hours before any breakfast and there is much work to do before then. I don't know about you, but this morning I will need all the energy I can get. I can share with you. We can break bread together, so to speak, if you like."

He looked at me and smiled, more with his eyes than anything else. "Thank you," he said.

I reached into the back seat, pulled my rucksack over to me and took out the bread, avocados, a knife, the thermos, cups and a couple of fresh scraps of cloth for something to wipe hands with.

"I know, it's like pandora's box, the endless amount of stuff I can stuff into a simple rucksack," I said somewhat apologetically.

"Actually, I was thinking of those Russian boxes, you know, endless boxes within boxes, that get smaller and smaller."

"It's something like that as well, I admit," I laughed. "I hope you don't mind this green tea. It does give equal energy without having to get it on a sugar high that ends abruptly, like leaving you high and dry in the middle of nowhere."

"No problem. Anything after that coffee.

Have you ever been left high and dry in the middle of nowhere?"

I could tell he was lightly teasing me, if facetiously. As a gradual sense of familiarity was developing between us.

"Yes," I said, without elaborating. "Goes with the territory. But so far 'Rubble' here, against all bets, hasn't let me down."

"Why 'Rubble'?", he asked.

"Short for 'Sir Rubble'."

"'Sir Rubble?'"

I could almost see his eyes suddenly narrow from the change of tone in his voice. Could he have somehow known that that had been Debbie's name for her VW bug?

"It just came to me. Probably from a long ago cartoon. This old crate was like held together with duct tape when I bought it."

"I'm sorry, I didn't mean to question, it was just the same name a cousin of mine back in the States once called her car, took me by surprise. By the way, this is really good bread."

"It comes from Beit She'an every morning very, very early, freshly baked. I'm glad you like it."

So he wasn't unaware of Debbie, of her life after she was "sold into Egypt". It filled me with as much apprehension as it plucked my heart strings. I knew it was sort of entering forbidden territory, this tantalizing desire to learn what I best keep in the bottle. That Avocado on the bread did hit the spot, and Reuben managed to down my green tea without grimacing.

We were just "licking our fingers" when in the rear view mirror I saw the dust being kicked up by several vehicles distant yet but coming closer. We were slightly behind schedule that morning. I wondered where was Stefan.

"Now we use our legs," I announced, laughingly, as I began to stuff things back into that bulging rucksack to take with us. "We've got to schlep this and the new equipment I got, plus my camera bag, up to the top."

"From up here, it looks like we are Lilliputian size atop the remnant of a large tree trunk sawed off close to the roots," Reuben observed, looking around him.

"Most newcomers at first sight compare it to being atop a coffee table, I laughed. "Yours is the more original by far."

An excavation site is laid out on a grid system - I went on to explain - made up of units of about three meter squares (or about ten foot squares); and when a new square is opened up, a grid line is again employed. With about a meter wide, 90-degree "earthen wall" called a baulk separating each square, each square being accessible via a ladder or a sandbag ramp of sorts the deeper it went. (Several, if not singularly so, designated by a letter of the alphabet, with the squares in each numerically numbered - all of which is recorded on a master chart - and whatever is found where is duly recorded.) Here at Tel Ronish, it was no different.

With my new equipment hauled up and ready to use, my cameras secured, most if not all of the others had arrived and we were about ready to lift the tarpaulins that pretty much covered our excavation area, a morning exercise that involved all of us, in unison. It took a bit of groaning on the poles, and grumbling, however good-naturedly, to get everything in place, standing and tied down. Perhaps we should have started earlier. The day was lighting up fast now, the sun a blazing yellow ball just clear of the eastern horizon, the air thickening already.

"Okay," I broke off. "It looks like everybody's here and ready to raise the covering."

Reuben, I noted, readily joined in, with a good sense of what was being done. For moments on end, our shouldering it, getting the tarpaulins with their poles upright, I'd put it out of my mind who Reuben was once to me (and perhaps still was if I allowed myself to go there). There was that part of me (or my brain) that saw it all as surreal - as if then and now had been superimposed on each other - though so very real it was, he and I here this morning - on an equal footing, though I had the advantage of being familiar with the territory - on a hilltop in The Galilee, in the trough of the Beit She'an Valley, he with the grownup me, he without a clue I was once that six-year-old to his what, six-teen-year-old, that summer on the Chesapeake Bay, a far cry from the meandering stream of a Jordan River barely a stone's throw from where we stood. But for the rising heat thickening with humidity.

"Time's a-wasting," I lightheartedly beckoned him, as I tied a piece of white muslin cloth I wrapped around my head against the sun, the dust getting into my hair, and my hair falling in the way of the camera lens as it would do. Otherwise I wore a t-shirt, my loose cotton trousers, with numerous side pockets, preferred to the shorts almost all the others inhabited at varying lengths - women and men both (my knees and legs uncovered having suffered one too many nicks and scrapes, gashes even). And my leather brogans, though sandals were favored by most. Reuben had on a pair of faded jeans and rolled up to his elbows a long-sleeve khaki shirt he'd left hanging out.

"And you might want to rub on some sun lotion, for good measure," I added. "On your face and arms. Best to do before you begin to sweat. In the lower pocket of my rucksack over there."

In no time, the site had become a virtual bee-hive - from a distance more like a swarm I could imagine, because everyone - from the archaeologist supervisors in charge of their squares, with clipboards in hand, to the nineteen-odd volunteers, tools in hand - had leapt to their tasks and were ardently engaged, wielding picks, lifting rocks, hoeing or shoveling debris into buckets to be hauled up and sifted, or were squatting in the dirt, trowels busily in their hands, or carefully scraping and brushing what was unearthed, multicolored heads bent down while fingers picked through the just-loosened debris, filling buckets of recognizable artifacts from large grains and bits of metal to sherds of broken pottery. The air itself filled with laughter and shouts, and here and there moments of bickering. (Stefan I heard would be coming out later with the IAA entourage.)

I had been walking around photographing everybody at work, catching them off guard - be it up close or in an overview, before the quickly fleeting "mellow" light turned abruptly hardedged - when Reuben caught up with me. Besides the artifacts, the human factor too was an integral part of the report.

"First thing I need to shoot today is the recently exposed stratigraphy in squares 'Gimel' and 'Hei'" I said. "We'll need to use those new light reflector panels we brought out with us. And a ladder."

I was happily surprised by his deftness with the reflectors, his grasp of my lighting needs even before I was. "I've taken a few photographs myself," he laughed. He correctly positioned too the step ladder I had to climb in order to shoot the layers straight on. The tall step ladder, always wobbly at best due to uneven ground to sit it on, he held firmly in place for me to get overhead shots - my two Leicas, a digital as well as my well beloved M3, dangling from my neck. (Though I'd have to tell him to get the horizontal and vertical metric scale sticks, where to place them; the signboards too, designating the particular area I was shooting in.) Where needed (and where possible), he'd lift up the ends of the overhead tarp, using an aluminum pole at hand, to give the area to be photographed more natural light. I had fashioned a trench-straddling "tripod" with a shutter release cord for directly overhead shooting; but Reuben it turned out was better at it than I am (I dare to admit) when it came to correctly positioning the camera on the first, but no more than the second, try. "When you worry too much over it, you get frustrated, thus repeating your mistake," he offered; he was right, ugh. I in turn would remind him that he had to drink water every half an hour or so, a near cardinal rule during the summer months here in this 600-odd feet below sea-level terrain, otherwise he risked finding himself all of a sudden seriously dehydrated, flaking out even.

We spoke at random while working, between my requests and his offering a suggestion or two. The accommodations here on Neve Rom for the dig's volunteers were reminiscent of that which had housed the seasonal volunteers on his former kibbutz, he'd casually remarked, a cluster of huts once servicing a long-grassed-over British airdrome of the latter Yishuv Days.

"We've had worse," I said, laughing. "On some digs there have been tents at the site, makeshift accommodations at their wildest. With the brush our privy. Though to be honest I didn't really mind them. Because in the elements there was no pretense of modern amenities, often in disrepair And we were at the site, which for my purposes was quite convenient. But I must admit there could be some royal pains for tent mates. Well, I was never the Girl Scout type, no big deal. Learned to lump it, I'd have to say. This year here, Stefan and I rated single rooms for a change, with attached baths. We are in the clover." But I wanted to redirect the conversation back to him, about him.

"Stefan introduced you last night as a long ago friend recently gotten back in touch with?" I asked him - a purposely vague if leading question, hoping he'd elaborate, without me having to be more specific.

"A long story," he smiled, mostly to himself. "I found him online, weirdly enough, one of those off-chance things. I had no idea he'd become an archaeologist, working here in Israel of all places. I remembered him as a poet, giving dramatic readings in local coffee houses. We last saw each other in Paris, I was on the way back to the States after two years on a kibbutz - this was some months after the 6 Day War - and he had been en route to Germany to check out the home village of his war years childhood. It was I who gave him the names of people on my former kibbutz should he wish to venture further east (I suppose I kind of insisted that he do so). He would write that Germany had been a not un-expected disappointment, and that he had fol-lowed my suggestion and had ended up hired as an English teacher at the regional kibbutz high school. And I had found myself disappointed over his feeing so much at home here among the young Israelis. When I hadn't, who were to me at the time but a disconcerting version of the roughnecks and bumpkins I'd grown up among, theirs being a far cry from the Jewish human-ism values of the Diaspora, from the Yiddish literature writers I'd devoured to Martin Buber and the proponents of 'Cultural Zionism', all of whom who had greatly informed me. We found ourselves in strong disagreement. I'm afraid I was rather harsh in my criticism. Made all the more so by my dread that Stefan had found an identity with the 'goy' I saw inherent in the Is-raelis in general that truly frightened me. That I likewise feared in myself. Because deep down in myself I knew I could too feel such an identity that I chafed against, that I morally and philo-sophically abhorred. Eventually he and I lost touch, I had been moving around a lot in those days, seeking answers rather than how to ask the right questions, climbing out of a lot of 'lows' after the 'highs', not realizing that there were no grand answers to be had, that the seeking itself was in and of itself the answer, like making oneself aware, if nothing else. We burnt the midnight oil last night catching up. Apparently he spent a summer on a dig in Jerusalem, and caught the bug. He is still a poet nonetheless. I was happy to hear."

"The only background I knew was that of a West Coast boarding school milieu from early childhood to age 18, having been orphaned at age 4 or 5," I hastened to add, should he ask, "when on an impulse I first came here, age 19, for a kibbutz work-study summer. That is, an ulpan. So I was laid wide open to all that was so new, without expectation. I was like a blank page in so many respects. I suppose I did encounter more than a few of your 'bumpkins', but most of even them were not so horrible once I got to know them. I was probably saved by an innate reticence, in that I could always step back in the nick of time to think before acting on any temptation to jump into the fire."

"I persevered on sheer stubbornness alone", he said. "I may have tottered a lot, but I always managed to hold fast. My single virtue, redeeming or otherwise."

"You mean, you were determined at all costs to have your cake while eating it?" I couldn't help but laugh, though I felt his pain. "Am I being unfair in saying this?"

"In retrospect, I wished I hadn't put all my eggs into one basket, that I hadn't put the cart before the horse. Desperate to demand that my preconceived notions match the reality on the ground, that left me awash in disappointments that I simultaneously refused to accept while battering myself for having them. I could have used some of your 'reticence' as you called it, rather than setting myself up for a lot of knee-jerk reaction knock downs. I would have come away with the same conclusions perhaps. But I would have opened myself up to a lot more besides. That which I'd only discover much later."

It was a sober answer, more so than I had expected.

"So what was it initially that brought you to kibbutz? To Israel? Not being Jewish to begin with." I hoped I hadn't had sounded flippant in asking, that cliche of a question so often asked here of the newly arrived, be they Jew or non-Jew, as if one is expected to answer standing on one leg - like I'd read Hillel had been ordered to explain Judaism to that Roman centurion. Not everyone could be Hillel.

"That is the subject of my last novel, *(K)hamsin*, as depicted by the quests of the several main characters that people its 1000 plus pages," he was boyishly grinning now. Much to my unanticipated relief. "Okay, its signature character in particular. In other words, yes, seeking 'utopia'. Well, a path at least. It was the times too. Where turbulence was the unacknowledged norm. My generation's thing. Of which I proudly, perhaps pleading mitigating circumstances, stand guilty as charged."

"And is this your first time back since then? Probably not, I would suspect."

"I returned for several months about five years later. During the time I lived in London. I was in Jerusalem most of the time, staying with a London friend and his wife who had recently gone on Aliyah. While traveling about the country visiting far-flung by then former kibbutz friends. It was just before I would return to the States."

"What about this trip, will you be staying on in Israel again for a while?"

"About 10 days, as of now. I have a meeting with a potential publisher early next week in Tel Aviv, not that I expect much to come of it. Anyway, I have prior commitments, and my companion awaits my return. It is usually her whose return I await, from her annual visits back home to Norway."

"Back to the States then for you, or is it London now, with your companion?" I asked matter-of-factly.

"To the States. Rebekah is established there, she's a portrait painter. I was in London to talk with publishers. Though I did live in London years ago, like I just mentioned. Worked on a magazine there, a Jewish arts magazine in which I was both a co-founder and co-editor. I miss London in a way, but it is not the same now - well, nowhere is, obviously. Where do you return to these days, unless you stay on here?"

"I have a summer escape place, along the coast of Scandinavia, I tell nobody about. On this island. For a couple of weeks or so, where I enjoy my little boat, rowing and sailing and shooting photographs solely for myself. Once things wrap up here for the season. Before my next assignment, if I've got one. And there is always one usually sooner than later to head out to."

I feared I'd tossed this out all too quickly to mask the sharp unsettling jab I felt upon hearing he had a one and only in his life, that I didn't really have him all to myself here, that "just us" thing, a one sided pretense that I obviously had begun to delude myself into thinking - when it would only be natural he would have had someone, a possibility I'd somehow kept at bay. What had I been starting to do? Get a grip, Deborah! Spying on one's past was fraught enough with the danger of stepping on emotional landmines. But finding yourself on a slippery slope sliding down into it. The past may not be passed, buried deep down inside us as it is, as well as in our particular time and place wherever, but we can't pick it up from where it left off for us personally and refit it to fill out some long-ago fantasy.

That which must have been weighing heavily on Gatsby's desolate heart that afternoon when George Wilson stepped out from the trees and shot him.

"I've been wanting to ask you about what first brought you to Israel," he said. "Other than being Jewish, probably. Which you have sort of answered. What got you into photography too."

"Later, Reuben, okay. I see Stefan has arrived with what looks like our 'guests' already."

Following right upon on the heels of Stefan with the IAA archaeologists came breakfast from Neve Rom, which had been prearranged for the occasion - much to the surprise of all of us. "Breakfast on wheels in the field," I said cheerily to Reuben. "You are in for a treat. And on your first day." As our visitors - two men and a woman (Avi Grantz, the senior of the two a stoutly seasoned veteran who had once co-directed with Stefan a dig down south, Naor Dan, a youthful personification of a steel-string instrument possessing an indifferent charm, and Nitza Harel, too a longtime friend of Stefan's, fiercely independent in her thought, often outspokenly controversial, whose stance I've often admired), being escorted by a didactic Stefan in his habitual weatherworn desert rat attire (the khaki cutoffs, a matching shirt with sleeves rolled to elbows, and a sweat- stained floppy brim hat) - poked about here and there among the area squares, braving the ladders to closer inspect what before now had been only read in the recent weekly reports. Or seen in my photographs. (Before coming out, I would hear, they had carefully perused our collection of latest finds not yet sent to Jerusalem - artifacts such as sherds of pottery, metal, stone; and eco-facts, that is seeds, pieces of animal bone, evidence of flora.) Meanwhile the crew from the kibbutz - the ever-congenial Benny, one of the older chaverim I'd gotten to know, along with two spunky high school girls working for the summer in the Chadar Ochel - laid out a sumptuous spread: boiled eggs, vegetables (whole or diced into a ready mix), fresh fruit and dates, olives, that freshly baked bread again, soft cheeses, pickled herring, whole carrots, Labaneh - always in those small sealed cups one often has to resort to using their teeth to open - with coffee, fruit juices and tea, and that chocolate spread no kibbutz breakfast can be complete without. Bottles of olive oil too and pitchers of water afloat with freshly sliced lemon pieces. Reuben had disappeared to somewhere, probably to observe some demonstration being offered on how this or that was done - or where whatever had been recently found in those newly excavated squares. While I occupied myself shooting the deft fingers nimbly arranging the foodstuff for our pleasure.

The tour at last concluded, the lot of us hungrily dived into the "smorgasbord" - if not quite as rapaciously as a flock of seagulls (but almost), before securing seats at our now quite crowded for all purposes long table, virtually on the brink of tottering from the squeeze. I'd topped my plate with a couple pieces of fruit, dates, olives (being an olive freak), a carrot, the pickled herring and Labaneh (though I would have greatly preferred yogurt instead). And as much as I love tea (but not kibbutz tea in a thermos), a cup of that lemon-flavored water as well. Across from me, Reuben went for the eggs, the vegetable mix (that he doused with a liberal amount of black pepper and olive oil), a swathe of soft cheese and more of that freshly baked bread. (Myself, I'd passed on the bread, having had my fill of carbs for one morning.) And (as if he had taken my warning to heart) he poured himself a large cup of juice, that he would refill several times.

It continues to intrigue me how people will involuntarily bond over food - whatever their petty differences be they personal or political (often enough it is both, though not often enough acknowledged). And it was no less the case this morning atop the Tel Ronish mound - where normally conflicting personalities maintained a jovial mood, be they the highly competitive archaeologists or the dig's colorful array of disparate volunteers. (I was reminded of what Stefan had said on the subject of collegial strife only a few days before: "I again marvel at something I recognized long ago, that all of us view the world differently, that none of us have the same opinion about anything, and basically all of us are in a totally separate universe of our own.") Or, perhaps it was simply our enjoying the lull of the relatively fresh air, however humid already, before it soon enough turned boiling hot. Theirs was a near cacophony of voices, occasionally a burst of laughter even, yet without rancor, just everybody attempting to get their opinion in all at once (like what else was new), be it in Hebrew or English for the most part, the collective babble. I watched Reuben - sitting there as if enveloped of a world of his own - realizing that he hadn't a clue about the shop talk that normally dominates these gatherings, that didn't include him, yet apparently straining to catch a clue nevertheless, his eyes unblinking as he quietly listened, a pensive frown clouding his features. One can feel ridiculously left out upon finding themselves in such a situation, I know. At once I felt sorry for him and yet I wanted to laugh; I felt like shouting across the table, almost irritably, "Don't waste your time!", as if to say it's not worth it, just relax, drink some more juice. Not that I myself can grasp the finer nuances of Hebrew while some of the terminology bantered about in English even decidedly leaves me cold, tuned out - on the other hand, it's familiar, I am "at home" here as much as I am anywhere, I might add, me and my camera.

(As one might surmise, we were a heterogeneous lot bunched together as we were around this plank-boarded table, of disparate ages, a paradigm of nationalities, ethnic diversities, bound by the project at hand for whatever reason personal or professional that had brought us here to be a part of it these few weeks of the year.)

While he'd only dropped into our midst the evening before, Reuben so far appeared to remain invisible to the others - as he sat there wrapped in his "aloneness" as it were. Almost as if he were an eavesdropper of sorts in plain sight. He was nothing but courtesy to a fault, I'd noted, but an engager in small talk he decidedly wasn't. My own personal curiosity aside, wasn't anyone even vaguely interested in this otherwise somewhat handsome stranger; other than his being Stefan's old friend, had anyone even bothered to notice him? Okay, he was obviously "accepted", much like the sun was rising, the daily weather forecast. Was it because I had laid claim on him right off the bat, upon his offer to help out, when one or more of the others might have held back, hadn't been quick enough? Perhaps it had been seen as a rather uncharacteristic if not a brazen move on my part, even without an inkling of any ulterior motive. And if so, what did it say about me, the perennial friend to all and buddy to none? I realized it was early in the summer so far, with each hovering yet among their own, just-emerging cliques as it wasn't that far into the season yet. So I shouldn't read too much into what I was perceiving to be their blithely ignoring Reuben's presence, I told myself. Then, was this too a self-justification masking a relief that I was so far not having any competition for his unswerving attention - so mysterious are the (often devious) ways of human emotions I continue to learn? It was during this but momentary preoccupation that I caught something out of the corner of my eye that gave me a jolt that I must have been unconsciously registering all along. Or was it my imagination that seated three people down from him, Sushila, a quintessential English rose of a student volunteer, was sneaking the odd glance in his direction, she of the violet blue eyes and long black hair tied back into a single braid. Normally shy, not one to be ostentatiously direct I would suspect - but when hormones kick in...... Well, maybe she'd read one of his books. Was that what it was with me too, hormones kicking in - me "the nobody's fool"? Was I fooling myself, tiptoeing so far along this surreptitious path I seem to be mapping out as I move? At the far end of the table, Avi Grantz and Nitza Harel were fielding questions from the volunteers close at hand as well as informally inquiring about the experience they were having in general on the dig so far. While Naor Dan, closer still could be heard exhibiting his charm before a contingent made up mainly of those young Scandinavian females seated by him. Breakfast was belatedly coming to an end.

It was like we, each in our own way, had heard the bong of an invisible bell as Stefan standing up pulled on his floppy brim desert hat, a fitting compliment to the long blond beard becoming streaked with gray. The table all at once began to stir, like a tremor during an earthquake; chairs were being pushed back, bodies began to intermingle. Several of the crew took the opportunity to greet Reuben, if but briefly, shaking hands with him - followed by Naor Dan who I heard say in English that he'd read his last novel, had found it "interesting" (Naor, a minute or two later, catching up with me, sought to airbrush me with his "charm" - which he knew I took with a grain of salt but couldn't resist doing anyway - while commending me on my photographs that accompanied the reports sent weekly to headquarters. Before I excused myself to go say goodbye to Nitza and Avi, who too have often complimented me on my work, often curious enough to discuss some captured detail, wanting to know the method I used to shoot it.)

"Back to the grind," I called out to Reuben. "There's more to be done before the heat begins to broil us alive."

"So, tell me," he asked, catching up with me. "Was this show just now more like face time with the field hands or what?"

"Yes and no," I started to laugh - he had a point. "It's part political, like it always is when the head honchos come around. But they do get to have their noses pointed to the ground, not a bad thing altogether. It's always good to take the pulse, periodically get the feel of a place, as the excavation under your auspices progresses. I think they are off to Tel Rechov next. That's north of here, above Beit She'an. It's a long, on-going dig and more important in the general scheme of things than Ronish, it being like a hub city of sorts from the mists of time. I think the jury is still out on where Tel Ronish fits into the puzzle. Is it but a mini outpost in the region, way down on the wheel's spoke - or something more? I have heard a buzz that it may be something more, thus we're here still, continuing to dig and sift away,"

"I read somewhere that somebody once called archaeology the most destructive of sciences."

"Hey, don't blame me," I laughed. "I just photograph the ruins, be they nature's or man-made. Or the destruction wrought by archaeology, if you will."

"I didn't mean it like it sounds," he said. "I realize it is like detective work, the fitting together these broken pieces of a puzzle for a greater picture. Nothing's perfect."

"Except my photographs. And we'd better

get at it before the sunlight obliterates us."

When I had called him over, he was being cornered by two of the Australians, the flaxen haired Vicki and Joely, newly minted literary groupies probably who'd remembered Stefan saying Reuben wrote novels, with the doe-eyed Sushila edging her way in their direction. They'll find him later, I felt for certain (my feelings about that suddenly in a muddle), but I really did need his help - and like yesterday. One square I needed to reshoot because the light now was just right; in two more squares, the reflector panels had to be moved to accommodate each angle I shot from - not so difficult, but bordering on the tedious - for Reuben, I suspected, undoubtedly so, yet he performed the tasks with good humor. I suspected he had been happy in a way to have escaped those girls' "come on", where he had to perform the published writer role, that while he enjoyed the notoriety it brought or wrought just as long as it didn't involve him personally - or was I merely thinking of myself in his place. I assumed he'd have found them attractive - in particular Sushila had she made it in time. Though they were half his age (Naor Dan certainly just had, Naor being Naor). But what I was beating around the bush getting at was simply who was he seeing when he looked at me - the bossy perfectionist, one who gave the impression of being brazenly in control. Certainly not that six year old girl he'd once spoiled (upon her demand) in the now shape and form of a grown woman gone 30 something already. (If he only knew, I dared to think.) One grown hardened to a certain extent, with steel-string muscles in more ways than one, beneath still soft curves and a wild mane of wavy hair. Any more than I see in him his 16th year post pubescent self. (In that ginger beard I'd spotted a gray hair or two.) Only I sense he is in there, at heart, profoundly so when I dare let myself admit it. Yes, but what does the he make of the me now, here like thrown together (and soon to literally melt in the already stifling heat), two strangers just met, a man and woman, flesh and blood. I'm not ready to go there, I grab myself. I'm Deborah Rosenfeld, the only me I am now, as I have long been.

I'd been tempted to raise my camera, sighting him there, but had refrained. Was it that I wanted him only in my frame - not shared with those two gushing Australian girls, with a single-minded, by her looks, Sushila bearing down?

"Last night Stefan gave me a snapshot history of Tel Ronish," Reuben broke into my muddled thoughts, as he was moving the reflector panels from one square to another, boyishly scampering up and down the ladders; I had been just about to tell him to take it easy in this heat. "That interest in it, much less any excavation plans, is relatively recent, in comparison to other tels in the area that had been come across decades ago, as far back as the 1930s, one of them."

"It's the same old story, there's only so much government money to spread around, so unless there is a private benefactor, be it an individual, a foundation or some university here or from abroad," I replied, a bit absentmindedly as I was juxtaposing in my head angles to shoot from vis-a-vis the light source. "And the others were proving to be such treasure troves already."

"You know," he said, on something of a whimsical note, "you stand here now, looking out over this lush, rolling landscape and imagine a panorama of history passing in review: Canaanite, Philistine, Phoenician, Persian, Hellenistic, Roman, Byzantine, Islamic, the Crusaders. The whole gang of of them, each thinking they'd consigned those before them to the dust bin. Who did I leave out?"

"Us Jews, but we were already here," I laughed. "Well, after the Canaanites, black flies and the summer heat, I reckon. And the heat hasn't gone anywhere either, which doesn't take imagination to see in those rising vapors yonder, and feel it. Did Stefan tell you about the discovery of a Byzantine period mikveh last summer? Which is why we are back here this summer."

It was an hour before noon now and the heat, like an invisible tidal wave, was already washing over us; we were breathing as if through a wet cloth pressed to our face. I've always found that keeping a steady pace while doing whatever I was doing I could maintain my equilibrium - and drinking water, which I again reminded Reuben to do. I could see he was becoming drenched with sweat, darkening his armpits and running down his face from beneath his hat. I sweat too, only not conspicuously so - thus for added relief I will splash water on my face and neck. But most importantly, breathing calmly however heavy the air. (I have seen people pass out upon becoming panicky.) Reuben, who had slowed down to pace himself evenly, was apparently aware of this as well. Throughout the excavation area, a general fatigue had settled in although the work continued, but as if in slow motion. Dripping faces were smeared from dusty arms drawn across them, bare knees in the dust had darkened as much as had the colorful array of tee shirts and head coverings. Myself, I merely lifted my hair and gave the back of my neck a few fans with the palm of my free hand where a bead of sweat would trickle down into my tee shirt.

"I grew up with summer heat that we thought rough enough," Reuben said, "but I have to admit this is in a league of its own. What one wouldn't do for a cool breeze off some body of water. Like where I grew up. And the kibbutz I was on was close enough to the coast for an afternoon breeze, and the cold water from the irrigation main too was a life saver."

"Where was it exactly that you grew up?" I asked, hoping it sounded in all innocence.

"Southern Maryland, on the Bay. Chesapeake Bay."

"Land of sky blue waters," I laughed.

"Something like that," he shrugged. "In the mornings it can be."

Having given my cameras a cursory dusting, I carefully packed them, my thoughts already on that afternoon back on Neve Rom developing the print rolls I'd just shot. While Reuben, only asking what went back with us and what stayed, hauled the equipment down to Rubble. I stood and watched him descend on one of his treks, a load on his shoulder, carrying another by hand, as his darkening silhouette in the sun's glare seemed to merge with his shadow. ("I can see how you can use help here, like you said," he'd spoken in a reflective tone of voice during our drive back to the kibbutz. "How do you manage it alone, as you obviously do, and get all the rest of your work done?" However awkwardly put, I realized he meant it as a compliment. "Keeps me slim and trim," I laughed. "I won't argue with that," he replied, my side glance at him catching what I took to an appreciative grin. So perhaps he'd noticed that I was a female of the species after all, me with my wild wet hair covered, clad in loose and dusty work clothes, my face perpetually squinting behind a camera's lens.) Meanwhile, the rest of the team too were in the throes of "breaking camp" for the day, going about it meticulously stacking or storing the various working tools before tarpaulin(s) could be "struck" for the night. It was only just past noon, it seemed such a shame not to get more done. But for safety's sake most of all, and to avoid carelessness (for it paid to keep a sharp awareness at all times - both to avoid injury and to not overlook some possible "find", however minuscule at first glance). The two of us were done just in time to help them take down the poles.

By the time we were collectively done, we were indeed a sweaty lot, many with smeared faces (from wiping brows with the back of arms) and grimy knees, with large dark splotches where t-shirts clung to breasts, armpits, and backs. What I'd have given for an old fashioned hand pump to stick head and body all under, as I pulled hard the handle and a cold water splashed forth.

That sudden sense of feeling at home here, me and my camera, that could surprise me in those unsuspecting moments Perhaps Israel suited me more than I nominally realized. Here where so many had created newfound identities to go with a new persona. To be remade. Escaping pasts best forgotten. Or, as in my case, transcending their pasts. Where they could lose themselves in a collective present established out of the shadows of a past.

Nestled within its copse of greenery, Neve Rom was an oasis if but in appearance compared to being atop Tel Ronish that morning, because despite the heavy shade from the sun the air was no less wet or thick. But inside my make-shift darkroom throughout that early afternoon its concrete walls had offered a respite (though it made a problem for drying the prints, with a small fan even). By the time I was done, fol-lowed by a quick shower at last, a change into lighter clothes, and a brief staff meeting, I felt more human finally, as if the atmospheric pres-sure had begun to lift, like the weight of the light itself. I hadn't given much thought to Reu-ben, or had pushed it away, in the intervening hours, until I bumped into him on the path to the Chader Ochel - he all spruced up and looking no worse for wear, his head of wavy hair now a mass of curly tufts - and we walked together to fetch supplies for the ritual four o'clock rendez-vous with the team over light food and drink.

"My becoming a photographer and my first trip to Israel, for that work study summer on a kibbutz, coalesced. I came across a flier about it on my local Hillel house bulletin board and ap-plied," I began, remembering my promise before breakfast to later answer his questions. After our initial greeting, he'd gone ruminatively si-lent as we'd continued side by side along the path and I suddenly felt a need to fill the void, to hold on to something I couldn't name but feared I might lose. "The fall before I bought my first camera, a second hand Pentax with a case full of lenses, and in between struggling with the vowel sounds in Hebrew and shoveling out the cow barn, the Refet, after milking, I shot photographs. It was a sparse, harsh place in the Negev, though the chaverim, hide-tough as they were, couldn't have been more warm and welcoming to a wet-behind-the-ears gawking American girl of eighteen, no nineteen I was by then. And once back in the States that fall, when I developed those umpteen rolls of film I'd shot I had been more than pleasantly surprised at what I'd captured, or to be exact, the way I had captured the ordinary, the mundane even, in the everyday life on the kibbutz - and its locale - in a startling black and white perspective. I showed them to a few people, and before I knew it some were published. Which led to a book, my first, *Deborah Rosenfeld: A Summer on Kibbutz*. It got my foot in the door, that book. Nobody was more surprised than I was. It was like my fate was sealed. I never looked back.

"I think I've seen a copy, actually," he said, in a rushed exclamation. "It had a grayish white cloth cover. I remember the up-close photographs, like intense portraits all, as if I was right there myself. The title reminded me of the title of that early Bergman film, *Summer with Monica*.

That's why it sticks. The likewise stark landscape and cloudless skies. And the name 'Deborah' too, from a past association. I had been tempted to buy it, but didn't that day, and when I came back for it, it was gone. It was in a second hand book sale, I'm afraid."

"It wasn't a big publication, though it went through a couple of reprintings. But like I said, it slowly led to other things, photographic assignments, and my reputation grew from there."

"Do you do journalistic stuff? Like ever covered wars, areas of conflict? Do you still?"

"I've never intentionally covered war zones, or sought out areas of conflict. Although upon several occasions I have found myself in such places or situations, where the scene changed radically, drastically overnight. And I have returned here during periods of conflict, the suicide bombings, waves of scud missiles, the intifada. To cover the people whomever and wherever, how they were holding up, to show them facing the challenge. That Pentax I continued to use until it was ripped from me at a border crossing, along with the film I'd shot. I was allowed to keep my life and the leather bag. In retrospect, I accept that I got the best of the bargain.

"That's when I bought the M-3, second hand as well, my forever standby print camera, be it for action or stills. And it has survived hard knocks, falls, and once a bus crash. I've kept using it even after going digital for most commercial work, merely expediency that. And here on archaeological sites it remains the best for reports and the archives. While the digital is useful for immediate printouts. My first digital was a Canon - the 'cannon' - I called it. It didn't survive its first crash. Though, fortunately I did.

"Otherwise, I'm a freelance photographer. I do commercial and magazine shoots, portraiture. I've shot promotional stills on film sets, worked for foundations, architectural studies, environment causes, archaeological site sponsors in conjunction with the local authority, often the case wherever I have worked, though here it is solely with the IAA.

"I have managed to be just 'almost famous', which suits me well. I get assignments, but it is my work that gets studied, used, enjoyed too, hopefully. Rather than me. For other reasons as well I've shied away from the celebrity bit. Which personally, I believe, has actually worked in my favor."

"But why archaeological sites?" He broke into my voluble reverie, for want of a better way to describe it; I saw he'd kept giving me unreadable side glances as I'd talked. "I can imagine the pay isn't all that great, is hardly as exciting as the other gigs you get. It is quite hard, exacting and tedious work under trying, even grueling, conditions. What got you into it?"

"I'm a sucker for punishment, you might

think. But I'm not really. The gains far outweigh the losses. That summer on kibbutz where I shot the photographs in my first book - I've published two other books since, personal stuff - I met Stefan. He had once been a high school teacher there before becoming an archeologist and was paying a surprise visit while working on a dig nearby. He was asked to give a talk to our ulpan class after which a visit to his site was arranged as a field trip. It was my first time at an archaeological site. I shot a few photographs, of him mostly exuding a dramatic intensity in his excitement, giving hands-on explanations. It was of historical importance, interesting, though not super exciting for me at the time, but what did I know then. Years later, I ran across his name. By then I had already done, I mean shot, a 17th century archaeological excavation in one of the mid-Atlantic states. So on an impulse, I found the address of the foundation that was sponsoring it, his dig, and sent him care of the foundation a copy of my book, including several loose prints of him with it, and a note telling him what I was now doing and asked about what possibilities were there in Israel for a photographer. It took a while for the book to reach him, I gather, but when it did he wrote me almost immediately thanking me, said he greatly admired my photographs from the kibbutz, and would let me know if anything turned up. It was almost a year later, I got another letter from him telling me of an opening for a dig photographer where he was about to work during the coming season, and that if I was interested, though the pay was near nonexistent, he'd heartily recommend me. The rest is history as they say."

I paused for a moment, while the two of us continued to walk side by side, shoulders almost touching, in silence, the only sound that of our footsteps on the path's coarse sand, his being a somewhat lighter step than my own I couldn't help but noticing, that reminded me of that of American Indians in movies seen quietly and swiftly stalking large game in a deep woods. Well, he was wearing those leather moccasins again. It almost made me feel ungainly, clumsy in comparison, what with my tendency to lope, even when not loping.

"I like archaeological digs - to shoot for them if hired to do so, to shoot around them when allowed to do so otherwise," I continued. "There is something elemental about them. And I like the people involved, their independence, their solitariness, their purposefulness, their ardor even, like with Stefan, both the archaeologists themselves as well as the volunteers, who are of all ages, from such diverse backgrounds, the far corners of the planet. They all have stories to share, their personalities I try to capture in my at large photographs. It's not the same, say on film sets, not even when out on location. There are always rank egos to deal with, in both places, but the archaeologists seem so much more elemental. I can see Stefan laughing now at me saying that. And when you make friends among them, they remain friends."

"Stefan says that you are the best photographer he's ever worked with on a dig, period. And you're always ready to 'shoulder the load', as he put it, come what may. He couldn't do without you. Besides, 'she's damn good looking too and to her credit doesn't give a fig about it. Has never used it to gain an advantage - yet at the same time she remains a 'mystery'."

"Stefan can wax romantic," I laughed. "And if you don't take this compliment of his with a grain of salt, Reuben Headey, I see I am going to have an awful lot to live up to in your eyes. And ultimately disappoint you."

He was shaking his head, smiling. "I'll take the 'mystery' part with a grain of salt."

I wanted to playfully reply like "Yeah?", but I let it pass. I'm not good at the repartee game, have no interest in playing it, and I had a feeling neither did he. But I found myself enjoying this familiarity passing between us, however superficial perhaps - as long as I didn't, on my part, allow it to go much further while at the same time wanting it to (both because I longed for it, as if behind my own back, while curiously attracted by the "forbidden fruit" it dangled before me).

They come to me in flashes, these memories, but the sheer elation they've always wrought lingers. There was water over the road from the marsh that bordered it that hadn't been there when we'd passed that way earlier - and I had balked, I was adamant - I simply wasn't going to take off my shoes and socks and wade through it barefooted like the others were prepared to do. (I was a little girl accustomed to city sidewalks, and never before such a phenomenon had presented itself before me. It was like an indignity or something.) Nicholas and Joy, my brother and sister, Nicholas especially ("stupid girls", Nicholas'd blathered), were all for leaving me behind - which had really angered me, had added insult to injury. That was when he, Reuben, turned around towards me, squatted and looked up into my eyes. "You don't have to walk, it's okay, I'll carry you," he said. "On my shoulders." There was a kind of mirth in his eyes, though his voice sounded assuredly matter of fact, practical. It had been the first time since our arrival the afternoon before that he had spoken directly to me, paid me individual attention, recognized me, I felt, as a complete individual and not as a family entity. It had been as if he'd addressed me as if I were a grownup, like an equal. A person in my own right. No longer the kid, at the bottom of the pecking order. It went straight to my head, needlessly to say. Instead of shrieking when he lifted me over his back, and gripping my dangling ankles, rose with me astraddle him, I experienced this exhilaration, as if I had gained a daring advantage of some kind - while my siblings sniped from below. When we cleared the water, he continued to carry me - for which I'd hardly complained. Like for the first time I was viewing the world from above - and not wanting to relinquish my exalted vantage point I had pretty much insisted that he carry me about whenever for the rest of our stay. Though Joy and Nicholas would continue to poke fun at him ("Oh, you are going to be in for it now," they'd teased), with my parents joining in with them. Let them, I had him all to myself, I supposed I'd preened. He hadn't seemed to mind, was always ready and willing, as if he relished accommodating me as much I did him doing it......And here I was now the taller of the two of us, as if somehow the world had turned upside down.

Was it because he'd acted towards me in so many ways like I was a grown up to him? An equal. Even if I'd made him my donkey, ecstatically so. In the way he'd enjoyed answering all my questions in detail, always as if he were giving a lecture that he took for granted I'd grasp. As if happy to share what he knew without qualification. I never thought what he might all the while be thinking. He was mine, mine exclusively (and consequently, I his). The rush it gave me was exhilarating.

We are all actors, us humans. We play many parts. Even those of us who are ostensibly whom we were purported to be at the outset. Chameleons to a one.

When I entered my teens, for some years already a "thrall" in my guardians' home, there emerged two sides of me out of that rebellious adolescent "sold into Egypt" - a sober, serious, pensive, even somber, side without and an effusive, silly, frivolous side within. Mine was the diametrical opposite of Anne Frank's as she so brilliantly postulated it in her "Diary", her future novel's first draft she often referred to it as being - a work I had held close to my heart as I fought to keep my head together in those turbulent years. (And while I'd eventually acquire a sense of humor - Anne's came to her naturally.) The "gray side" of me, I called it, this holding the lid down fast on the other me, the buried child. The side that wanted to enjoy the crazy irony of everything, with a kind of gleeful gusto. Early on, I realized I had better start to merge them. There was nothing bad, wrong, with either side per se. Each was valid as long as they didn't drift into the extreme, becoming diametrical sides of the same coin. I needed that coin to be whole.

"Do you consider photography a visual art form, like sculpture and painting, film making even, or do you see it as more a form of journalism, well a kind of record keeping?" Reuben suddenly asked as we walked back together on the same path, carrying several items between us for the tea. "If I haven't put my foot into something."

"The medium is a craft, same as writing is, that can be used to create a work of art. Beyond that I take the 5th. That argument is a bottomless pit. Do I think of myself as an artist. No, I just take photographs. Like a painter friend I once knew just painted. For the love of painting, the joy of creating anew with each canvas, the constant stretching herself, of offering something others would enjoy. Of course, you try to do your subject justice, you just don't point the camera and indiscriminately shoot. It requires a certain amount of discernment. Me, I think of myself as an inward observer of the outward. Well, I do study faces that might find themselves within my frames. There is an entire universe in a person's face."

"I think of the writers who have spoken to me, one in particular who opened something up in me I hadn't known was there. What about you?"

"In that college town on the East Coast I ended up in coming east there was a film festival, part of which showed 'Jewish films' and I quite by chance caught this documentary about a young Jewish woman photographer - she was young still at the time the film was made, in the 1950s - who excelled in shooting scenes of the streets, in startling black and whites, here in

Israel, the capitals of Europe, and in NYC, that were like intimate portraits. I enjoyed the rich texture of her photographs, with their haunting quality. They touched a chord in me, I could almost taste them. It was like they touched a nerve, triggered a 'hunger' to be exact that, like you, I'd never before realized I had. And it looked like a really fun thing to do - to find the frame that captured the gist of that which one normally sees wherever, whatever, that unconsciously causes one to remember a particular 'sensation' one has carried away from a scene encountered. There's something 'romantic' too about the process. It was not long afterwards passing a camera repair shop I'd often passed before, out of a nudge of curiosity I entered. Cameras I knew nothing about, but I remembered the looks of the camera the young woman in the film shot with. Immediately, my eye was caught by what turned out to be a Pentax 1000, with its portrait lens already attached. Holding it to my eye and adjusting the focus, whatever I framed had the same vibrant close-up intensity - like as if electricity had shot through me, tingling, throbbing - of those photos in that film. It was like I was seeing through a third eye. The camera, I really liked the feel of it in my hands too.

"Her name was Ruth Orkin, that young woman photographer. And she was from California also. In the late 30s, a teenager still, she rode her bike from Hollywood to New York City, taking photographs along the way."

"That's a great story," he said. "I mean it is cinematic. Like a scene from a film. A girl emerges from watching a movie about a photographer, walks down the street past a camera store, sees a camera in the display window and on an impulse walks in. What with the irony and all in it."

"There was another film I saw in that series. It was set in Israel, somewhere near the sea, on a kibbutz. Michal Bat Adam wrote and directed it. Even played her grownup self in it. I seem to remember date palms and cypress trees, the light seemed so airy. I can't say how much it influenced me, though six months later I applied for that summer ulpan. What mostly resonated with me at the time was the story. Was like my own in many ways. A young girl accustomed to her independence is sent to live in a communal setting - the Beit Yellidim, the children's house on a kibbutz - she'd feel so out of kilter in, her parents having gone abroad for a year to work, as doctors in a danger zone. It may have been autobiographical, like characters she created and played in other films, they seemed so personal. And the cinematography capturing beauty and harshness be it in the landscape or in the characters portrayed never pandered to sentimentality, was never shot for its own sake, was always in service to the story."

"Were you disappointed when you discovered that the kibbutz hosting the ulpan didn't match that setting? Or maybe I'm simply imagining how I'd have been. As I had been."

"At first sight, I suppose I was. There were no palm trees - although I had seen them en route. But it was all so wildly new. And I was feeling my way. The nature was harsh, in retrospect, if it had been picture perfect I probably wouldn't have been inspired to shoot the photographs I did. As I have always found the picture perfect in real life to be deceptive, when not a monotony, ultimately boring. Anyway, us ulpaniks didn't have time to dwell on aesthetics. We were thrown into our classes and the work right off the bat. It wasn't easy, both learning Hebrew and the work, but I was determined to prove I could do it - that, and with the sense of acceptance I felt offered reassurance. Because I felt included for the first time in my life, not accepted but included, for my sake. It was a weird sensation, yet a pleasant one, a satisfying one. I suppose it helped that I took the work and my classes equally serious. I wanted most of all to do a good job. Which I'd discover was truly appreciated, respected. Whatever the politics were didn't dent me. I survived my stay with flying colors. And I'm still coming back here, Israel warts and all."

"In my case, it was to have been for the rest of my life. I realized immediately I had made a colossal mistake, that had cost me in so many burnt bridges just to get there. How was I going to become a writer in Hebrew when my language was English to the core. And that was besides the warts I hadn't expected. For a long time I was too ashamed to admit it. Like I may have mentioned already." He said it with a tinge of bitterness, if not regret in his voice suddenly gone weary. "I was very angry. Perhaps more so at myself, blaming myself for my disappointment, some inherent weakness I hadn't overcome."

"It sounds like you brought a lot of baggage with you," I offered. "I was fortunate in a way in that I had none."

"It looks like just about everybody is here," he said extemporaneously, as if to avert the subject, as we emerged out from under the trees to find more or less most of our archaeological team either circled in plastic chairs or sitting on the close-cut grass - while a close-by folding table already appeared to list under the weight of the laid out goodies. He quickly adding before greetings commenced, "I think you are right, I definitely had."

With the eventual breaking up of our afternoon "tea" (in Hebrew, "Aruchat Arba", literally translates as "snacks" or "snacks time"), the platters of open-faced sandwiches left with crumbs, pastries devoured, and the thermos of tea emptied, I said to Reuben in passing "L'hitraot" or "See you later", he being a former kibbutznik I knew he'd know. I wanted to keep it light, almost nonchalant, nothing binding. After the intensity of our discussion earlier on the way there, I needed to establish a certain space, if only for the time being. To take a deep breath. I didn't want to press too closely, or draw him to me, if only by accident, too tightly. Not before I knew where I was going with him - if indeed anywhere. Not before I had defined a few things to myself. I had to check on my drying prints - and with the digitals to sort and choose from to include with the morning's outgoing reports to Jerusalem.

Reuben throughout the tea had nibbled on a tomato and cream cheese sandwich while drinking tea, looking pleasantly thoughtful as he appeared to listen attentively to the small talk buzzing around him, mostly in English here, once or twice smiling, almost laughing once. It was a learned act on his part, I suspected, in order to keep the world at bay. With that studied unobtrusiveness of his, I wondered if he would make a good spy. Inconspicuous as he was in plain sight. Me, I felt no need to either stand-out or to disappear in full view. In a strange way I often turned up on these occasions just to relax in the company of others, nothing more. I had no desire to be garrulous. I'd just be Deborah. I'd never turn anybody away who wanted to say something or had a question. The others had gotten to know me in my designated role and felt comfortable with that. They recognized that I might just twiddle my thumbs throughout or at any time just jump up and leave. All the while I was taking a pulse of my own. That I could share with Stefan, should he ask, or I could file it away, say for "a rainy day".

Sushila had been conspicuously absent, I found myself noticing, until someone mentioned they thought she had a headache. And Reuben had taken a seat on the fringe, as had I, while Joely had sat hemmed in amid the thick of the gathering.

I thought too of going for a swim in the pool, as the air was still cloyingly thick amid the trees, but it really wasn't my thing, swimming - and I can take but so many minutes of fresh water in my eyes. Thus I found myself on the threshold of my studio and the die was cast.

I had hoped to have been done with Aruchat-Erev, the evening meal, before too many people, including those from the dig team, arrived. Which was why I'd come early, right upon my finishing up - to my perfection - those prints from the morning. But upon entering the Chader Ochel, the dining hall, I saw that that was not going to be the case. At the second table, beneath the parade of large, square windows along the far wall that sat eight, were five of them, and as kibbutz decorum required that each table had to be filled before the next table could be sat at, I had no choice. It would have been too conspicuous for me to have turned and left, alas, having already been sighted. So I strolled over making it look as nonchalantly as I could muster. There at one end was Stefan - with, an older volunteer, and Rafi, one of the Israeli student archaeologists; and at the other, Reuben, managing quite well in appearing calm at the center of a vortex - that is, with Sushila (who must have recovered from her headache) leaning close beside him and Joely hunched forward directly opposite. I flopped down next to Joely and poured myself from a sweating stainless steel pitcher a tall glass of ice cold crushed fruit juice. I could have sat next to Rafi, whom I was fond enough of, but the three of them were deep into a discussion of Vaclav Havel. ("Havel's plays are marvelous in their originality. They have a disintegrative quality about them," Stefan was saying. "Everything goes along normally, and suddenly reality disintegrates, and nothing is as it seems...") I chose to not break the train of thought here and on a whim joined "the kids" (Did I really write that - "the kids"?), sliding down beside Joely who hadn't noticed at first, so intense was her attention upon whatever Reuben had been saying - something about how he finds the word or two at the outset of a piece of writing that give him the end of a "thread" that he can follow - much as one who has descended into a cave might follow a thread trailed from the entrance so that he can find his way back out. Sushila too appeared to be held in rapt attention. So I was hardly going to disrupt anybody's concentration by joining their coterie instead. I popped a radish or two into my mouth from the common vegetable platter, and served myself - there was chicken soup with carrot slices floating in it, potato salad, bread and hummus. Bread thickly smeared with hummus and soup sounded good to my by now groaning stomach. "What's this?" Rafi, who'd at last noticed my presence, called out in English, "Devorah does not bring her work load to finish to the dining table, maybe she is not well?" And I bantered back, "Nope. Finished it in the 'Beit Shemoosh' before coming here, thank you." Then Joel, laughing, chimed in: "Ah Deborah, ever the workaholic, no matter doing what. No matter where, she puts us all to shame. Right, Stefan." I grinned as I bit into the bread - the hummus, freshly made and thick, with just the right amount of garlic and lemon, really tasted good. I turned my attention to Reuben - between spooning my soup, a tad watery but okay - who continued to field questions (if not quite fend them off simultaneously) from his literary - if unintentionally so - inquisitors. (I don't think I imagined a certain look he ever so surreptitiously gave me in moments of pause, catching his breath.) Sushila, her big violet blue eyes wildly full of an earnest concern, queried him excessively about what I gathered was his first novel, its scenes of emotional "child abuse", the boy protagonist's parents' self-destructive addictions, its rural southern 1950s social and racial divide she had been painfully aware of having existed, if but theoretically so. (She could only think of the toll it must have taken him to write something so richly described, so honestly and understandably, and with humor to boot. I wanted to roll my eyes, but mercifully didn't.) I found myself being envious of her, she obviously had read it so thoroughly - when I, myself, had never ever seen a copy. Out on the Tel, he'd only spoken of his last novel, in its relation to his first time in Israel, couched as it had been in theoretical phraseology, however interesting, to the point of sounding "bloodless". On the other hand, this earlier work, poignantly delineated back to him by Sushila's ardent desired to impress while teasing out of him some nitty gritty, however academically expressed, caught my attention. Suddenly I was all ears, putting aside what I saw was her attempt to make herself attractive to him by whatever route she needed to take - it sounded like it touched on the world I as the something of a precocious runt of a Debbie had known him from, who had no less sought to make herself attractive to him at the time. I'd have to ask Stefan if he had one or both of these books. "It's just a story, partly truth, partly fiction, to use that line from a Kris Kristofferson song," Reuben said at last to a disappointed, trying not to show it, Sushila. While I had to laugh inside, he knew his way around things better than I would have guessed.

3

Last evening when returning from Neve Rom's club house where I caught up on reading that week's issues of *The Jerusalem Post*, Israel's English language daily, and had enjoyed a tolerable cup of expresso, I stopped by Stefan's room in hopes he had a copy of Reuben's first novel, the one Sushila had so zealously questioned Reuben about at dinner. Stefan didn't have a copy (well, he had a hardback original - the one Reuben had sent him - back home in the States), but he did have *(K)hamsin*, in a massive thick paperback. Stefan had flashed me an ambivalent look, before smiling as if to say, "Ah hah, you too." I sighed, "Apparently I am about the only one on the dig who hasn't read him. I am beginning to feel left out of the conversation. When we were talking this morning he mentioned it in the context of why he came here to kibbutz way back when and his subsequent disenchantment. But the more he said I got the feeling he was painting an ethereal picture in the sky, as if to blur the particulars. And you know me, once whetted, I want to gnaw on the bone. Not literally, but to bite into the nitty gritty." Stefan rather solemnly reached over to the bookshelf beside him and pulled out this hefty volume. "I hope this won't become some sort of competitive sport between Sushila and you, of all people," he said, handing me *(K)hamsin*, the cover a flaming reddish sky against which stood out the title in a dark print. "Don't worry about me, Scouts honor," I grinned largely. "I can't help but be curious, can I. He being your friend. Thanks." (Thanks as well to that expresso, I'd been able to stretch several hours in which to "peruse" Reuben's lengthy tome - that is, near feverishly, searching through it, reading here and there, as if for a needle in a hay stack, I hoped I'd recognize when I saw it - before I was ready to drop like a log.)

I ran the foregoing through my mind as through the nether light I drove Rubble out to the Tel, with Reuben again seated beside me, we having gotten an early start before the break of dawn. If I were to deduce that its central character, through whose experiences drives the story, was based on him - the flashbacks to earlier periods in said character's life and background I'd carried from my childhood self, admittedly gone a bit fuzzy with age, being so different from that which had emerged out of the rich personal and social tapestry his words wove. It was like in a dream where you recognize the people in it but don't know them. Or no longer know them. cause you never knew them - for themselves, you realize. So who was this instinctively recognizable to me - and he was indeed that, to the core of my being I had to admit - stranger sitting there next to me as we bumped and pitched along? I knew I had to do a lot more reading to find out, if ever I found out then. Nothing is ever that simple as it may appear at first sight - nor should it be. I wondered what Deborah would have thought of Reuben's novel? But I was Deborah now. As much as I had been Debbie of old.

But don't think I wasn't tempted, in our quiet moments together like this, to confess to him that I was once the little girl he remembered, courting the disaster it would inevitably have wrought. The scenario I imagined might go like this, ruinous to us both: "Do you remember a little girl you once called 'Gigi'? Tell me about her, if you do. What was she to you?" I'd ask him, out of the blue. He'd be caught off guard, puzzled, no, bewildered, possibly 'threatened' even by it. "Deborah, how do you know that?" His voice suddenly sharp, like thrown off key. "How could you know that? I never, I mean we just met for the first time two days ago." I looked at him calmly, not to give anything away, before answering him. "I was her." He looked at me like he couldn't believe what he had just heard. Befuddled, he blurted out incongruously, "You were Debbie?" It was almost an accusation. "She's dead. She was killed in a car accident when she was sixteen. What is this? Why?" I'd continued to look at him calmly. "Almost seventeen, to be exact, shy of three weeks. Deborah died in my place and I became her," I'd never dared take it further, I hadn't a clue how to. Even as a fantasy, I knew, there was an element of selfishness on my part I didn't like.

"You know, I hadn't quite taken you for an American that first evening," Reuben broke into my reverie, "when you came in late, what with your, well, graceful, at-ease demeanor - which is the only way I can describe it - nor did I quite take you for an Israeli either despite the Israelis calling you 'Devorah'; yet I thought, no I felt, I recognized you, strangely enough, though I knew we'd never before met. Not that I believe one knows someone from like another existence, lifetime, but as a metaphor for the irrational. Not that I am the most rational person on the planet."

"I think it is called cognitive intuition," I laughed. Inwardly though, I froze like an animal caught in a headlight beam. Could he have read my thoughts at that instant of "recognition", when I had likewise "recognized" him? A great part of me at that moment ached to confirm his "suspicion" with all my heart, while what good sense I still possessed kicked me hard in the shins, saying clearly "Don't be ridiculous!. Ultimately, it is Deborah he sees. You are walking through a minefield here and the wrong step will blow up in both your faces. "But 'a graceful demeanor' I've never before been said to have."

"It is the irrepressible romantic in me, I realize," he seemed quick to amend. "Or so I have been often enough told. Whatever that says about me. It's just you move with this kind of ease. I meant it in a complimentary sense, please take it for that only. So, what is first on the agenda this morning, after the raising of the canopies so to speak?"

Though he'd yet to put it on, Reuben had with him that floppy-brimmed desert hat, holding it on his knee. Likewise the brogans. He wore the same jeans too, but a fresh khaki shirt with big breast pockets that hung out side of it. He wore his clothes comfortably loose, wherever he found himself I imagined, unlike the teenager whose picture I carried in my mind. As for me I'd wrapped my piece of white muslin around my head already, to save time, both against the sun and to keep my hair out of my camera's lens. In another place we might be film extras heading out to the on-location set. Not so long back I did have such a gig, ferrying back and forth the stunt crew, the minor stars as well, on a film where I had been hired by production to shoot stills.

"I want to reshoot some more in square 'Hei' first thing before moving on." I answered him. "Talking with Stefan last night I realized I may not have gotten a few particulars that got them excited yesterday morning; it being a new area, its findings yet to fit a pattern remain random issues yet. It was a preliminary shooting. I mean it is like a work in progress. Nevertheless it's back to the grind to cover my backside in case. Won't take long."

It was shortly before our return to Neve Rom for breakfast; Reuben and I were working in an exploratory trench for me to finish up some preliminary shooting in it, where more or less we were alone together: he asked me "What is your background? I know you said you grew up more or less in an orphanage, or rather as an orphan in that private school that in all but name only was an orphanage in your case. What I really mean is, your people, your parent's, their family's background? Ashkenazim, I would think. Was it a Jewish orientated school in which you grew up?"

"That was a mouthful!" I wanted to cry out. I started to laugh, and to catch my breath I had to lower my camera, as I was three quarters the way up the stepladder shooting with Reuben on the other side holding it steady as he spoke, in an inquisitive but a nonintrusive way. I sensed he was quite earnest, wasn't just passing the time of day. But I couldn't help but laugh - like where did I start to answer him, for I had researched Deborah's background quite thoroughly, as a background, but not her family per se, having nothing to go on but her parents' names on her birth certificate. And that photograph of them with her a toddler still. Deborah herself had never spoken of these things, other than a chance remark. I would surmise she didn't know herself. I once remember her saying, with an uncharacteristic hurt in her voice, "At least you can remember your mother and father".

"Yeah, I must seem to you like a 'Little Orphan Annie' with a sugar daddy or two in the wings," I said. "With what must sound like with quite a privileged education. The school fostered an Ethical Culture milieu, and consequently had a considerable number of Jewish students in it - or to be more precise kids from a Jewish background, like me, with little to no knowledge of 'being Jewish'. I suppose it left us out on a limb so to speak, though I speak for myself here. Therefore, I will risk surmising that us Rosenfelds are definitely Ashkenazim, the name is more German-Austrian Jewish but we could be from anywhere between Warsaw and Odessa. The period of their arrival on American soil is anybody's guess. I wish I knew more, therefore I've had to create my own 'legend'."

"And how would you rewrite your family history though?" Reuben asked. "I know I'd like to rewrite mine. We all do, I guess, at one time or another."

"Well, I have a clean slate remember. I'd be a descendant of fiery rebels having escaped the repercussions of the 1905 revolution in Russia.

Or Babel's Benya Krick in Odessa was a great-granduncle. Let's see, who else. A Talmudic sage or a Hasidic rebbe, for a contrast, as described by Martin Buber in his *Tales of the Hasidim*. Or best of all, Morris Rosenfeld, the famed Yiddish 'sweatshop poet', for my great grandfather. And I.B. Singer a distant cousin. (As far as I know, Morris might very well have been a relative). And Ruth Orkin for a big sister. Okay, an aunt, I guess. Then there is always that warrior judge from days of yore, my namesake, who stung like a bee. Well, like a hornet it must have been to those unlucky Canaanites at the bottom of the hill. That is Mount Tabor, if you remember your Biblical history. You can almost see it from here, I've always wondered what she really got up to with Barak."

"You've certainly done your reading."

"You too, I see. But then I thought you would have. You with your 'Old Testament' background," I said, smiling down at him. "So much for fairy tales though. I'm afraid my ancestors were most likely naive bourgeois Germans, until, with the rise of Hitler and Nazism, their world came crashing down and one of them caught the boat in the nick of time - and wasn't sent back upon his arrival in the U.S., as had happened to others in those years. In the States, when people hear my name they think 'She's a Jew', here in Israel it's 'She's a Yeke'. Either way it gives a jab. It was something I'd never experienced before I tossed my few belongings into an old VW bus, it being the first thing I bought with the money in my trust fund, once I came into it, and headed out across country - leaving that vicarious womb behind.

"My parents, I was told, died in an automobile accident, leaving me with that trust fund administered by a distant cousin, or his bank rather, on my mother's side I believe, who I can never remember seeing. All of which sounds really weird, I know. Being a Jewish family, of sorts. But it's California, I guess. The school did a fair job of being a surrogate parent. I was about five at the time. I have no real memory of them, nothing I am cognizant of. I think they might have had something to do with the film industry. I could never find an obituary, only a short piece in *The LA Times* of the accident, kept very vague. All I can recall, in a startling vivid way, is finding myself suddenly abandoned, inexplicably so. I think all of us at that school felt abandoned in varying degrees. I suppose it is the one thing we all had in common, became a bond of sorts. After what I gather was a difficult period of adjustment I found an abiding interest in learning, in many respects a form of escape I would suppose. Immersed in my studies I'd go long periods without even thinking about my parents, or the lack of them in my life, they were never real to me. But for a photograph of two young people with a toddler between them.

I see their names on my birth certificate, their ages, but little else (their address they gave no longer exists). It is almost as if they never really existed. Maybe their names weren't even Rosenfeld. And by the time I came of age I no longer much cared. I was simply alive and it was a brand new day.

"So, yes, I grew up in California, if you can call it that, the 'growing up' part, I mean. Orange groves and in the canyons coyotes and no end to the sun - or freeways. Like here - including a semblance now of those freeways - not counting winters, only milder, almost sweet. And I left it without regret."

I couldn't believe I'd just made all that up, right off the top of my head - well, with its basis in a few details Deborah had offhandedly mentioned. And it had poured out of me like it really was my own to tell, to embroider if I wished. I'd truly felt it I realized. Again, I ached to tell him my real story, Debbie's story, I wanted to tell him about me, in whatever guise it took - and Deborah was me now.

"That's quite a story," he spoke after a thoughtful minute had seemed to pass. "A very painful one, Deborah, as it played out. I suppose a very American story too. I have heard too much about my family background, back to the Civil War period at least. But how much of it was actually true? Let's say, in my retelling of it, in fiction, I improvised. And in that I like to think that the truth came out."

"We are all actors, Reuben, us humans. We play many parts. Even those of us who are whom she or he were originally."

On the drive back out to the dig after breakfast Reuben began to tell about how his Israeli roommate, Avi, an archeology student with us as an assistant, had tried to teach him the rudiments of backgammon (or "shesh besh" in Hebrew), apparently to no avail. "It's this one's theory verses that one's theory until I could no longer see the woods for the trees. It became a session in comparative philosophies, each contradicting the other," he chuckled as if under his breath. "And people complain that chess is complicated."

"Do you play chess?" I asked, as offhandedly as I could manage. It was the moment I had been waiting for, laid at my feet without any muster on my part. It could burn out like a shooting star or lead me into water way over my head. I was 'fishing' and I could very well end up with the hook in me.

"Well, I, yes," he began. "I used to play, when a teenager."

"But you didn't keep it up?"

"My once enthusiasm dissipated. Like with a lot of teenage things." I felt I could almost hear an inward sigh mixed with a certain sense of the ironic on his part. "It was after I got beaten by a six year old girl - this little cousin I never knew existed before, visiting with her family for the first time from the city - not once but three times in a row she checkmated me, and I had only just taught her how to play, at her insistence. That's what did it, more or less. I realized that I did not have the patience, much less the power of concentration required, not then, not now either I suppose."

"Surely you let her win?"

"If I remember correctly, when we began the first game, maybe I gave her a little slack, not that it would have affected the outcome, to see what she would or could do. Only right in front of my eyes she had gained ground, giving up nothing in return, before I really realized it, she was always thinking two moves ahead of me, pushing me into corners, laying traps for me to trip into. It was as if it came so natural to her. I was amazed. I can almost see her now, on her knees in front of the old hassock in the living room upon which the chess board sat (I believe she had the red pieces). And there was this grin in her eyes, followed by a suppressed giggle when out of the blue she checkmated me, having locked in my king with nowhere left to go. How had she done it? Like I just said, I had only just taught her the rules. It was like she never forgot anything, she never had to ask twice. Her concentration was impeccable while outwardly demonstrating a certain nonchalance. She gave no quarter. For her age, she really was something else."

As the years passed I'd begun to think I must have dreamed this, though I remember it well enough, in certain detail, but like you think you can recall a specific dream that rational thought will conclude over time that you've had to have embellished. But hearing Reuben describe it, so intimately here if you will, a kind surge swelled up inside of me, overwhelming me in a way. It was like a flashback, a still shot, photographically vivid. Suddenly I was in that room again, with its polished 1940s furnishing (there were Venetian blinds at the windows behind deep yellow curtains), the floor was covered by a rich green carpet my bony knees dug into, the sole light a warm glow from a tall, standing lamp to the side of him as he sat on the edge a plush armchair bent over the board (I'd had the white pieces; I remember I had insisted on having them) on that hassock between us, with a puzzled frown on his face as if he couldn't figure out on the board what I had done, like if I were teasing him or what. I would continue to play chess, once I got into high school that is and joined the chess club. The trouble was I beat everybody until nobody wanted to play with me.

"Whatever became of her, this little girl cousin?" Okay, here goes I told myself. "You certainly remember her well."

"She died in a car accident of some sort when

she was sixteen. Her name was Debbie, well, Deborah of course. But everyone called her Debbie."

"Some sort?"

"It's said she slumped over the steering wheel driving along a suburban street, and the car struck a utility pole, with no explanation as to why. And the impact supposedly ruptured this heart valve, the aorta."

"I'm sorry to hear that," I said, hesitantly (In a flash I could see Deborah in the doorway, in my clothes, her long hair pulled back in a pony-tail like I wore mine, my billfold and car keys in her hand, off to take my place in that class). "It sounds like you were deeply fond of her, even if she bested you at chess. Did you keep in touch with her after that visit?"

"For the first couple of years, after that sum-mer," he began thoughtfully, though it would soon evolve into as if he were retelling a story he'd probably told to himself many times over. And I would hang onto every word - however ex-hilarating, however torturous to bear too. "Her big sister Joy and I became pen pals, and Debbie would scrawl notes to me to be enclosed in Joy's letters, about how well she was doing in school, maybe she was in the second grade already, later the third grade: the brains in the family Joy would call her with a certain wistfulness. She'd also write that she 'loved' me, 'missed' me, and that I had better wait for her to grow up so we could marry. All of which Joy found quite amusing ('You are all she talks about,' Joy had written early on, 'driving the rest of us nuts.'); the whole family did actually, except her brother Nicholas who was seemingly jealous, spitefully so. (But then I'd never been close to my own brother.) I found myself a bit embarrassed by her ardent declarations, I mean I was ten years older than her, in my mid-teens (who was forever developing crushes on girls my own age, one even older), while at the same time I was earnestly heartened by her affection, that at once seemed so intense yet utterly genuine, without guile. I guess we essentially bonded during that initial visit, despite the age difference. I might add that despite my losing at chess to her, I read voluminously to her, at her insistence (stories in a batch of advanced children's books she'd brought with her that she could read very well herself), and answered her seemingly endless stream of questions about everything under the sun while talking to her more like I would to a grownup than to a kid, because she wanted answers in detail. Much of it had to do with her being in the countryside for the first time ever, which was like a whole new world opened up to her I came to realize. While the city girl in her could exhibit a surprisingly street smart sophistication to a still pretty much country hick like myself. I felt we really did communicate on a certain level that defied the age difference, not so much knowledge-wise obviously, but a with a mutual sensibility about things that defies definition. Like I said, she was something else. She was so much more than just a cousin. A twin sister somehow? I don't think I've met anyone since quite like her. Certainly no child like her. But then, subsequently, I could have been looking too hard for it and missed it right under my nose, as can happen when you look 'too hard' for something. Rebekah comes awfully close, I suppose, but then I am a different person now - or am I? Happily for me, Rebecca is a grownup." Then, he added, "You probably think I imagined it all, made a mountain out of a mole hill. I wonder myself at times."

I wanted to say, "You were looking for a kindred spirit, even if only that found was in a child more or less, much as that little girl was probably longing for the same in a grownup; or in another person, to be more specific: both of you bonded," but instead I asked: "How come for only a couple of years you kept in touch? If you don't mind me asking."

Because, I sensed, he wanted to tell it, and I didn't want to disrupt the flow by getting him bogged down in particulars, not yet (later perhaps). I wasn't really sure how much more I'd be able to bear hearing, not in one go, but I had asked for it. I sought to take it as dispassionately as I possibly could.

"Her father, Uncle Seth, would have a heart

attack that Christmas and the family's economy went downhill. He and my aunt hadn't much money to begin with since years before they had run through his small inheritance and he'd been working like two to three jobs, meanwhile my aunt's already poor health took a nose dive. Aunt Victoria was my mother's much younger sister. So they were unable to return the following summer as hoped. I'd wanted Debbie to come at least. But that was scrapped due to my father having just gotten out of the hospital. Aunt Victoria thought it would be too great a burden on my mother having Debbie visit. But the real reason had been my parents' ongoing acrimonious relationship she'd witnessed firsthand the summer before. I went with my mother to visit them that Thanksgiving, which was where I would meet my cousins Kathy and Kerry for the first time in years, the daughters of my mother's older brother, who would sort of captivate me to some extent, much, I felt, to Joy's chagrin, they being my age and quite pretty in the bargain, when Joy had felt that I had been her find, though she didn't mind sharing me with Debbie (yet there was a jealousy building up there as well, I would at times sense). Teenage rivalries, you know. While Debbie, in the midst of it all, seemed to distance herself at the same time, like ignoring all that was coming down around her as if it had nothing to do with her, seemingly cool and exceedingly confident in her own private sphere. Like the afternoon during that visit she walked into Joy's room to find us teenagers lolling on the bed doing the kissing cousins thing. Which was all very mind-blowingly new to me, who'd never before kissed or been kissed. But instead of being incensed at being left out, as I'd feared she'd be, she merely joined us in the pile and before I knew it she and I were lying face to face, her with a laughing pleased as punch grin. Well, Joy didn't write me off, not yet any way; we continued to correspond periodically, her letters full of the family's woes (and they were very real woes indeed), with an occasional note from Debbie, that might include a school photograph, about how well she was doing in her studies (school I think was her escape, where she could immerse herself in her studies vis à vis their tumult at home). Only that winter she'd come down ill with rheumatic fever that apparently lingered on for quite a while. But by summer, when I'd last have any length of time with her, she appeared fully recovered, though terribly thin as I remember (due to her having grown taller, I thought). It was the summer before I went off to college. I reluctantly applied for several summer jobs in DC where a high school friend now lived, and while waiting to hear I beat a retreat to the door of my uncle and aunt, at their invitation I might add, though my father opposed it (Aunt Victoria though took my part against my father when he demanded I return home and take a job on a bread truck: once she stood up for me - it was during that Thanksgiving visit - to her beloved big sister as well). I had my high school graduation gift money to help pay my way, but I'd thoughtlessly burdened them no less: not that they ever indicated such. Everybody was happy to have me at first, Debbie in particular. While she no longer insisted I carry her about piggyback, she was still full of questions, wanting answers, and liked for me to read to her. Nicholas resented it, I could quickly tell, as I continued to pay him scant interest, I'm afraid. And soon enough I was caught up again in the rivalry between Joy and those sister cousins, Kathy and Kerry (not only were they 'rich' and 'pretty' they 'stole' from her any boy she found just because they could do it, she'd accuse, including me). And before I knew it I was 'persona-non-grata'. I'd betrayed her. At the time I was angry, hurt, though much later I came to realize that I'd asked for it, that I had been insensitive to her situation. I am not certain how much Uncle Seth and Aunt Victoria were aware of all this, Aunt Victoria being sick in bed most of my stay, with Uncle Seth tending to her hand and foot (who continued to call me 'a gentleman and a scholar' in the way of a compliment). Debbie too seems to cool towards me in the end, I felt. Whether it was Joy, the hot weather or my charm had diminished with familiarity, I don't know. In any case I had too long over stayed my welcome. And once back home, I would head off to college in the fall as planned, getting caught up in all that sudden sea change of scenery, things happening, my falling in and out of love, finally my flunking out. I would hear no more from Joy. Uncle Seth would die within a year and Aunt Victoria two years later. Joy would marry, after putting Nicholas and Debbie up for fostering. At the time I was told that Nicholas and Debbie had been adopted out of state by a Christian minister (who I'd readily assumed to be the Bible Belt fundamentalist type) and his family, as neither my parents nor Kathy and Kerry's parents would take them in (though I would learn in time it was much more complicated than that). As for me keeping in touch somehow with Debbie, I was told by my mother that contact with her former family wasn't allowed (which was not quite true), that she was being well cared for and was happy in her new home (again not quite true), a 'good Christian home' (as Debbie had been 'left to run wild' during her mother's long illness). What with my being so inquisitive, maybe it was suspected I had some unnatural interest in Debbie, given our age difference and all. Meanwhile, I too was going through a tumultuous period, wearing my heart on my sleeve, felt hopelessly inept; it had been all I could do just to keep my head above water. In the back of my mind, I told myself that one day when Debbie'd 'grown up', was on her own, free of restriction, I'd find her again. Because in my heart I wanted to find her again. I wanted that connection with her again. There was no one in my family I'd ever felt so close to. Had always hoped to have some word about her, but there wasn't any. It was seven years later, after kibbutz, the war, New York City, when I was living in London, having founded a magazine there, I would get a rather pious, woebegone letter from my mother saying Debbie had been killed in a car accident on her way to school. I couldn't believe what I was reading at first. The words didn't sink in.

He stopped abruptly, though it was more like he reached a finish line out of breath. "I'm sorry, Deborah,' he exclaimed, shaking his head, attempting a smile that didn't quite make it. "I've gone on for far too much. I get carried away. The writer in me, I guess."

"No, Reuben, I'm intrigued. Really. But we are here now and we'd better hit the deck running, if you don't mind. I want to get a head start on that new trench."

As the two of us scrambled to reach the top, lugging equipment in hand and bumping shoulders almost in our ascent, Reuben gave me a glance that I caught out of the corner of my eye and turned my head in time to catch it, the two of us breaking into impish smiles, as if to say his making me privy to a buried pain I'd allowed him to unburden himself of, at least for the mo-

ment of his telling it, had henceforth created a
further intimacy of sorts. Suddenly I wanted to
hold him, press him to me, if he only knew the
half of it - anything beyond that I won't go into,
no I won't go there I assured myself. I was feeling
more than simply battered numb underneath. It
was like I was aching for some kind of closeness,
an all-embracing warmth. Inside I was the little
kid he'd felt so deeply with, as I with him still
to the depths of my being, I realized, as it was
at that time. From his recollection I really was,
just like I'd imagined I'd been. If it was true and
Debbie wasn't merely a figment of his fantasy.
I don't recall that bedroom scene in particular,
but I don't think he made it up, I know I was like
that - before that pesky kid was sold into bondage, to use a pertinent Biblical metaphor. Before
I had had to go underground and play the roles
assigned me on the surface. But my mother's
suffering in those last years, hearing her cries,
burns within me yet, I know, strikes a fear in me
as it did the time I had that bladder infection.
And the loss of my father, the kindest of men,
before that. As Deborah I have recaptured, resurrected much of that earlier me Reuben'd just so
acutely reminded me of originally possessing. It
was like being another allowed me to reclaim
so much of what was the original Debbie, had
sprung the lock to the trap door so to speak.

What I hope he didn't remember from that
last summer was my sleep walking nights, as I

often did then, into Joy's room - it had to have been that last time he stayed with us - and crawling into the bed where he lay, Joy having given up her room to him those weeks he had stayed with us. I have no idea what he thought upon awaking and finding me there because he never mentioned it to me, though I remember Joy apologizing to him, told him not to worry about it. I hope I didn't pee in the bed any of those times, I don't think I did. But the one instance I came close for certain to peeing on him was like one of those nightmares you awake from having for years afterwards. We were all happily packed to the old family Mercury one hot night at a drive-in movie, he with Nicholas and Joy in the backseat with me on his lap, well more like on his knees actually so I could look out over the front seat between my parents' heads to see the screen. When I had to pee badly, I must have twisted and squirmed forever until at the last moment I leaned over and whispered desperately into my mother's ear, who sharply ordered a grumbling Joy to go with me to the toilet. Later, on the way home, I'd fall asleep nestled up against his chest. I hadn't thought about that in years already, not since way back when. I had to have felt pleased as punch at the time anyway my having had "possession" of him so to speak, much as I'd felt on top of the world the afternoon two years before I'd sat on his shoulders while he carried me through the water on that road

- or another time (it had to have been during that last visit as well) when out sightseeing, he'd laughingly carried me in his arms up this steep flight of stairs (while Nicholas had carped and Joy had mercilessly teased him) after I'd balked at walking up them myself. What a calculating pest I had been, deep down. (And still was, considering how I was now "playing him".) The wonders of nature, our animal-in-the-wild instincts at whatever age emerging as they do with the occasion.

"So the last time you would see Debbie then was that summer before you went to college, when you and her sister more or less fell out?"

Though it was necessary to capture it in its preliminary stages, I meant to work around and in the midst of the excavation in progress on that aforementioned "new trench" (working in the way was more like it), which for those involved is essentially an exploration process (that could be compared to looking for a new vein of ore). Basically the volunteers were sympathetic towards what I had to do, even if Aharon the supervisor was himself having a bad hair day, a couple of times coming close to shouting at us - at me for Reuben having caused a minor obstruction while manipulating those reflector shields at my pleasure (in Aharon's version of it), until I told him, in English to take a powder for his toothache or whatever it was bugging him,

The volunteers about began to laugh at the way I said it, and he, Aharon, broke down and laughed as well. So by the time Reuben and I were done, and we'd found an isolated spot on the far end of the new baulk in the making in order to catch our breaths (and drink a copious amount of water, only to feel it immediately gush from our pores in sweat), everybody, including us, was vastly relieved. Reuben had been a little concerned that he'd precipitated bad feelings between Aharon and me, but I had laughed and told him to forget it. Tempers would flare here among us occasionally, considering our working conditions, the fucking heat, our oversized egos - just as long as we didn't take it home with us so to speak.

"Yes, well, no actually,' he stumbled a bit to find the words to answer my question. "It was at my aunt's funeral. Where I last saw her, but from a distance. I was still chafed by what I felt was Joy's betrayal, who I felt wouldn't have wanted me to come closer. My mother was there, not in the best of conditions, along with family members, who I saw were all given short shrift by Joy, who I figured remained embittered towards us all. And I had come on my own, from a nearby city, so I sort of hung back fearing rejection - by even Debbie by that time. Which I would come to deeply regret, in light of what would shortly become of her. But the Debbie I saw that day was almost unrecognizable. She'd grown so much taller for one thing. After all, two years had passed. I had this sickening feeling that she probably would no longer remember what it had been like with us, quite apart from my fear that Joy had long turned her against me (that and the inexcusable fact that I had never tried to keep in contact in the interim).

"Besides having grown taller," I couldn't help but ask. "How had she changed? Well, physically at least?"

"She looked like a 'wild child' wanting to break free of her restraints, which were in the form of these two stout, matronly women dressed in black, one on each side of her holding her by her arms as she tugged against their grip. She looked really out of it, like as if she wasn't connecting with what was happening. Like she wanted out of there, to break free and just run, never stop - like she had become a feral animal. I expect she was inwardly snarling. This was a completely unexpected Debbie, yet an understandable one. Her hair, but for the bangs on her forehead, and even they were now falling into her eyes, was longer than I remembered it, was pulled back in a loose pony tail, with strands having broken free to fall loose over her ears. Being already ridiculously ashamed, and suddenly being afraid of being rejected as well, I was simply too chickenshit period to approach her. Then, when she died, when it hit me that I would never have the chance of finding her, of seeing her again, I doubly regretted that I hadn't gone up to her that day to let her know that I cared, that I had not forgotten her (like she must have thought I had), that I would not ever forget her, as if that would have helped matters much, practically speaking, and without saying it outright in front of those two women what she meant to me, would always mean to me. (And this was before I would learn she'd been adopted or fostered rather by this minister and his family. Before I feared she may have been lost to me forever, would have been indoctrinated into their church, brainwashed or whatever. I had so little trust in her innate resolve, I guess, in the Debbie I knew.) I should have put aside my stupid pride and gone up to Joy too. Even if she might have out and out spurned me, remembering her previous viral bitterness. Because we had been friends. Anyway, putting my own ego aside, my selfishness as it were, I thought her death at such an early age was downright unfair, like why her, why not me instead, as she was the best, the smartest of all us cousins. I believe she would have gone far once out into the world at large, that it was a tragedy. I was angry too, at what my mother wrote (or the way she wrote), that in so many words 'poor little orphaned Debbie has gone to a better place', that it was 'for the best' and 'God's plan', 'God knows best' and all that claptrap, besides how 'pretty she looked' in the fucking coffin. Between my sobbing and wanting to throw up I started to laugh uncontrollably. Before I slammed my fist into my desk top. I was in London still, editor of that new Jewish arts magazine. It was a bright summer morning, I remember and I was sitting my desk in my room as I slit open the envelope, wondering who's dead, sick or married now, the long-accustomed order of my mother's epistles that she never deviated from. And you know what struck apart from that she had died. That she had been old enough to drive, my little Debbie."

I had somehow totally forgotten that day of the funeral, had long blacked it out of my memory, probably from the outset - until his description brought it back to me, if but in spades. I almost wanted to hate him for it, knowing I wouldn't, couldn't actually. I had felt so deserted, by one and all, felt I was suffocating, a trapped rat flinging myself like against the bars of my cage. Why the fuck hadn't he, of all people, come to me, rescued me, ridden me off on his white horse, or something, like in the fucking fairy tales I guess. I must have felt that, though had never formed it into any coherent thought, much less words. I wanted to grab him now, shake him, how can he tell me this shit as if he wanted absolution, my sympathy. Only he didn't know it was me he was confessing this to - which I had admittedly churned out of him much like some interrogator not above using torture in the form of striking an exposed nerve to get the results something perhaps dark in me craved (and from him especially). When I know now that he obviously still loved me - or his memory of me as a child. "Bloody hell" - as that English boy, Daniel, working that morning in that new trench with the Danish Jonna liked to exclaim - where was I going with this?

"Don't beat yourself up so, Reuben, as obviously you still do. Debbie wouldn't have wanted you to. When she grew older she probably understood, more than you realize. Having been there herself by then. You were at a tender age, remember, what were you, twenty? Where were the grownups in the family, aunts and uncles, for Joy too? And her brother. What happened to him?"

"I was told that everyone was quite self-satisfactorily pleased with the arrangement, seeing that she would be incarcerated, in my opinion, in a 'God fearing home' and not running wild in the streets like she'd been allowed to do, I'd been told, during her mother's protracted, final illness. Nicholas too was fostered, but later, much later, I'd heard he'd run away, he being almost of legal age by then, to live on his own. I would eventually discover that things were not quite like this, at the outset, not by a long shot in Debbie's case. But that would be nearly fifteen years later. When I went searching for myself. Once I myself had acquired a more stable life. Had already written my first novel. Felt secure in my own voice, the voice I'd created in order to tell the story, any story."

"You make it sound that after the lull of so much water under the bridge, you had an epiphany. But I'm sure it was more complicated than that. So what did happen?"

"I had this dream'" he said, looking quickly away from me as he spoke, as if uncertain how to proceed (or if he should, and perhaps risk sounding foolish). Only to suddenly look distracted, as he continued to gaze off into the far distance, with a puzzling frown forming with the squinting of his eyes against the sun.

"What the hell is that coming this way," he said. "That swirling-about rising cloud of dust over there?" As I turned to see what he was talking about.

"Shit!" I exclaimed.

Jumping to my feet, with my right hand planted on my hip as I pointed with my left, I cried out in what must have sounded akin to Brando's Anthony barking "lend me your ears!" in the movie *Julius Caesar*, for the benefit of those clustered far and near. "STEFAN! STEFAN! DUST DEVIL! OVER THERE! A TSUNAMI OF ONE! LISTEN EVERYBODY, SECURE WHAT YOU ARE WORKING WITH. AND GET OVER TO THE CLOSEST WALL, COVER YOUR HEADS WITH WHATEVER YOU CAN. AND PROTECT YOUR EYES.

WE'VE GOT BUT SECONDS BEFORE THE TARPS COULD RISE UP BEFORE COME TUMBLING DOWN ON TOP OF US, POLES AND ALL!"

I felt the air change - a searing at my back - as I leaped back down in the trench, ordering Reuben as I did so to collect the ladder and reflector shields while I hurriedly began to shove my cameras into that old leather case of mine, before bending to give him a hand, "Up close to the wall everything!" I reiterated. He quickly did what I asked, without question, for which I was thankful, as there was literally no time for explanation. In every direction I glanced, I saw the volunteers and supervisors bend double as they rushed about, the air thickening with dust already, the overlaying ends of the tarps wildly flapping to the rising tune of something akin to a whistling roar descending from overhead.

"Get down, you idiot!" I yelled to Reuben, he having straightened up to see what was happening, holding his hands out to shield his eyes, with grits of sand already biting into his skin, the brim of his hat having flattened against its crown - as I yanked hard on his arm to pull him down, with him falling on top of me in the general confusion the very moment the full blast of wind struck and the world around went suddenly haywire. It was not unlike an artillery shell having exploded in the air directly above us.

Within seconds the world went black, the

tarpaulin with its poles had collapsed on top of us, or across the top of the trench that is. (At least we hadn't been run through by a pole plummeting downwards into the trench, - even if they were but aluminum poles, yet poles nevertheless turned into projectiles - and as I hadn't heard any sudden screams, only some yells and none too few expletives out of the near distance, I was hopefully assuming that went for the rest of the crew as well.) I continued to lie there, just as we'd fallen, with Reuben straddling me, our bodies seeming glued together with a mutual profusion of sweat oozing through our grimy wet clothes. Cheek to cheek, a warm hand covered the other half of my face pressing it close as if to protect me from any falling debris in the confusion, while my arms around his back held him tight to me. It was almost like I had forgotten how good it felt to have a man's body against mine - and of all the men in the world, his body. I ached to wrap my legs around him right that moment, clutching him to me, never letting go ("shocking" to some extent even my less than modest inner nature, considering who he was). But the weight of his body wedged me down - and there was this loose piece of rock jabbing at my back. I brought my hand up to his face, touching it.

"I'm sorry I called you an idiot," I whispered. "You okay?"

"I've been called worse," he chuckled.

"Otherwise, I think so. And you? Okay, I mean. I must have fallen on you like a ton of bricks."

"Yeah, I'll live. But let me try to crawl out, if you will. We've got to get out from under all this. Once I've found my camera case."

"I stashed it against the wall, just beyond our feet I think."

He moved to the side until I was freed enough to be able to sit upright and clutch my knees before crawling on all fours to the wall, feeling my way as I moved forward - We were in total darkness.

"Jonna! Danny!" I called out to the two volunteers whom I'd last caught sight of near the far end of the trench, rushing about with Aharon to hold things down. :Is everybody there? You too, Aharon?"

"Beseder, tov!" mumbled Aharon in Hebrew, then in English. "We good. I see some daylight, will crawl out to it. Can you there?"

"No light I can yet see," I said, just as my hand clutched my cameras' leather case and I heaved a sigh of relief. "But the edge of the tarp was but a few feet away before everything fell. Reuben and I will follow one of the poles until we come to the end. Danny, Jonna, you two stay put for now. You could break an arm or leg if you try to move about in the dark where you are. Aharon is a soldier, he has training. I have been through a couple of these mishaps before. With enough of us on the outside, we will raise the poles again, just as we do mornings."

As long as I believed I had confidence I could act on it, hoping that it would hold until we got underway, well, clawed our way out would be more like it. I'd done it once before. It was not that we couldn't hold out where we were, though breathing eventually could be less than desired. I did not want to make a rent in the tarp unless there was no other choice, I imagined Aharon hadn't either. Reuben had by now sat up as well. Some in similar situations sink inwardly into a quiet panic, others simply hyperventilate. Then there are those, once they have got their wits about them, who are ready to act, thinking fast about what they can do to extricate themselves (and others, if there are others with them). I was seriously counting on Reuben to be among the latter.

"Ready to move?" I asked. It was more like in a whisper. I just hope he would sense the steely determination imbued in it and take heart, if need be. I was most likely going to need his help.

"Lead the way. Unless you want me to go first?"

"I'll go. If I can get myself up and over under the tarp, can find where I can raise it enough for us to crawl and find that pole that will lead us out to the edge. Should I need a boost once I've got one leg over, don't be squeamish about giving my butt a hard shove. I am going to stand up and feel for the top of the trench then go for it.

You hang on close behind me. It's going to be a squeeze, but we'll make it. So, here goes."

It had been a year since I'd last hoisted myself up and over the gunnel of my boat on its cradle in the winter slip, but I got my leg over none the less - yet I had a feeling I was sliding back as I dug my fingers into the hard dirt for traction, though most likely I wasn't. Nevertheless I cried out, "Reuben, give my ass a hard push, like now!" Which he did, with one hand under my thigh to shove as the other under my knee lifted - and I was up and over, with both knees firmly on a hard-packed flat surface so as to raise my torso and the tarp weighing down tight against my back.

"Your cameras, they are at my feet. If you stick out your hand, I'll put the case strap into it for you to grip." Which he did.

"Thank you," I offered, stashing it behind me. "You now. I can pull you if need be. But meanwhile, I want to keep as much of the tarp as I can high enough for you to lift yourself over." It took him two tries, but he made it, joining me in the hot dust. I could feel the tarp getting hotter to my back. That is when I remembered the air following in the wake of that previous dust devil rising as much as ten degrees. Another reason to get the tarps back up and those trapped under them into at least fresh air whatever the temperature.

"I've got my right hand on a pole, feel for it

and you'll find it too. We'll crawl along it, it can't be more than five or six feet to the end if you remember."

As we emerged into the glaring sunlight and what felt like a furnace blast of heat, giving our eyes some moments to adjust, I quickly surveyed the damage, as we leaned against one another for support once we'd gotten to our feet. All of the tarpaulins, with their poles, lay supine across the excavation areas. But none had blown away, that is off the Tel. Those under them were calling out, complaining about the heat, saying that breathing was becoming unpleasant to downright difficult. Aharon I saw had extracted himself quickly enough, as I figured he'd do. At the opposite end of our excavation area, Stefan was beginning to organize the lifting of the tarpaulins over that section. And he had obviously made a call to Neve Rom for help. Five or six men I recognized from the kibbutz were coming onto the top of the Tel from the direction of the car park below.

I quickly reached down into my camera bag, reacting on pure instinct, and pulled out the digital and the M3. "Reuben," I almost commanded as I straightened up, "Steady me, if you can manage, I need to get some shots for the report." Which he did, hands firmly on my hips. Whatever pleasure I might have otherwise derived from his touching me as he did, I hadn't time to think about as I fired off one frame after another, holding one or the other camera by its strap as I did - first with the digital (I was glad I had left its sunshield on, even if the light bearing down now was almost directly overhead), then with the manual M3 for more in depth coverage by my manipulating the settings, trusting those Leica lenses to compensate under the circumstances that so often in the past had saved the day.

"Ready to help out?" I asked, turning my head towards Reuben as I spoke. I knew I had to look a comic fright. My unruly hair feeling gluey and knotted no doubt looked it were I to free it from the muslin cloth still wrapped around my head, with falling strands of hair plastered to my grime-smeared cheeks and forehead (it was as if climbing over that top, with what felt like a pair of strong hands almost into my crotch giving me a final shove, I'd literally kissed the dirt, if not quite having swallowed a peck of it in the bargain). My sweat-drenched darkly stained tee shirt had to be a total see-through already. (I didn't much care about that, I was wearing a halter bra for what it was worth, the little I actually needed one.) My trousers had been already filthy. And as if my feet weren't hot enough, dirt had gotten into my brogans - I could feel it roughly gone squishy between my wet toes. Reuben had had his desert hat pushed back to where it hung from him by its neck strap. While rivulets of water, running down out of his curly tufts, had left streaks in the coat of dust on his face down into his beard. But his eyes locking into mine, their soft blues more than ever exhibiting an intense curiosity, silently drew me into them - as if to say we'd just had some kind of existential moment, hadn't we, however solitary it may have been to the other at the time - but that we'd had it nevertheless whether we chose to acknowledge it or not. Despite what his eyes told me, was he actually aware of it, as much as I was fighting against recognizing it in myself. It was as if he knew it was me, without knowing me, when I knew all along I was falling in love with him even as I was wanting him to fall in love with the me that was Deborah who deep down had known it was the Debbie in me that turned him on.

"Ready,'" he smiled at me so knowingly, putting his arm ever so briefly round my shoulder, giving it the slightest of squeezes. "But afterwards maybe you can tell me what the hell just happened. A 'dust devil'?"

"And you, that dream you had."

The damage to the site overall was minimal, considering - and most importantly, there had been no serious injuries, just a bruise or two (I had thought for certain I'd have had one considering Reuben's feeling in the dark with that abrupt grip upon my inner thigh when giving me that shove up), besides the overall general discomfort and confusion experienced upon having, so to speak, the sky to fall and the lights go out. And consequently the sudden rise in the temperature when it had already been at the broiling point. But in no time flat we had the tarpaulins "resurrected", much thanks to that extra help coming from Neve Rom - to at least shield us from the direct blaze of the sun.

We were a weary crew calling it a day once we'd secured the site, en total, leaving it prepared to be picked up from where we left off come bright and early tomorrow morning. A battle-weary bunch of disheveled stragglers is how the lot of us must have looked as we at last trudged down to our vehicles for the ride back to the kibbutz - for some lunch, showers and a well-deserved rest, before the washing of the artifacts and afternoon tea.

The parking lot at the foot of the Tel looked swept by a sudden sandstorm, but Rubble being no worse for wear on account of it, just covered by a fine layer of yellowish dust. I yanked open the rear door, dodging a spill. I didn't have a broom, a couple long pieces of thick cloth would do. I tossed one of them to Reuben.

"You take the passenger side windows," I laughed at the perplexed frown on his face. "We'll whack it off." Giving the rear door a whack, sending dust flying, upon closing it.

"You'll have to admit that your old Rubble,

sorry, vintage Rubble, does look now like the quintessential Land Rover in whatever movie, having just lumbered across the Sahara, if not the Sinai. Straight from the central casting garage."

"And if we don't clear these windows of this dust, like yesterday, we risk melting into pools of butter, or whatever one melted into some ridiculous nursery rhyme."

Myself, I had developing to do first and foremost. But I had too to figure out (get a grip on) what the hell I was doing in this evolving relationship with Reuben, the long-ago cousin I had idolized as a child who had no inkling that my Deborah Rosenfeld was actually her. He who had descended upon me two days before like out of a void - a genie's magic lamp it may as well have been, for all the bizarre reality of its possibly happening - in the guise of this old friend of Stefan's. (That's about as objectively as I can put it.) I indeed felt I was now on that "slippery slope" I'd warned myself against, what with my resurgence of feelings for him intertwined now with a fast- growing physical attraction (that had always been there lurking just below the surface, hidden as they say in plain sight). Which I suspect was mutual however separate the direction it may be coming from. (I mean, I suspect he has yet to acknowledge it to himself.) I knew I risked opening this Pandora's box what with my getting him to talk, by subterfuge, about the

Debbie he had known (as well as what he had subsequently may have learned about me in the wake of "her death"). Curiosity seemed about to kill the cat. Because as Deborah I didn't really need to know this. I'm doing just fine with what I already know I am, I told myself. Which was already a surplus of enough.

With what prints I had from the morning's shoot both stacked as well as hanging up to dry, and me in my ankle-swishing India cotton skirt, my favorite for this sticky, thick weather, as it leaves me free to unconsciously stride, and an off-white top, I strolled from under the arcade that fronted my room; my dampish hair not long out of the shower and shaken free felt tons lighter bereft now of that gluey sweat, as did the rest of me - physically at least. I had tentatively resolved to give my curiosity, along with whatever else I was feeling, a slight reprieve in order to take stock of the situation once removed. A resolution that lasted no longer than the time it took me to reach the circular path. When I saw him approaching through the trees. In that kind of slow motion gait of his that belied his adroit swiftness in action. Because there was a certain reticence about it that portrayed an innate charm he was totally unaware of. I saw that he too had washed up and had donned a new set of clothes: a pair of pale blue jeans and one of those Sunny Surplus shirts 60s activists wore like a uniform of sorts proclaiming their militancy in umpteen b&w photographs of Civil Rights and Anti Vietnam War demonstrations. Of which he was a veteran, from what I have so far read into *(K)hamsin*. I hadn't seen him since we'd returned in Rubble earlier from the Tel; I'd immediately gone to lunch, wolfing down falafel in pita - plied heavily with tahini that ran deliciously down my chin with each bite I took - before making a beeline for the studio.

It was as he came closer it struck me, as it never failed to do, that I was now the taller of the two of us, when once he'd seemed a giant to me and I had sat giddily (and giggling) upon his shoulders. A sort of bashful grin appeared to go before him before turning into a smile. But always like something he found humorous only he was privy too, unconsciously so, I'd begun to suspect and had chosen not to pay it any mind. Who knows what he saw in my face, my entire stance, as I stood there resolutely at ease, my head cocked slightly to one side. I never took my eyes off of his for one second - and neither did he off mine.

"You look lovely, Ms. Rosenfeld. If I may risk saying so. But you always do. Even at your sweat-streaked, grimiest best. And never more so than when this morning you leaped atop that baulk and took command. You were amazing."

"I simply did what had to be done. There was no time to think."

"And a good thing you did. Otherwise, quite a few of us most likely had ended up with a serious injury. Myself included, especially if you hadn't pulled me down when you did. Now you were going to explain what a dust devil is. But before that, the reason I came over was to ask about this river I'm told runs through the kibbutz somewhere. I tried to find Stefan but he's in a powwow with the nobs, the maskurut."

"Yes, there is a stream rather, fed by underground springs, that they call a creek here - though hardly a creek by your standards," I replied sort of offhandedly, before I'd grasped the opportunity it offered. "In past summers I've enjoyed going there and sitting beside it, in the little park that borders it on both sides. But I've yet to even check it out so far this year. Fancy a walk with me? It's a little ways from here, on the far side of Neva Rom, beyond the original part of the residential section."

Reuben gave me a slight bow, as if to say I am at your command, while with a motion of his arm gallantly indicated for me to lead the way. All the while smiling as if unto himself as if to hold back his wanting to smile directly at me - or into my eyes rather.

"A Dust Devil?" I began to speak as we strolled. "The night cools the air on the top of the eastern mountains, which then rolls down the slopes and out to sea in a westerly direction. During the day this air heats up and rises, and by midafternoon there is a strong breeze towards the east, as the hot air is sucked back up and into the mountains. Every day this goes back and forth. Dust Devils, I don't know where the term comes from, form when a pocket of hot air near the surface rises quickly through the cooler air above it, forming an updraft. Well, that's how it starts. It ends up in a vortex, as a spinning chimney-like funnel, through which more hot air rushes, and, eventually, with the friction wrought, a forward momentum is produced. And if I say one more word, you'll realize how much hot air I am expelling. Let's just say it is something like that."

We were both laughing by now, enjoying a moment of the ridiculous.

"Yeah, it sounds pretty anemic in theory, compared to the real thing on the ground," he chuckled.

"I will just add that it likes hot flat surfaces under a clear sky to refuel itself. And the area surrounding Tel Ronish, as well as the Tel itself, under today's sky, was perfect in this respect."

"Kind of like a mini tornado," Reuben's voice took a serious note now, "But it was that cloud of dust it kicked up and carried with it that appears to be what caused the most damage. Reminds me of a micro burst at sea when this sudden wind - I can't remember what conditions creates it - picks up the water off the tops of the waves - thus producing a driving rain effect. It can swamp a sail boat, even with just one sail up and reefed at that. Like what happened to *Pride of Baltimore*. It was the weight of all that dust in the air that essentially flattened the tarpaulins like it did. But you'd experienced one before, didn't I hear you say?"

Yes, I know I was going to give Debbie a rest. But he had been on the threshold of telling what he knew of Debbie's life during those "lost years", as I sometimes look at them. Besides what he knew, or had though he'd found out, I was curious as to how he found out, who had been the oracle of this information (or had it been misinformation deliberately put out by "the informer". Because I couldn't imagine anyone, other than say Deborah herself, who'd had no way of telling anything to anyone, who could have even begun to "know" me at that time). Did I dare then let myself in for a shock, though most likely it would be a disappointment?

"It was on smaller scale, nothing quite like what occurred this morning on Tel Ronish. Which reminds me, just before it struck, you mentioned something about having a dream. You'd only just finished telling of your reaction to Debbie's death, and saying that the anguish you hadn't been able to shake would eventually lead you to search out for yourself what really had happened to her during those intervening years. Unless, of course, you feel you've talked enough about her for one day. Or forever perhaps."

He turned and looked me. I saw in that soft blue of his eyes now a burning something that brimming tears, had there been any, could not have extinguished. Could he see in mine - behind their glittering green I am told they can give off - my sudden fear, well, a sudden uncertainty rather? That, if I let my imagination run wild right that moment, would surely give me away.

"I dreamed of her writing me a letter. Or, to be more precise, I had this dream in which she was writing me a letter. In the dream. A long, intricate letter. That she was reading aloud as she was writing it. It was like a voice over out of a movie. And it was the voice of a thoughtful young woman, I might add, not a child's voice, that I would remember. Don't laugh, or think I am looney." It was as if he were asking, while simultaneously breaking into a narrative I sensed he'd a long time wanted to tell. To a sympathetic yet detached party. "She was saying that she wasn't dead. And although a long time had passed, she thought of me always. And that she missed me. She had sent letters to me care of my mother. And wondered why I had never answered them, if I had even gotten them? As she had been told that I was out of the country. All the while she was speaking I was trying to read what she was writing. It was again like out of a movie scene, where you see the handwriting, but not quite the words close up to read them for yourself, all the while the voiceover is continuing. And though it seemed to be going on and on, the visual was becoming blearier, like the paper it was being written on had grown 'thinner', the voice simultaneously beginning to fade, like the battery in a radio running down. By that time I'd grown desperate to hear, to see. I was losing her. It was disappearing, like gossamer. Until it all suddenly just evaporated. And I awoke to find myself sitting up in the bed in a sweat. It was in the dark of night, about 3am I think the clock hands said. Fitzgerald's 'very dark night of the soul' hour. It was so vivid still, and I was trying to hold on to it, to remember everything I'd heard, in particular that from the fade out. It hadn't really happened, I told myself, though it seemed like it had. It had been a dream, had not been real. In the morning when I woke up, my recollection of it had grown all the dimmer, had receded much as had the final lines during the dream itself. Like the harder I had tried to see them, or hear her voice, the more both disappeared from me. Leaving me shaken, baffled, and ultimately curious."

I had to resist the impulse to reach and take his hand in mine. Why to, by subterfuge, communicate to him that Debbie hadn't died, if only unto myself - as I could never tell him that it had been Deborah in my stead? As if I might via physical touch communicate it through subconscious vibes or something? Though that letter had come from some something deep within him, that ostensibly may have had nothing to do with any memory of me, but had nevertheless ridden piggyback on whatever. Before I became Deborah I indeed had thought of him, not often but with a longing, a tug at the heartstrings when I had. He'd probably forgotten all about that little girl he called "Gigi", having grown up and gone out into the world, as I learned from Kerry he had done (where in the odd daydream I might wish I could have gone, if not with him, then likewise on my own - as I would inevitably do, if in the guise of a new persona I have fashioned out of the proverbial clay as I went along). Okay, if I were to believe in telepathy, so to speak, then, yes, that letter in his dream had been a long-delayed post having turned up at long last.

"I hadn't thought much about her in some years before this dream, really thought of her," he continued, as if having had to catch his breath. "Not after the initial period following her death, when I would at unexpected moments be gripped by this grief and sort of lash out in sobs. I'd filed it all away, in some deep recess of my mind, as I got on with my physical survival, my spiritual odyssey as it were, attempting to pull myself back up out of a void of my own making. And, at long last start writing my novels - once I'd found my voice to do so. She'd become a blurred image, growing fainter the harder I tried to keep a picture of her in my mind, of the child I had known, had loved, really loved. Whose own 'love' had meant so much at that time in my life. While earlier I had been able to recall her well enough. It was like I had drawn a curtain, if but a diaphanous one it seems. When I did think of her, I merely felt myself foolish to do so."

"Could it have been telepathy, a radio wave?" His tone changed again, becoming sharper with self-reflection. "Or a voice from the dead - or the beyond like in that seance stuff? It was something you cannot intellectually rationalize. No, I'm not a believer in the mystical, except perhaps as a poetic hypothesis. Certainly not in the occult. It's all a figment of man's imagination. Maybe I dreamed she was writing to me out of some buried memory, who knows. That suddenly burst. Am I really like Heathcliff? You know, like his seeing and hearing Cathy, his other half, outside that window begging to be let in? Only it was Cathy who really was Heathcliff - or more Heathcliff than Heathcliff. Or maybe Emily herself was? Dealing with her own demons as she wrote."

"During that dream, Debbie never actually said it was her. At least I don't think she did. I just knew it was her. It'd all sounded so, it had all seemed so, natural. I guess I just made it up inside of me. Yet long after that dream, when all the rational thought in my being told me it had been just that, a dream, I could still have moments when I'd suspect it might not have been a dream after all. That maybe it hadn't been Debbie who had died in that automobile accident. That she still lived out there, somewhere. Crazy as it all sounds. That dream really did rattle me at the time, coming as it had out of the blue."

We'd walked a good ways already in the direction of that "river", at a steady amble, as Reuben continued to ruminate upon his dream, almost as if he were alone and talking out loud to himself. As I simultaneously absorbed his words like a sponge - as if literally through the pores of my skin, the very sinews of my body, to hold for later reflection, being unable to respond for fear of sounding like I was trying to speak while under water. That he was laying a heavy trip on me he had no way of knowing, just as I had no way of telling him. Instead, I really wanted to simply yell, "Shut up, you moron, here I am a flesh and blood woman, walking close beside you - and who tunnel-crawled through dirt and sweat together with you a few hours earlier - whom you can't see for this hang-up you have on some long dead child." All the while just wanting him to get on with it, get it off his chest - that I understood he had to do before he reached the part where he began that "search" for her he'd spoken of. And, of course, what he'd ultimately found (and from whom). Which had been my rather devious plan from the outset, hadn't it. So,

I'd best shut up, perhaps have mercy for him if anything. Only I was fucking falling in love with him - or something - right in plain sight, and couldn't bloody well help myself, as I saw it.

"I'd always told myself that one day, when she had grown up, I'd find her again. When there would be no prohibition, as I had been originally told, against her being able to be in touch with members of her family. When she'd be of legal age to choose for herself Although I'd find out that she had been in touch with certain family members all along - her sister, Joy, and Kerry, a mutual cousin.

"Some time back, I saw an old B&W movie called *Love Letters* from the 1940s and set in England following WW2. While still in the army, Joseph Cotton wrote a series of letters for a fellow soldier, a cavalier sort of guy, to send to his girl, Victoria, back home. Cotton, or his character rather, put his own heartfelt feelings into the writing of them as they had become a subterfuge for some girl he wished he, himself, had, in order to write to with deep, heartfelt emotions. Later, after the war, in England, Cotton's character will inevitably meet, by chance, this Victoria (played by Jennifer Jones) who had fallen in love with the writer of those letters (whom she'd tragically learned wasn't the boyfriend). Being a romantic love story of the period it all sorted itself out in the end. But Victoria's recognizing a kindred spirit in the writer of those letters, as had he with the person who had replied to them in hers to that boyfriend, had for some reason reminded me of that dream of Debbie writing to me all this years ago.

"It was not long after that dream I dared to ask my mother, during a visit, and she swore Debbie had never written to me care of her. I searched through the desk in the living room anyway, where all sorts of family stuff always got stuffed and came across this enlarged black and white photo of a beautiful, long-dark-haired girl in what appeared to have been a high school graduation photograph, accompanying this minister's rather pious self-serving eulogy for a 'Debbie'. And yes, it was Debbie, my mother affirmed it. The photograph, and a copy of his memorial sermon, Rev. Marston, Debbie's guardian, had sent to all the family members. I was amazed that this could have been Debbie, one so poised, so serenely 'beatific' as was this young woman actually in that photograph. It hardly jelled with that minister's description of a tormented searching-for-faith teenager, so at odds with herself. Whom he'd had such a struggle with.

"And it was this what belatedly inspired me to search for what had actually become of Debbie, to find out who really was the young woman in that photograph. In relation to the beloved little cousin I had known."

By this time we'd reached that "river" and were sitting together on a rough-hewn bench nestled beneath one of those spindly trees full of entangled branches that thickly lined both banks of what amounted to a torpid, moving brook of crystal clear water. Although, the nearest kibbutz housing was but a whistle away, we may as well have been secluded in a nature park - which it was - a mini park that is, a certain rarity in these parts at least.

"The spring that feeds it is just upstream a ways. That water is ice cold, by the way, in case you have thought of sticking your toes in."

"Coming back from Tel Ronish this morning, it would have been more than tempting." He laughed."

"You could write a story about Debbie," I offered, "present her as a fictional character - starting with that dream, then going backwards and forward, fill in all you personally know interchangeably with whatever it was that your search turned up. Because it sounds so much like you really want to, what with all the passion you obviously feel about it. I get the impression that it is screaming inside of you to be told. Don't just scatter it on the wind, Reuben."

"You are probably right. I would just have to find my voice, like I was saying to Sushila last evening at the dinner table in regards to my first novel - and everything I have written since. I guess I dumped a load on you, didn't I? A bad habit of mine, I know."

"Don't apologize, I'd asked you to. I know what it is myself to suddenly open pandora's box. Can't shut myself up. I hope whatever it was you were able to discover about Debbie brought you some closure. Oops, sorry, that's a dumb word."

"I think I know what you meant. No, it only filled my imagination, well, with more things to imagine, about her, like who she really was, or had been rather, behind what everybody was telling me about her. I guess that is where the real story is, seeking her out that somehow lies buried now beneath the contradictory stories of others about her."

"You are making me curious, Reuben," I laughed. "You know you shouldn't do that."

"I don't mind talking about it, Deborah, especially with you. I get the feeling that you really listen. But, you are right, I need to get a focus on it, instead of just gushing it all out, like I've just done. When I do though, you'll be in for it."

The dappled light seemed to be playing tricks on my eyes, the silently moving water before us. It was like unto the unreeling of a film on a movie projector. I thought I might be experiencing a sort of claustrophobia that had crept up on me unawares. I bent towards him and gave him a brush of a kiss on his temple, as I took his nearest hand in mine and leaped to my feet. Before he could register a surprise.

"Come on," I said. "It's about afternoon tea time, Aruchat Arba, and I am famished. What about you?"

"After this morning I think I'll never be able to drink enough liquid again."

4

I slipped away early from that afternoon tea gathering and did my "disappearing act" that I knew no one would much notice, they all knowing my idiosyncratic habits, except perhaps for a "puzzled" Reuben who I left sandwiched between Sushila and Jonna, whom by now I felt he was relatively "safe" from. That is I retreated to my room, foregoing dinner only to emerge for a late evening walk, briefly stopping by Aharon's room in reply to a note he'd left on my door earlier: he and Stefan had scurried up some plastic pipes to replace the few aluminum ones that had been bent out of whack by the dust devil and had tied then to "Rubble's" roof rack in the meantime, for taking out to the Tel in the morning. I vaguely remember walking between the trees and shrubbery along the pathways, bathed intermittently by a flood of lamp shine, simply enjoying the solitude it offered. Had I hoped I might accidentally run into Reuben also seeking aloneness with his thoughts, whatever they could be after laying himself so open as he had to me that afternoon, in the morning too, before that dust devil had intervened to throw us so physically together as it undeniably had done - and changed our courses - I was still not sure how or where it would lead us should we together hold to it. I knew I was being driven by this inner dynamic where the emotional brake linings had worn dangerously thin. It was one of those once-in-a-lifetime opportunities (to see yourself in the eyes of others as if through the eyes of another who was indeed oneself no less) yet a gift, as it were, so obviously beset with its own trojan horse. I craved for answers to what I didn't need to know, that might burn me badly - and equally burn him by my putting him in the role of being the purveyor of those revelations: in that it was bringing us together in such a way that there was nowhere to go (a knowledge that I alone was privy to, I could absolutely not share with him ever, that I had to bear alone). So not only was I beating around the bush with myself, I was feeling my way through the dark as if by my fingertips. I should back off, cut any tie with him however much skin would be torn off by a hardening glue - for both our sakes. If it wasn't already too fucking late. "Deborah!" I wanted to scream aloud into that black emptiness of the night enclosing me. (I knew it was no use appealing to the Debbie in me who was in this case I suspected the willful catalyst.)

All the while I had been inducing him to talk about Debbie, it seemed amiss that I had not asked him about his immediate family, when I had given him a rundown on Deborah's (upon his asking me), however much fiction had been built upon scant facts. What of his mother, my aunt, and there was a younger brother close to my brother's age - long-ago people to the Deborah I had become, who had already seemed from a distant past to Debbie at the end, people to be politely asked of those few times I had spoken with Kerry. But these thoughts were again flitting across the periphery of my groggy-yet wakefulness as I drove my rattletrap of a Rubble, by now accustomed to what I supposed was Reuben's introspective silence in the seat next to me, over the back roads out to the Tel that morning. When he asked me all of a sudden, "I wonder why you aren't better known for your photography. It is like you are 'almost famous' like you said, yet remain in the shadows, as if standing on the threshold of a doorway?"

"I like that 'in the shadows' part, fits me to a tee." Quite taken aback - I hadn't expected that one so early in the day - I'd pulled the first thing I could think of out of the air, biding for time until I could fabricate something of a coherent answer. "I simply don't want to be known. I'd rather remain a mystery. It gives me 'freedom'. That is, an inner creative freedom for certain. I want the viewer to enjoy the photograph. To see whatever the way I do and use their imagination. Even when doing work-related photo shoots, like here on an archeological dig, I don't want Naor Dan to just see a sherd, I want him to see 'the sherd', as if it exemplified all the sherds in the world, found already or waiting to be found. With nuances of light and angle of lines. I want to make it a visible object where one can see the whole of what it had originated from."

I left him to ponder that, as we'd arrived and immediately began to unload my equipment before tacking that bunch of pipes on the roof rack - that would be needed first thing in raising the tarpaulins. I was feeling irked for no apparent reason and knew that I could be testy that day, after a restless night (for what good that walk did me, other than stretch my legs). I didn't want to let "the fog" in, give it an inch and it'd take a mile. Yet, until I'd heard what Reuben had unearthed in his search for that former me, my wretched curiosity would be as torturous to live with as whatever he might divulge, yes, right down to the dregs.

I saw the rise of dust from several vehicles growing larger in our direction and I called out sharply, I realized, trying to curb myself: "Reuben, let's get down that piping already. Some of the troops are almost here. I'd like for them to lug it to the top while on their way up; we have enough to tote. Because they can't get started getting up several of the covers without these replacements."

Today he had on a pair of canvas shorts,

with one of those long-tail blue shirts hanging loose over his belt, the sleeves rolled up above his elbows. He had strong legs from what I could see of them, as he swung himself up gripping the bars of the rack while stepping on to the threshold rim of an opened rear door, with muscular calves, rather lovely legs for a guy I thought (must have come from all those times of his hoisting me about like he did, I wanted to chuckle) as I stood by Rubble's hood waiting for him to begin handing them down to me.

"It's uncanny, Deborah," he began, as he hoisted the bundle of pipes over the rack's bars, at the same time turning to look down at me, before tilting them in my direction, "how right this minute you look so much like as if that high school year book photo of Debbie could have been of you at an earlier age."

"Fuck!" I almost said aloud, if but under my breath (I knew it was bound to occur to him to make the comparison sooner or later. I had brought it upon myself, hadn't I - I who had studied the novelty of the human face through countless framings through a camera's lens knew it was inevitable that he would, almost as if I really had wanted him too), all the while maintaining this coy grin frozen on my lips as I looked up directly into his eyes, before speaking.

"I'm me, Reuben, not Debbie." I said it, almost softly, yet as deliberately as I could.

"Of course you are, no doubt about that. It is just that with certain expressions, from a particular angle or two, it's a feeling I get, I got, that's all. I hadn't seen her in person since age ten, and from a distance at that, until I came across that photograph. Hell, I didn't mean to insinuate, (he was partially grinning, but with a certain pain I could detect close to the surface behind it) I mean what with all my going on about her yesterday I'll probably start seeing traces of her in Stefan even. I know, that's definitely a stretch. Maybe Sushila though. She has that 'dark, west country' English look. That's where my mother's family hails from in ye ole country. Whom Debbie in that photograph exemplified. But there was this touch of the Slavic she'd had from Uncle Seth, who may or may not have had some Jewish ancestry. I know, I'm talking through my hat. I'm sorry."

"That's okay. Here's Aharon now coming for those pipes. Hand them on down to me. We can talk later. Remember you were going to tell me what your search for her turned up, the belated search touched off by having come across that photograph."

Once the tarpaulin covers were raised, several of which were sturdier than ever thanks to those replacement poles, the excavation site was as pulsating with fervent activity, as if yesterday's abrupt disruption by that Dust Devil was a thing of the distant past. I had the inter-rupted job in that trench to complete, and Reu-ben was inarguably there to help me get it done, once we'd lugged over the ladders and the re-flector shields, working up a sweat already in the sweltering air. It was important to have a visual record at the outset of a new section - for what it might show unseen initially to the naked eye before a "find" is uncovered just beneath it, or behind it. And for that a reflected light is es-sential, for which once again Reuben proved his adroitness as if it were he himself who was peer-ing through the camera's lens. As we deftly navi-gated in and around the several volunteers this morning - Joely and Candis, who was a Canadian student, having joined with Jonna and Daniel - and Aharon, forever with that clipboard in hand. So intent upon what they were all doing, we more or less happily went unnoticed. It is always a dance, a minuet if you will, working as it were in tight quarters. The trick was to remain "invis-ible", like the friendly ghost (as opposed to being the dig's equivalent of a detested paparazzi). It continued like this up to breakfast time and our return to Neve Rom. I regretted I hadn't brought the makings of breakfast out with us so that we could have had this trench to ourselves, and I might have wrapped this part of the shoot by the time everybody returned.

I was leaning forward on Rubble's steering wheel as we bumped along, elbows akimbo, staring ahead, my mind more on the photographs I just shot, or the something in their imagery I couldn't put my finger on, rather than on Reuben's intense (or so I felt) silence beside me, when he at last spoke. Cautiously as he often would begin before working up to a torrent of words - much like Ravel's *Bolero* does. (I wondered what he'd make of that comparison if I dared tell him?)

"Debbie's guardian, foster father or whatever, this Reverend Marston, his seeming obsession with what he fancied was her 'struggling for faith', that she was deeply troubled, that she was 'afraid of love', didn't trust it when it was offered, and that if she saw Jesus in the room with her she'd be scared shitless - I have struggled with ever since finding the memorial, along with that photograph, and reading it way back when. In short, I don't think he had a clue about what made her tick, and that he was merely projecting his own self-serving fantasy of an explanation upon what might have been just an above-average teenage girl's angst at her age, that given what she'd experienced, had come through being all the more acute, let's say. Hers was more of a search - rather than a 'struggle' as he deemed it - I'd say, a search for that which would ring true to her, that she could get her teeth into, and whether she realized it herself, it wasn't what he had to offer her. Whatever fear on her part there might have been was that fear deep down of the unknown we all have at that age, that she could only hope that she'd be able to recognize when she did. Now, I am probably projecting my own teen's travail, only I think hers was more grounded in reality, in the actual, than mine was. I haven't put that very well, have I? Just demonstrating my own grappling with straws."

I ground Rubble to a halt, having pulled it over to side of the road, switched off the engine, turned and looked at him. He had it so right, in spades. My heart was thumping loudly, I could hear it in my ears like an echo, like a seismic rumble from the depths of my being. The sense of it he had right, I mean. For I had truly wanted to buy into my guardian's bag (not the words I would have used at the time) - because I had begun to feel so hypocritical having sincerely paid lip service to it for so long, once early on I'd decided to go with the prevailing flow and act out what I perceived to be expected on me - as I knew I was in it for a long haul, without an exit, until I reached the age of consent that is. I even took it to heart eventually, fully throwing myself into the spirit of things, finding a certain elan in my oftentimes overly ardent participation. But I was changing inside of me, and not just the woman emerging out of the cocoon of a female child, if only into the confusion it wrought in a teenage girl: my mind began to be plagued by self-doubts, having played with an untruth for so long by adhering to what my immediate society had come to expect of me, because of the lie I'd been lying to myself to maintain. No, my foster father, much as I have come to dislike thinking of him as that, didn't have a clue. I could almost feel sorry for him, if I let myself. With whom I often enough played a kind of devil's advocate role by my not daring at that point to come clean with what I really felt, essentially because I hadn't yet articulated it even unto myself - that Reuben's analysis here cut to the quick of. I'd merely lashed out then with kind of self-abnegation, the fear of Jesus, the I-wasn't-good-enough, wasn't worthy stuff (like as if I were a spiritual Dickensesque orphan). Fucking excuses to hide what I didn't know how to say, that I possibly wouldn't have possessed the courage to have said if I had known. But it is true the part that I feared to trust being loved, both because I'd had it snatched away from me early on, even before having been sent away from the only world I'd ever known, felt familiar in, and because of the pretense with which I'd learned to live amid my new surroundings that, as I've already said, had become more and more a moral challenge to maintain. To live with myself performing a charade - not that I knew to call it that, yet needless to say one that augmented any sense of my worthiness in and of itself.

"Or grasping at straws," I gave him a grinning smile, holding back a laugh that would only have been to shield from his view how a nerve in me had been struck. I saw the sudden bafflement cross his face following what must have seemed to him a sudden dramatic move on my part that he was unaccustomed to seeing. "Either way, you'd be wrong. I think you have ever so precisely hit upon the gist of the matter. Essentially he was, as you implied, projecting his own ego upon the vulnerability of a rootless young girl. Perhaps it being his only source of reference in this case. You'd mentioned earlier, the words in that memorial or whatever hadn't jived with the image of her in that photograph that could have been me at her age."

"Alright, I'm sorry about that," he kind of laughed, "was doing my own projecting, I guess. But, yes, to your question, it was more than just that photo alone. It was my own recollection of her if from a zillion years before. It just didn't sound in character with the kid I remembered any more than it did with the look on her face in that photograph. He portrayed her as one broken, hapless. She may have been 'troubled' but hapless I couldn't imagine. I have this small color pic of her she sent me when about eight or almost, from the spring before I visited them last. She is looking squarely into the camera, with all the natural self-assurance in the world for one her age, her eyes laughing with a mischievous, I won't dare say, an openness, on an equal level with the viewer, well, a directness that says everything and maybe says nothing. In that other photo, she is posed, looking to the side, that is you don't see her eyes looking to yours. But there is a stubborn determination you sense about her, that the women in my mother's family seem to have in abundance, She was nobody's pushover, nobody's fool."

"You know, you've asked me about my family, but I have been amiss, don't you think, not asking about yours," I said as I started up the engine and wrenched Rubble into gear - to give Debbie a breather, "Your parents...?"

"That's okay, Deborah." he laughed. "Thanks, but I've taken no offense, far from it. I had it in bushels with Roni and Sushila asking me about the prototypes for the family in my first novel. My father is dead, my mother is elderly yet living on her own still in her house, a suburban tract house in a small village up county, as they say in those parts, from the old farm place of my paternal grandparents by the bay, where my brother and I grew up."

"And your brother?"

"He lives with his latest love in a small town in the area. He and I were never that close, and we are even further apart now. He's not a bad guy, we are just entirely two different people. He once called me 'a daydreaming communist'."

I didn't remember his brother, from that one summer visit to the country, just that he and my brother, Nicholas, were about the same age. About what became of my brother I really wouldn't want to know - when I was little he hit on me and when I protested to our parents he'd say it was because I was a pest. And later he became smarmy, when not outright accusing me of having it better than him. Joy neither did I want to know - Joy who sent me away because she wanted to marry, only to fawn over me summers when I was allowed to visit - I would never know which was the real her. (The Reverend had it right: I learned not to trust love, to be wary of it when offered). "Does it seem strange to return to what is no longer there?" I asked; I'd pulled that one out of thin air, not sure where it was headed, he no doubt wasn't either given the look on his face, "I mean the old farm setting, by the water, where your boyhood haunts were located?"

"I gotcha. Yes, in the beginning, but I seldom go there nowadays. I find no beauty in the world I come from."

"You feel estranged from your mother too?" I blurted out rather blatantly, before catching myself (I just remembered she was my mother's beloved big sister, who sent us gifts).

"Not quite," he laughed quite freely, "Not that she doesn't ask for it at times. Since Rebekah and I have gotten together, we visit her about twice a year. We would do it more often, but when we are with her most of the time is spent by her bemoaning the fact that we don't. At least by now we can share the same bedroom, which wasn't the case early on, with another. Rebekah does like her, and she Rebekah. Family life, perhaps you are fortunate at least in that you are spared that."

"But you spoke of a 'search' when you said you had not been satisfied by how she'd been more or less defined by her guardian, that foster father minister? I took it to mean you'd dug further?"

"First of all I wrote to the minister, this Rev, Marston."

"You really did that!"

"Yeah, I did, believe it or not. I explained to him I had lived abroad for a long while, had been abroad when Debbie died, that I had only just come across a photo of her and his memorial sermon with it - it being the first I'd heard about her after so many years - at my mother's, who had been Debbie's mother's big sister. I told him of the super bright kid I'd known, that she though the youngest of the lot was by far the smartest of all our cousins on hers and my mother's side of the family, possessing this vibrant, curious personality like none other. I guess I laid it on thick, while trying to hold down the rage I felt from having read the picture he'd painted of her. Of the troubled soul struggling, with his help and prayers, to find this almighty behemoth, 'faith'. All the while questioning his obsession with it, maybe 'anxiousness' is a better word for it, to be fair. To give him his due though, he did write

⌐ anxiety ?

132

that she had this personal charisma that could light up a room, the giving of herself to others, in that she had the rare ability to radiate hope in spite of her ongoing struggle to fully 'believe'. Worst of all was his contention that in death there was a 'victory' for her she hadn't known in life. Then on the return flight from her funeral, he saw the throne of God in a cloud formation that told him Debbie was with Jesus. All's well that ends well, neatly tied up in pink ribbon with a big bow."

"Did he write back?"

"He did, quite cordially, yet decidedly impersonal. Not quite cold, definitely not warm. Very guarded, I'd say. And later I'd learn from Kerry there was a reason for that. In essence he repeated the greatly troubled teenager with great gifts though plagued by doubt, you know, the struggling to find faith bit, like all he had to do was switch on the cassette in his head, sprout the old party line."

He would, as I remember well. I could never penetrate that wall of his, with the least thing personal it could come down with a thud, though normally it was a silent drop, the entrance sealed off before one realized it. My reaction to this was to pull his leg - like saying if Jesus came into the room where I was, I'd be frightened, stuff like that. Perhaps I ought to have been ashamed of myself, mocking another's belief, but when that one can only see another in the context of their own framework of reference, therefore denying that other an existence apart, well, beyond that frame of reference, they are fair game for the me that escaped, if you will, that frame of reference, by becoming Deborah Rosenfeld like I did.

"Kerry is one of those cousins, whose sister's name is Kathy?"

"Yes, one of the 'kissing cousins'", he grinned a little ironically. "One of the times I went to Norway with Rebekah, we stayed over at Kerry's home the evening of our arrival back in the US. And the next morning early while the two of us were alone still sharing a few cups of coffee I asked her about Debbie, if she knew anything. I remember well her first comment on that 'memoriam' piece. It sounded to her like Reverend Marston was basically relieved to have Debbie out of his hair, as if a burden had been lifted off his shoulders. To which I reluctantly agreed, because what he wrote both in the memoriam and more or less repeated in his reply to my query, his laying it on thick with the sob-story of finding redemption in death, was truly protesting too much. A sensation I had not been able to shake, sad as I feel it to be. But Kerry had a lot more to tell me, more that I could have ever hoped for."

"And I want to hear it, do you mind?" I cut him short as I pulled up behind the Chadar Ochel and switched off the engine. "But first let's eat, and if we, as the Brits say, tuck it in quickly enough, without choking, we can beat the others back out to the site and get a head start on things. Barring another 'Dust Devil' I'd like to wrap up those trench shots by noon."

I was not so sure how much more I was ready to hear, how much more I could bear. I was beginning to feel as if an autopsy was being performed on me, guided by my own hand as if I were holding a mirror above me while the pathologist went about the grisly job. In any case, I had to give it a rest, for now. I had to catch my breath, as I was stretching the framework of the boundaries I had believed I'd been prepared for reaching here, if just, without having given any thought to just how far this might go. I could imagine it wasn't going to be any easier for Reuben as well, given the depths of his feelings for the girl I once was - even if his only memories of her are of her as a child. With this sense of identification with her that was clawing at his innards.

Back out at the site several hours later, following breakfast, we had finished my shoot, momentarily (every facet of work on an archeological dig is "momentarily", ongoing), and having almost emptied our canteens (I'd wetted my face as well, allowing the water to trickle down my neck and under my tee shirt), Reuben and I had hoisted ourselves upon the baulk furthest from the volunteers feverishly chipping and brushing away at a portion of earthen wall I was keeping my eye on (that I had earlier photographed), my digital camera hanging from my neck. He'd removed his hat and with his fingers had vigorously ruffled his hair. By now that insatiably curious side of me was aching to ask what happened next, what more had Kerry, whom I remembered as living in the shadow of her twin Kathy, had told him.

"It wasn't true, what I'd earlier been lead to believe, that Debbie wasn't allowed to have contact with her family," he began (as if had read my thoughts), breaking a strained quiet between us. "Or as it was told to me directly that family members weren't to have contact with her. Or that as time passed, restrictions were lightened. Kerry told me Debbie'd call them twice a year, from the Marstons, and again when she'd visit Joy in the summer. When she'd call from the Marstons she'd come off as being circumspect, demure. But from Joy's she was almost always exuberant, enthusiastic, full of life. It was like she was two wholly different people. And she'd always ask about family members. In that, in Kerry's words, Debbie was invariably polite."

"'Did she ask about me?' I dared to ask. 'Oh yes', said Kerry, 'whenever she'd call, and the time later on when she visited us that once'. Only none of them knew where I was exactly. From my mother their mother had heard I was living in Israel, on a kibbutz; there was something about me studying at Tel Aviv University of all things, as if my life wasn't full enough already. Which Debbie thought was 'cool', was how Kerry put it. Then I was either in Europe or living in England they'd further heard, by that time she'd visited them. She'd always ask them to say 'hello' to me from her, if they saw me or heard from me. But, of course, they never did either. I hadn't been in touch with them in years, though I'd learn later that my brother had been, only he knew little more than they did at the time. Debbie must have really felt that I'd forgotten about her. If only I might have somehow known.

"That visit to Kerry and family took place in the summer a year before she died, she having out of the blue phoned a day or so beforehand, which Kerry took to mean that the Marstons probably at the last minute acceded to her request, as apparently their mother and Rev. Marston had been loggerheads over his guardianship of Debbie from day one. And upon arrival, the Marstons had sat in the car in the driveway for the duration of Debbie's visit. At first Debbie had been shy with them, but soon became her natural self, Kerry said. The first thing that had struck all of them was her height. Debbie was close to six feet tall, 5 feet ten or eleven I think she told them. But that she stood straight, as if unconscious she was the tallest person in the room. She was naturally graceful, physically, was how Kerry put it. She sat straight as well, very dignified like. She radiated this inner beauty, was how Kerry described her. She had an inner beauty as well as an outer, physical beauty. She was dressed casually, wearing jeans. The only sense of any tension, Kerry felt, was the way in which she gripped her fingers together while she sat with them. (No doubt their mother, Aunt Reba, had grilled her about how she was being treated and all, though with good intentions, and it had probably sounded like being given 'the 3rd'.) Otherwise, she'd remained calm throughout, had been reserved to a certain degree, sort of detached with bursts of enthusiastic responses. Kerry said she spoke openly, directly to you, no less, that she was definitely articulate. (I'd asked). But most of all, she likewise spoke with her eyes. When Debbie smiled, Kerry said, she had curious, laughing, searching, mischievous eyes that looked at one directly, without guile. That she literally talked with her eyes.

"The Marstons tried their damnedest to make Debbie feel guilty as hell, Kerry went on to say. But apparently it hadn't really worked. The way I see it, Rev. Marston and his wife sought to make Debbie feel she wasn't ever 'good enough' in the name of keeping her in her place and not allowing her natural intelligence to go to her head. Or to question their bag, that is think independently from them. But maybe here

I am guilty of conjecture as my father never considered me 'good enough'. At the funeral, Kerry'd said, Reverend Marston had spoken as if he had done Debbie a great favor. Kerry described Marston as a cold fish, tall with blond hair prematurely graying at the temples, a long rigid face. His eyes had a steel glint in them. Though Mrs. Marston was a 'regular human being'. I'd always pictured him like the preacher played by Robert Mitchum in *The Night of the Hunter*.

"'Debbie had been a rather spoiled little girl', Kerry'd gone on. 'With Uncle Seth and Aunt Victoria, she always got her way.' Which I'd accepted, reluctantly. Because, if anything, I spoiled her too. Only I don't really see it that way. She was naturally the brightest of all of us cousins, I had been careful to counter. Certainly smarter than all of us at her age as her school reports indicated from day one, that Joy would brag about with a certain self-effacement. But with Joy and Nicholas there was no contest that I could see. In school she outperformed them in leaps and bounds. She appeared to really love to study, and (as I said before) had this amazing ability to concentrate, to see, that is think, ahead. Then too, Joy was the ugly duckling when compared physically with Debbie, because it had already been quite obvious that by the time Debbie was Joy's age she was going to be a beauty (Nicholas though would probably turn out to be a good looking guy). Which wasn't Joy's fault, her looks. It did seem that just about everything for Joy fell through, boyfriends and the like. And she really hated having to wear Kathy and Kerry's hand-me-downs. Which never did much for her in comparison to their looks. I remember being sympathetic in my letters, but couldn't help being put off by her forever self-pitying. Then the family's ill health didn't help matters. Which was 'unfair', yet it sounded so redundant, harsh as it is to put it like that. She had so little self-esteem, it hurt too that she'd become so bitter. And she lied so, I'd learn the hard way. I ended up being totally put off by that. And when she hated it was with no holds barred. From early on, I'd realize in retrospect, she'd been Joy Jekyll and Joy Hyde, not unlike my mother can be. What a family, my mother's family. Though I really had no right to judge her harshly, I became very disappointed in her, that's all. And that was long before she gave Debbie away."

With an eye still focused on what Jonna and Daniel were doing at that wall, joined now by Aharon, with Rafi and Joely, I listened in a sort of distant way to the sound of Reuben's voice, which I found the easiest way to absorb what he was saying in that earnest intensity of his - which I have to admit did touch me, turned me on - so as not to fall victim to a knee jerk reaction that would break the thread of his thought. Because the way in which he was relating what were to me both revelations mixed with the half-remembered to the vaguely recalled - was as important as what he actually said.

I suppose I did wonder, belatedly, why I heard from no member of my erstwhile family at the beginning of "my exile", as I slowly emerged from the state of recalcitrant solitude into which I had withdrawn belligerently in my blatant refusal to accept the fact that I was at the mercy of the powers that be, and began to piecemeal a plan, if not quite cognizant of it at the time, for my eventual escape. All through which I had clung to some hope that Joy'd take me back- until it came to bear that that too was but a chimera, like a smell the source of can never be reached. I suppose I simply feigned acceptance of a "separate peace". Joy had been but a pacifier periodically offered for the real thing forever out of reach.

Yes, at Christmas, I was allowed, it being Christmas, to call my Uncle Raymond's where I would speak to Kathy and Kerry, and to Aunt Reba who'd hog the phone plying me with questions I'd have been reluctant to answer outright, out of this inner reticence of mine, even if I had been alone in the house. With Joy too there had been this prevailing tension, given her history with Aunt Reba, as much as I understood it and with the twins which I'd come to understand. But given Joy's history with me she couldn't outright deny me - and though she may have smoldered underneath she wanted, I felt, to keep the

connection open. At Joy's too I felt the require-
ment to be circumspect, to a degree, when
speaking of my life with the Marstons, as it had
been she who had consigned me to my fate so to
speak, thus sensitive to any inferred criticism
even when I might forget and make the odd remark (which, unable to bite my tongue, I could
do). But with the twins, more so with the im-
pressionistic Kerry than with the more rational
Kathy, I could forget myself enough, once
warmed up, to drop more or less the shield of
pretense for moments on end, though I could
never open up with them like I would be able to
do later with Deborah. Thus Kerry's describing
me as being "exuberant" when calling from Joy's
isn't an exaggeration (and at the time I was exceedingly grateful of the opportunity afforded
me). Did I ask about Reuben each time I phoned?
I always asked about family members, as a rou-
tine, so perhaps I did, though it was in combin-
ation with my dutiful queries in general (though
I think I was consciously careful not to make
him sound more special than the others), not
that I wasn't in earnest in my asking, as news of
any one I remembered gave me this kind of sub-
terranean lifeline to that lost world of my
former existence: that I hadn't really just imagined it. He had been a big part of that world I
had lost, as had been my father and mother, as
had the uncensored sense of freedom they each
in their own way had allowed a rambunctious

child. I had not heard of him or from long before I was sent into exile, before that door was summarily closed. Until this day I had not heard what had gone down between him and Joy (other than Joy's accusation that he favored Kathy and Kerry) that had precipitated the sudden break in relations. Or why he'd just dumped me as it were. Anyway, I was preoccupied with growing older, becoming myself, burying deep within me all that stuff I'd once felt for certain people and things, in order to find my feet on the rungs of the ladder one must climb as we unconsciously begin to cast off former shells, in the process of emerging from the cocoon. I suppose too I simply didn't want to remember the silly little girl that had been me only a couple or more years earlier. But there were times I did ask about him in particular, for one reason or another. I had been thinking of him prior to these phone calls, something had brought my memory of him to the fore. I'd buried him deep in my heart, with something like a lid over his memory. I think I missed him and I knew that was a futile thing to feel.

What I do remember is that visit, how I had lobbied for being allowed it, and it is quite true that it was not decided in my favor until the day before we left, as it was somewhat out of the way of the intended destination. I was to be given an hour, thanks to my foster mother's out-of-the-ordinary intervention; while I saw that it was making my foster father nervous, for all his last minute smiles offered to save face. The thing between him and Aunt Reba I sensed was the crux of the matter (whatever this thing was - beyond Aunt Reba's having wanted to take me in as well, as she had Nicholas for while). Which I suppose was the reason why he refused to go in - not that I wanted him to - when he was uncharacteristically rude, or almost rude, when Kathy and Kerry came out upon our arrival with the invitation from Aunt Reba. Once inside the house and seated (it wasn't going to be made my fault that the Marstons were going to swelter in the car), Kerry for some reason chose to sit beside me when I was certain Aunt Reba was going to claim that spot, instead of sitting across from me with Kathy. Their eyes focused upon me, like I'd suddenly come back from the dead (it had been five long years, in spite of the phone calls). I realized I was as much a stranger to them as they suddenly were to me, for all the familiarity we shared. How I appeared to them I couldn't begin to fathom. I felt Aunt Reba looked pretty much like I remembered, a small bundle of intensity wearing those same rhinestone rimmed glasses, but hers was the voice on the phone - definite in tone, abrupt, unswerving in the exactitude of her words - while Kathy and Kerry no longer looked like the teen princesses Joy so hated (and envied), but young women, though I sensed a certain anxiousness, uncertainty in their outward demeanor. Of course, they had all commented on my height, which by then I'd come to accept in the natural order of things (my father had been tall, so was Uncle Raymond - who much to my regret, with some misgiving, I was told was unable be there; my mother too hadn't been exactly short), so yeah, I stood straight, for it had never been in my nature to slouch, and when people complimented me on my demeanor I thanked them with a smile and went on my way thinking no more of it. Of course I'd changed, much more so than they actually had. Besides my height (Kerry did ask out of the blue and I told them, much like she related to Reuben), I was a woman already - in appearance pretty much so, of which I was perfectly cognizant - well, on the cusp of becoming one. And I had been living a double life for so long, like playing an established role in one of those daytime soaps, having made a truce with duplicity.

The Marstons seemed to always let me know, in sundry ways, how much they'd done for me (maybe that is how their foster parents had raised them), that they had literally rescued me from the street, if not quite some den of inequity. (It was a far from a "structured" household I'd come from, an abnormality to the core of their thinking I'd quickly find out - in short, in their eyes, I hadn't been housebroken as if that were one of the proverbial deadly sins.)

That I had been a show off, like Kerry said, I

suppose I never really thought of it as that, I was just happily exuberant, like when I got a good report card (I had worked for it, only I never considered study "work"), admittedly full of myself, the runt of the pack's prerogative perhaps. They got enthusiastic over stuff too, with the Twins it was new outfits uncle Raymond had bought them or their favorite pop idol latest hit; Joy usually got head over heels about some guy (which, alas, never lasted). I don't believe Kerry or Kathy ever caught wind of my "infatuation" with Reuben; the few occasions during that time period when they'd breeze in to visit it was all about them and their latest - after all they were the brightest stars in the firmament; I left it to Joy to envy and resent and Nicholas, callow youth that he could be, to make the odd sneering remark. My family though did bear the brunt of it, and while my memory is vague on details during the fall that followed that first summer (it was just before my father's first heart attack), the emotional charge "my conquest" had given me bubbled over during most of the hours of those days. (That, unnerving me, had come rushing back at me the moment I saw him, even if I didn't know that it really could have been him sitting there next to Stefan as Stefan's old friend, even if I had been unable to put my finger on it for minutes on end - right up to the minute he introduced himself to me upon my, thinking back on it, somewhat audacious approach.) Yet set against this self-hubris was my family's rapid decline from then on - my father then my mother's illnesses, with little money, dependent upon Uncle Raymond's largesse - that I would rather blithely sail through, being the little kid I was, while Nicholas was more often than not angry (and taking it out on me, who royally countered his punches, his kicks, his cutting remarks). With Joy growing more and more dispirited, slumping bitterly into bouts of self-pity. I found it all suffocating, so I retreated into my own little world - I would study hard and Reuben would come to my rescue. I would be all grown up, because he would have waited for me. It was a fantasia with streaks of sunshine breaking through the clouds, with him lifting me to his shoulders and the two of us, me astride him, entering it. I didn't appreciate it that my father, biting back his own pain, had to take care of my often incapacitated mother, us kids to boot, normally without uttering a word of complaint. But then he was gone, and Joy had to take the helm, when just a teenage girl simply wanting a life that was not to be. My mother would desperately complain to Joy all the while praising Joy's "sacrifice" ("The apple of my eye," she called Joy - who otherwise was "ungrateful", "selfish"). My mother was in such pain towards the end, it really did become unbearable to hear her cries. All the while, bemoaning what was going to become of us. People we knew (and some we didn't, well Joy did) came and went doing what they could administering to us, Reverend Marston one of them, their words full of sentiment (no wonder I hate that word and all it implies), their advice, the inevitability to it, frightening to both Nicholas and me most of all (by that time Joy had found Alan, whom she was determined not to give up, not to lose come what may). I began to disappear, to walk the streets, staying long at the library doing my homework, when Joy asked me to help I turned a deaf ear - Joy telling me to do this or that, telling Nicholas too (who found his own "refuge" wherever). Years later, when suffering that prolonged bout with cystitis, my mother's screams pierced the solitude of my nights, haunted my waking hours, until I was certain I would end up like her - carted off to an unfeeling hospital to die alone where no amount of medicine applied seemed to quell her final pain. All the while, Reverend Marston prayed for me to find "hope", as if my being dubious of 'hope" was synonymous with struggling to find "faith" as he saw it. It was in the midst of this that Deborah came bursting into my life.

Seated next to Kerry as I was, I may have turned to her and asked that if they ever heard from Reuben and to say hello from me if they ever did. (I had only recently watched the movie, *Gigi* - long before I'd read Colette's novella - that had readily brought to mind the nickname he'd given me.) It would have been the natural thing to have done under the circumstances. Once his name had come up while I was asking after various family members and once again no one seemed to know anything definite about him or his whereabouts. He was living in London, Aunt Reba seem to remember his mother telling her the last time they'd spoken on the phone. "He doesn't seem to stay in any place too long," Aunt Reba had seemed to summarily dismiss him, adding, "He got in with the Jews and turned into one of those hot heads." That I felt I sensed both Kathy and Kerry visibly shrink from, though they said nothing. Over the years, in one of my phone calls, when I might have asked that same question, I remember hearing he was living in Israel on a kibbutz among other things. Of course I knew of Israel, the Biblical Israel in particular. But of modern Israel too. The Six Day War having not that long ago occurred. Kibbutz I must have looked up at some point, reading that it was a communal farm owned by the members, where everyone was equal socially and financially, which must have sounded to me like somewhere east of the moon (somewhat analogous with Adam and Eve's "Eden", I suppose, though I don't think I went so far as to wonder if everybody went naked like in a nudist colony I'd heard about, even Christian ones. How much all of this would, a couple of years later, as Deborah, influence me to apply for a place at that kibbutz ulpan for that first full summer out in the world on my own? It probably did, as much as did the cinematography in that Michal Bat Adam movie did. And I was by then already a Jew, by osmosis. In that it was where I had found myself to be, having become Deborah. Which I chose to embrace. The irony is so had Reuben, if coming to it from a diametrically opposite direction. In that he had made his choice up front, while mine had come after the fact. What could it be in our general make up, what germination we mutually share, that had brought the two of us separately, independently, to take on this responsibility. No, I am not going to wax mystical about it, I'll leave that to the cabalists if not quite to astrology and the like.

"And that photograph I found was possibly her junior high school photo," I heard Reuben say, "not a senior class photo, though that is what it looks like. As Kerry understood it, Debbie was a junior still officially. Though she had almost enough credits to have graduated that spring. And had been trying to finish high school that summer, while she worked, by taking equivalent college courses towards that goal. Because she'd dropped a class that spring either due to a persistent infection Marston alluded to in his letter or depression or both. So if that photo is a senior class photo after all, that would explain why it was taken."

All the while, with growing interest, my eyes followed the mounting excitement at that wall on the far end of the trench. They'd found something - or thought they'd found something, not an unusual occurrence on any dig, with whatever failing to pan out (so you suck in your disappointment, feeling just a little foolish and get back methodically to the humdrum). Meanwhile, all that Reuben had surmised was surprisingly accurate. It was almost that he had the ability to perceive me, embody me - but then he was a novelist, although that doesn't quite explain it. What he'd hadn't known (couldn't have known otherwise, his crystal ball notwithstanding), was this was when Deborah entered my life. That she would take on my cause as her own - and one might say, died for it.

"As for photographs, Kerry said they had had one of Debbie from later that summer when she was at Joy's, where she and Joy are standing side by side, in which Debbie was head and shoulders taller. Only it was lost in a fire at Kathy's.

"Kerry said that Joy was devastated by Debbie's death. She'd been roundly accused earlier of selling Debbie. At the funeral, Joy said she deeply regretted giving Debbie to Rev. Marston."

I knew Joy was troubled by her "selling me into Egypt", having weathered the storm of accusations from certain family members far and near, Aunt Reba being the most vociferous of the pack, of which I'd feign ignorance to maintain any semblance of equilibrium during my annual visits, as Joy still wore her slights on her sleeve. As for any regrets after the fact, sentiment comes easy to express upon such occasions - only to be able to do it all over again when it came to the crunch.

"Reuben, we need to check out what is going on over there," I broke off his revelations, or reverie I'll refrain from calling it, "fascinating" however much it really was (no matter, I had long felt a certain choking sensation in my throat), with a wave of my thumb in the direction of the far wall. "I think they may have found something - or think they have, Aharon appears to be taking it serious, Rafi too. I'll need to get pictures in case."

Perhaps we both had been sitting long enough, the way the two of us leap into action as if it were a kind of celebratory relief to have escaped a rut of sorts we'd been passively digging in our mind. I to grab my print camera, Reuben one of the reflectors (but when he looked for one of my ladders, we saw that Jonna, in spite it's wobbling under her, was in a rush climbing it, a trowel and a short pick in hand, her long blonde braids bobbing against her shoulders.

"I hope some will hold it for her," Reuben said as he caught up with me, "it's treacherous to get a good footing amid all the rubble."

"Rafi," I was about to yell to not crowd that

ladder like they were doing, in their individual fervor to expose what it was embedded in that wall, as if to be the first or something (I had been shooting them, standing back a ways to capture fully the tension that can precede some significant find, squinting through my camera's lens much as might one studying in minute detail the position of each participant both individually and all together), when I saw Jonna, in the precise moment of overextending her reach, with the already tilted askew ladder beginning to topple, as belatedly she tried to correct herself: in vain.

"Shit!" I cried aloud, rising from my crouch just about the moment the thump of her body hit the ground below, following a short cry, a fall of not more than six feet from where she had been perched, followed immediately by the metallic clatter of the ladder - but there was such a resounding echo (of finality in it) that I would remember it for long afterwards.

I was on my feet before I knew it, racing towards her - with Reuben, I think, right behind me. It was one of those instinctive things one does, without aforethought. My eyes were riveted upon the inert body lying there unmoving on its left side; had her head struck a rock being my primary concern. While those about her, recovering from the initial shock moved back as Rafi and Aharon bent towards her - like in slow motion, it would seem - though but a matter of seconds in actuality. "Jonna," I spoke softly, wedged between the two guys, the three of us on our knees, having restrained them from their attempts to arouse her by shaking her, along with barking at her in an overly anxious Hebrew - then to Aharon as in almost a whisper I too spoke in my Hebrew, "Better go call for an ambulance, because even if she comes to, she's probably damaged her hip and shoulder and won't be able to walk. But even as the words were coming out of my mouth, I could see that he'd had the same thought. She was breathing, that much had been ascertained. And there wasn't any blood, that I could see, around her head.

"But don't move her," the soldier in him almost ordered, "I will have Stefan come to you, meanwhile."

"Don't worry, I've had a course in emergency care," (Which I had taken extracurricular in preparation for a summer job outside school I didn't get), I said before turning my attention again to Jonna.

The essential thing was to keep her calm, to speak quietly around her. I asked her if she could "hear" me, as sometimes one can hear an external voice penetrating the mist that has enveloped us, the initial balm of a shock. I told her there was nothing to fear, but don't try to move just yet, breath slowly, help was on the way, these things happen to all of us at one time or another, only try not to drift off, think thoughts about how you can help us help you, don't feel regret, just stay with us. I was beginning to fear I was over doing. I didn't know Jonna all that well, just that she was a university student from Denmark and spoke a perfect English on the dig (as the Norwegian and Swedish volunteers did not understand Danish) without any discernible accent.

As I rambled on, in that monotone of sorts, her eyes began to flutter, then open. With a frowning smile crossing her face, with a certain bewilderment as what had happened began to come back to her. Before she could open her mouth, I said:

"Don't talk, Jonna, not quite yet. Aharon has gone to get aid, just in case. You took a tumble, but you are going to be alright."

Then, suddenly, Reuben was beside me. "Deborah's right about you not trying to talk. Yet you'll need to keep alert, in case there is a concussion. But if I ask you a question, can you nod or shake your head, just slightly, if it doesn't hurt you." Giving him ever so slight a smile, she nodded. Another of his literary fans, no doubt.

He proceeded to quietly ask if she was in pain - in her head, in her shoulder and arm, in her hip or leg, anywhere in her back as well perhaps. And if so whether or not it was sore-like pain or a sharp pain. All of her answers added up to a dull "soreness". The same when he went on further, asking her to try to move her left arm and legs just a little. And her head too. She was more alert now. I was afraid she was going to ask if this meant she was off the dig, if only for a very short duration, for Jonna was one of those volunteers who wholeheartedly set their teeth into the whole of things once she got involved. All the while Stefan I knew was going to pull his hair out by tufts worrying about the insurance company, any possible lawsuit made against both the IAA as well as the director, himself, and the supervisors. Quite apart from any care and concern for Jonna's well-being.

"What is it you think you've found, Jonna?" I asked, essentially to keep her alert now that she was.

"The base of a portal of some kind" Jonna suddenly beaming as if momentarily forgetting her predicament, "It appears to be too large for either a house, or maybe a municipal building. I can imagine it being a town or city gate, only not that far into antiquity because of the lack of depth, yes. But far enough back, I hope. It begins close to the bottom of the trench here, rising almost to the top, you'll see. When there is enough uncovered so you can start photographing it. My first belief was that I must have hit a wall." Then adding, "I'm sorry for all this trouble, If only I hadn't been so overly anxious. I hope I won't have caused too much disruption. It is so exciting to have found an artifact of this size, which perhaps will be of importance."

"Here's Aharon, back with Stefan," I heard Daniel say, and we all turned from hovering over Jonna to see a solemn-faced Stefan climbing down into the trench. I could hear what he was feeling even if he'd never come out and say it: "Yesterday a dust devil and today this, I'm scared shitless to think about tomorrow at this rate," before rebuking himself in mid-sentence, upon seeing Jonna lying there in certainly an uncomfortable position if not so obviously in pain. Standing, I stepped back, as did Reuben and Rafi likewise, and before Stefan went to her, kneeling, I quickly gave him the particulars as I saw them. (Apparently no concussion - but that remained to be seen of course - with possibly torn ligaments, certainly bruising with the risk of blood clots. Broken bones, not apparent. Her spirit is good, but disappointed.) About the potential "find", doubtless Aharon had already filled him in.

"Is the cavalry on the way?" I turned to Aharon. "You know, an ambulance". There were moments there when I had been turning the scenario over in my mind of me behind the wheel of Rubble, with Jonna laid out in the back, if we took a seat out, and crying out with every lurch, every bump struck.

"'Mah-dah' come, but may be with helicopter, from Afula, 'Ha'emek'" he quipped in English for the sake of all of us anxious to hear. "There is terror alert. We didn't know." ("MDA" is the acronym for Magen David Adom, Israel's National Ambulance Service. And "Ha'emek" being the estimable medical center in Afula. It being much closer than Tiberias, certainly Nahariya over on the coast. Jonna wouldn't be that far away.) But a "terror alert"? It couldn't have been that great a threat or the area would be crawling with soldiers. The border hereabouts had been incident free for years, and we were by far a stretch from Lebanon. (Though once on a dig further north I had been sleeping out at the site when one night a rocket landed in the adjacent field, with sirens in the distance. I think I cried out "Fuck!" before turning over and going back to the sandman. Some recent splinter group flexing its muscle most likely, not unlike little boys doing the daredevil thing.)

"If any one has any water left, give it to Jonna," I called out. "You can later supply from the tin in the back of Rubble."

Within half an hour, a brightly painted chopper dropped down out of the sky onto the parking place at the foot of the Tel. At a distance it appeared like a colorful toy that one would have expected a kid on the ground with a remote to have been guiding in. And before we knew it two girls and a guy, wearing their green flak jackets and carrying a case and what looked like a yet folded stretcher, appeared over the top of the mound, the sun glinting off their dark glasses, and headed quickly towards us, followed by Stefan and Rafi. Nurit, Gal, and Boaz they said their names were as they began to minister to Jonna, like without a moment to waste. I watched on with a certain relief as they adroitly ascertained what I had earlier concluded. A concussion (I knew a thing or two about concussions) having been my primary worry, while a broken vertebrae or two I thought remotely possible though she hadn't been experiencing any piercing pain. The rest of us too sort of hung back, our arms hung slack at our sides, in that sense of helplessness mode while the professionals ignoring us performed their tasks, with the almost noon air seemingly heavier than ever with the heat. Or we were more conscious of it rather, under the circumstances. Reuben, his hands cupped behind his back, was scrapping at the loose dirt with the toe of his right brogan. Stefan, when his hands weren't on his hips was wiping his face with a wrinkled bandana. The khaki shirts both wore showed widening dark patches of sweat. I hadn't wanted to think what I looked like, a manikin coming unglued most likely. At the outset, when there had existed a likely possibility I might be the ambulance driver, I had given considerable thought to how first of all to lift Jonna intact out of this trench, without inflicting upon her further injury, worsening her condition. In a pinch I've seen people with broken bones lifted up between two ladders, all the while keeping them supine, miraculously so - even participating in one such rescue myself, my heart in my throat throughout.

But I need not have fretted. I should have known that when push came to shove the Israelis would take it as if all in a day's work. And that they did. With smiles all around for those para-medicals. Jonna on that stretcher unfolded was "levitated" without incident. The taller among us, which included me, were conscripted to lift it up and over the edge, where a second team hoofed it to the waiting chopper - and Jonna, mercifully secure inside and not lashed to one of its runners, was off (which I dutifully photographed from atop the Tel). In good hands the lot of us felt reasonably assured for whatever might come.

"What do you think it could be that Jonna found?" Reuben asked as he and I began to collect the photography equipment, he having already lugged over the ladder Jonna fell from. I'd made him drink the remainder of my canteen, though it was warm enough to steep tea. "Remains to be seen," I answered cryptically. "But whatever I'll have to be ready to shoot it as it emerges into the light, I imagine the very first thing tomorrow morning. We both will, I mean. My egotism does get the best of me when all work on an archeological site is a team enterprise. I of all people mustn't forget that."

He laughed. "You were really good with her, in the way you got her to forget herself, as if in a normal conversation, as you sought to ferret any injury she might have sustained. To forget that initial fear of the worst that is born of shock. She'll probably never forget you, how you were there with her. With all of us for that matter, because we were all in a state of shock, if by proxy, by just being there witnessing her state of sudden helplessness."

"Sounds like you may have been there once yourself."

"Once," he said quickly. "Only I was very lucky, luckier than perhaps I deserved to be." "Well, you are here right now, And that's what counts, what's important. Certainly fortunate for me."

The tarpaulin covers hurriedly were coming down and, upon stashing the equipment, Reuben and I went to join in. Calling it a day was not a moment too soon that day. (And this is coming from one who is normally inured to the heat.) Without the slightest semblance of a breeze, the air was a solid wall of humidity one had to wave off to catch one's breath. Which may or may not have been the contributing factor in Jonna's fall, rather that her impetuosity. But more or less we'd come up to speed following yesterday's debacle.

"Did you ever learn more about the cause of Debbie's death? Or rather what caused it," I asked him as we walked down to the parking place, lugging the equipment. I could see that the cars, and Rubble likewise, had been given a dusting whipped up by that chopper's blades.

"The official reason, according to the newspaper as well as her death certificate - yes, I had a friend look at them and sent a copy to me - was that her chest struck the steering wheel and it caused her aorta to rupture. The driver of the car behind her said she had been traveling slightly under the 25mph speed limit when she suddenly slumped over the wheel, her white Beetle rode up on the sidewalk and at a greatly reduced speed already, and struck head-on a telephone pole. She was pronounced dead upon her arrival at the hospital. But curious about this purported aorta bursting, I read about probable causes, one being aortic aneurysm. And a cause of that could possibly be a bout of rheumatic fever during childhood damaging the heart valves. That was when I remembered Joy mentioning that Debbie had had rheumatic fever in a letter to me the second winter after we met, had awoken unable to get her breath and all."

"You did mention that a couple of days ago, but only in passing, in another context. So do you think that is what caused her heart to 'burst'"?

"Reverend Marston wrote nothing of this in his reply to mine. He said there was nothing wrong with her physically, it was just that she was depressed. He mentioned nothing of black-outs either that others said she had been experiencing. I got all this too from Kerry much later, who'd had it from Aunt Reba. Apparently, Mrs. Marston readily admitted to someone at the funeral that she regretted that Debbie's heart had not been checked."

My bugaboo, yes. But Deborah's? A mystery. As for those "blackouts" a subsequent gynecologist laid the blame on the cocktail of antibiotics I had previously been prescribed. I suppose I was taken to a doctor way back then for that fever - it was scary as shit for the first few hours; I suppose he gave me something to quell the initial on-slaught - but I never once heard any mention by my parents about possible heart damage. In that regard I can hardly fault Lucy Marston.

As we climbed into Rubble, careful not to touch the scorching metal (any more than we had to) and rolled the windows down (old habit of mine brought from the States, my rolling windows up whenever parked, leaving only a crack at the top for air to circulate), Reuben turned to me. For some reason I hesitated putting the key into the ignition, after having pulled out the choke. There had always been that boyish youthfulness in his face belying an "old soul" (a phrase I'd come across many, many years later that even as a child I might have applied to him had I known how to articulate it). Because in many ways he had never been a child, as perhaps I hadn't either.

How I had wanted to capture it, what with my digital still hanging from my neck, only the moment had passed too quickly. And to have raised the camera to my eye, in our close quarters, would have spooked him even faster.

"I hope this won't sound ghoulish, macabre even," he began, "but I got the name from Kerry of the cemetery she was buried in - I had forgotten its name - and found her grave, Rebekah and I did, not all that long ago actually. It was just a flat stone with her name on it and the requisite dates. It was located in this vast rolling acreage of a necropolis south of the city, near the airport, in a rather forlorn far corner near a wall. Nowhere near her parents' graves. The utter loneliness of it cut me, like she had long been forgotten. And there was nothing I could do about it. I felt so useless, helpless. I did this Jewish thing. I'd brought with me this small stone, and I laid it by her name. I guess I was hoping she'd know somehow. But that is all fantasy, just my fantasy."

Looking away, I just stared forward, not wanting to show that I was biting my lips. To distract myself, I turned the key and the motor sputtered then growled to life as I stomped on the accelerator pedal a couple of times, pushing in the choke as I did it before the roar deafened me, deafened both of us. A ritual of sorts normally done without thought. I switched on the windshield wipers to clear off the dust, allowing several swipes of the blades before turning them off. Somewhere in my fantasy, in my wishful thinking, I'd assumed I'd have been buried next to my parents. Or Deborah rather would have been. I didn't want the picture Reuben's words had implanted in my mind that in my own way had left me as gutted, empty as he'd felt believing it was Debbie: that was me buried there, his Debbie (as Deborah was my Deborah). Deborah deserved a better fate than that. In that far, forlorn corner, left unattended, forgotten. It was as if she'd never existed, apart from my memory, of which I was the sole guardian. There would be no stone for her, with her name on it. But then, she hadn't died, Debbie had. Deborah was still alive. She was me. Her name that became mine due to our "switcheroo". That I would carry forth into the world, write in amid the stars, engrave upon mountain tops - well, in other people's memories at least. "All we ever possess between birth and death is knowledge and memories," wrote Albert Camus I'd read somewhere. Or that he'd written something like that at any rate.

"She won't be forgotten, Reuben," I said at last. "She lives in your memory of her. And in my memory now of your memory of her."

Following lunch, I made myself scarce to everyone - even to a couple of knockings on my darkroom door (to whomever they could possibly be, Whatthefuck, it's a darkroom, where, if I were there, I'd be working - which I was of course, printing that morning's shots. I must have snapped the shutter in the split second I saw a tottering Jonna and my leap up to run towards where she lay. It was a dramatic photograph, the perfect contrast between light and shadow, the frozen-in-the-moment, captured figures within its frame caught off guard as if on the threshold of what was about to occur - while Jonna herself was poised just on the verge of realizing the pickle she was in, undeniably so. Depending upon the extent of her injuries, I wondered sillily if she'd ever want to see a copy. I imagine the IAA certainly would, should her insurance company make a fuss.

The portrait of Debbie that Reuben had been painting, even if guided to a certain extent by my unseen hand, had left me feeling blood raw inside, as if I had been crazily running, relentlessly so, without letup, until I'd about fallen to my knees out of breath. I needed a break - and tomorrow sundown Shabbat began. It was a good time for me to jump into Rubble and take off for somewhere, anywhere - just me, I and my cameras. I did have a couple of questions left lingering, but Reuben wouldn't be leaving for several more days.

With the afternoon tea time approaching,

our Aruchat Arba, and I having showered the dust out of my ears among other crevices, physically and mentally I might add, and changed into a flowing summer dress, I strolled casually (for a change) in the direction of its daily setting. (For a change too I brought along my digital, it hung from its strap around my neck.) I was still somewhat hesitantly formulating in my mind what I was going to announce or rather how exactly I was going to put it (which could make or break this half-baked if not totally fatuous "scheme": I was going to risk all on what would amount to a throw of the dice). Me, who could be so famously cautious - except for those few and far in-between occasions when I wasn't. The sun was still high above the tree tops, if the air tolerably lighter, for a change at this hour. A full crowd had gathered, it looked like, probably on account of Jonna's accident, each of them naturally being both concerned and curious. I slipped in among them, as inconspicuously as possible (what with my wearing that dress - that Sushila of all people would compliment me on), my eyes and ears alert for the temper of the moment, smiling greetings to this one and that one as I made my way to the afternoon's spread. The immediate question was, of course, how serious were Jonna's injuries and would she be able to return to the dig before the season was out. Several of the volunteers asked me, to which I could only reply to both queries that it was early to tell but that Stefan was in touch with the hospital and would let us know when there was something definite. The second question floating in the air naturally concerned "the find", which had generated a certain excitement, of anticipation of what the morrow might bring once it was fully "dug out", with a potpourri of fanciful speculations bandied about. I overheard one or two mention the terror alert, its possibly implications for the excavation, only for it to slip into oblivion.

Reuben arrived late, along with Stefan and Rafi. The news was that Jonna had had a mild concussion of sorts, with a seriously sprained leg and a torn ligament or two in her left arm, near the shoulder, along with a sustained shock to her body in general. She wouldn't be in the hospital for long, but she would need physical therapy to help her quickly regain full use of those affected limbs. Which was about what I'd figured. And now that Reuben was there - for some minutes I'd been afraid he wouldn't be coming - I could look for the opportune moment to make my offer.

As I sipped a concoction akin to a limeaid drink, I did a cursory appraisal of this summer's gang, congenially socializing about me as I kind of slunk into my own, becoming-invisible-in-plain-sight mode. (Hoping to capture something of it, several times I raised the camera to my eye, with no one seeming to notice.) Apart from the last couple of days (and Reuben's arrival earlier in the week), it had been, so far, a friction-free season here on Tel Ronish. None of the faction-forming contention among the volunteers that had rent previous summer periods, in my some years of experience on this job - the petty jealousies, preening egos, political grand-standings, sexual tension with its attractions-distractions that can wreak havoc among the volunteers working together - with Stefan or any director having to expend time and effort being a kind of counselor- referee. The supervisors too could stray across boundaries, though normally that more often befell the student supervisors, getting the hots for a particular volunteer or conversely a volunteer going for a supervisor - even the dig's director upon the odd occasion. (Stefan has this one story I'll leave untold here.) I too have had the temptation or two, as one encounters over time such a wide variety of personalities on these jobs I take. But that is just it, I'm on a job - and among any number of considerations cardinal rule number one is that you don't crap in the work place. I've always felt it important to maintain a "neutrality" among my work associates and the dig volunteers. (Because under what pretext can one carry on a special friendship, much less one as lovers, and still avoid whatever affects the work and one's relationship with others in such "tight quarters". Stefan was right to be concerned about Sushila's wearing it on her sleeve with her interest in Reuben, thus his jokingly giving me fair warning like he had.)

Was I now about to break that rule (forget about the mitigating circumstances involved here)? I suspected there had been "talk" about my continuing to keep Reuben assisting me on the Tel - with our rides in Rubble to and from the site, it would only be natural - some giggling as well (since we were often seen often engaged in deep conversation while we worked), which is why I have always kept the relationship out in the open and ostensibly aboveboard. And I have been careful about our encounters back at the kibbutz - lunch together, a dinner once, perhaps walking a ways together on a path, with seldom an eye contact during Arachat Arba. He, himself, appeared to have taken it in stride - had never sought a more private rendezvous as one might have suspected him to have gone for. Perhaps he instinctively understood the situation. Perhaps he was afraid of things evolving into a step further, into. He sensed the mutual attraction as strongly as I did, I was certain. It was almost as if we had intuitively agreed not to outwardly acknowledge it, each keeping it our little secret like something sweet to suck on to ourselves. And his was a more complicated situation what with Rebekah in the equation. I don't think he'd ever found himself in such a predicament before, or he'd never let it go this far in his feelings, I would speculate. And whatever I was doing or going to do might be merely based on a will-o-wisp on my part after all. He might simply have found me to be but a sympathetic ear. All practical wisdom told me I should leave good enough alone - but there was something so unresolved between us. (Or was it between him and Debbie?) I was going to play with fire. My "curiosity" had simply gotten the best of me.

I detected a lull among the gathering, as if sated they were waiting for someone to be the first to leave.

"Hey everybody," I spoke up, "I'm heading off tomorrow afternoon in the direction of the Kinneret. To shoot photographs of something other than stratigraphy and pottery sherds. Anybody want a ride somewhere? Don't speak up all at once."

"Don't tell me Deborah that these black flies bite better there?" said Joel, one of the South African volunteers, to an applause of laughter.

"If they do I can always bring some stowaways back in Rubble," I replied. "Will you be going as far as Tiberias?" asked Siri. "I have a friend there."

"I'll be looking for an overnight camping spot by the lake either just before or further north of Tiberias. As I meander."

"What about the terrorist alert earlier?" Daniel, the English guy who'd worked with Jonna asked.

"I haven't heard any more about it," I tried

to answer calmly, so as not to create a mountain out of a mole hill. "Hereabouts it's akin to a storm watch. The possibility exists, based on information received, is not to be taken lightly, I might add. So far, as Neve Rom hasn't gone into security mode, we'll see,"

"I've always wanted to visit Kibbutz Deganya, to see the Gordon House Museum," Reuben suddenly mused. "But it is not open on Shabbat. Long ago I visited Tiberias with a Jerusalem couple I was staying with. They went for a wedding. That night the three of us slept out on the lawn by the lake just down from the hotel where the reception had been held. Woke up the next morning with the sunrise. That was a sight I won't forget."

"You could hang out somewhere until Sunday, when the buses are running again." Steve, this older American guy, offered. "Hell, I'd join you. Only I've got be in Tel Aviv."

"I'd need to be back here early on the afternoon of Shabbat, as I have to leave early on Sunday, Yom Reshon. Even that's cutting it close. I don't want to just dash back in here and dash out again."

My grand ploy hadn't seemed to be working. And I hadn't remembered Reuben had mentioned something about meeting a publisher about a Hebrew edition of *(K)hamsin* the first of the week. I suppose I'd been under the delusion I'd have him there forever, of course knowing better. Well, I'd paid out the bait and he hadn't bitten, so far. If ever he would. Perhaps he too needed a cover, so as not to be obvious. And I had not quite taken that into consideration.

"I'll be leaving right after lunch tomorrow. Well, no later than midafternoon," I lastly announced with a bit of a chuckle ("Deborah time" it has been called before), as several were rising from their chairs. "In case, anybody? And I plan on being back by nightfall following Shabbat."

I was half way to my darkroom, having moved steadily but not exactly in a rush, when I heard someone behind me on the dirt path I'd taken, as if whomever it was was making a belated attempt to catch up; I stopped and turned, more curiously than cautiously, to see Reuben now gaining ground between us. Had I expected this? Had I hoped for it? He had a serious expression on his face, with almost a frown between his eyes, as if he were squinting into direct sunlight in order to make me out. He still wore the khaki-colored canvas shorts from the morning, but the shirt, a fresh one of a robin's egg blue hanging freely, I realized I had not before seen on him. That boyish bounce to his step was always so him. I almost expected him to reach up and run the fingers of one of his hands through those wavy curls.

Though at a distance yet, I started to raise my camera, but couldn't. "Deborah," he called out when he was close without having to shout.

"What is it, Reuben?" I said dispassionately but with a light smile. Not to let on just how much I suddenly wanted him to take me into his arms.

"I'm sorry for back there with my fumbling for an excuse to take you up on your offer," he said, without disguise. "I sounded pretty lame, I know."

"Reuben, you are welcome to come with me. No subterfuge necessary. I'd like you to. And we'll be back in good time."

I saw a half smile begin to break across his face, for all the caution still in his eyes as he slightly nodded in acknowledgement that words spoken aloud were not needed here between us.

"But," I added, "come first thing in the morning we've got to get onto whatever it is Jonna almost broke her neck over finding."

5

I don't know who was the more surprised, myself or the two soldiers having a smoke at the foot of the Tel when I looked down to see them sitting there, their rifles propped against their knees. They were on a foot patrol, I assumed, given that alert mentioned the day before. I merely nodded, like all was cool, and one of them gave me a tentative smile before I turned to go help Reuben coming up from the parking place with my equipment. As I'd yet to wrap that piece of muslin around my head, I guess I just looked like any tall Israeli girl with a lot thick dark hair.

We'd gotten an early start, the last stars of the night were just fading out by the time we'd arrived. We pulled carefully back a portion of the tarp lying over the trench in order to enter it and at my direction scrambled down, with the ladder in tow - to place it on the spot where Jonna had had it. I shot a few frames of the wall behind it already illuminated by the growing daylight. Though Jonna had been using it yesterday, I hoped someone would think to bring an extra one from storage that morning because I was going to need it to record the action, as that was my job to do. But first I needed to check out the scene so as to know from which angle to shoot from once things got hopping here. Climbing up, with Reuben steadying the ladder, I took a peek at what Jonna'd begun to unearth before her fall, and while it was tempting to make use of the brush she'd left behind, I knew that that would be going beyond the boundaries of my territory. But I could see by its outline that it was a sizable block, full square, the likes of which the dig had yet to come across since my association with it. And its importance in the scheme of things would depend upon its location in antiquity. That I'd leave to Aharon, to do the drawings and note where it was found. My job was to capture in photographs its before, during and after extraction. For which I took several more preliminary shots.

"What do you think?" Reuben asked, looking up at me.

"Considering its position, here on this side of the Tel facing in the general direction of Beit She'an, and given its apparent size, it is possibly a segment of an important gate. Possibly. Only it is not my job to speculate. I have seen the best archaeologist, when firing from the hip or lip in these circumstances, full of enthusiasm, make embarrassing assumptions."

Meanwhile I'd spotted dust rising in the distance.

With the tarpaulin covers raised, each member of the team returned to the respective tasks they'd left off from yesterday before the disruption brought on by Jonna's fall, but not before a number of them, their curiosity wetted, edged close to try and catch a glimpse at the exposure, and possible dislodging of whatever it was that Jonna had "found" - only to be shooed back by Stefan, his hat in hand as he wiped his forehead with the back of an arm ("In good time!" he barked. "Meanwhile we all have work to do, as we do here, and work with however minuscule the results is equally as important to the whole - remember that. Archaeology is romanticized by the big finds. But, overall, it is a process of elimination, separating the wheat from the chaff. The real find is precisely that, recognizing which is the wheat and which is the chaff."). Joining Daniel, Rafi and Aharon at the wall of the trench, besides Stephan, was Joel and, for some reason, Sushila, who'd become Aharon's "Girl Friday", taking notes. They worked expeditiously, taking their time, mumbling among themselves much like a team of doctors bent over a patient on an operating table as they picked, pried and loosened with utmost care, brushing as they went - while I photographed: over their shoulders from the ladder held by a diligent Reuben (lest I ended up, if lucky, joining Jonna); I shot from beneath their elbows at a crouch as well, from wherever I could edge my way in among them. (My height, that I've never complained about, has often served me well, also has had its disadvantages - like when I need to be inconspicuous in the midst of some action.) But I got my shots, in particular of Stefan's sharp profile, often in dramatic relief vis-à -vis the anxious grimaces upon the faces of the others in any particular frame, as all in various poses bent to the task of freeing this block of stone from the compact soil surrounding it - and especially the one capturing the anxious moment of elation that showed in Sushila's eyes staring out from behind the fall of her dark tousled locks - frames that should overall please those in Jerusalem for publicity purposes, political ones as well, yet might raise the ire of a few envious egos no less. (Stefan having always been something of a "maverick" in certain staid eyes at IAA.)

The previous evening as I was again working late, Stefan had caught up with me as I was leaving the darkroom. He acted like it was coincidental and began telling me, as we walked, that *Algot*, the official journal of the Israel Antiquities Authority, was about to publish an article by him on floatation, only he was certain they would slash his text yet publish every drawing as a consolation prize. Although I sensed this was but a beating around the bush before he got to his reason for wanting to see me - and alone at that: Reuben. As I'd begun to suspect, people had begun to wonder what it was with us, what with this veil of exclusiveness, however in plain sight, we'd drawn around ourselves at the Tel, as if we were a conspiracy of two, our heads always together so to speak, being deep into conversation as we worked as if nobody else existed.

"You and Reuben seem to have a lot to talk about," he sort of floated it out into night air, as I had expected he would eventually work around to doing. I let it hang there, for some steps ahead. The two of us were close to the same height, with me being but a couple of inches shorter. While Stefan was a very private person he exuded a familiarity that invited one to come close but not too close. I kind of let out a soft chuckled, as if unto myself.

"Yeah, I guess we do," I said. "He's been telling me this story that for certain reasons I have felt compelling, have found intriguing. It has multilayers that keep unfolding. It all began with his telling of a dream he'd had. I'd mentioned something I'd read on our way out our second morning about the effect of dreams on our waking conscious. And some while later, while we took a breather, he began to tell of his dream of this young woman, who was some years dead, a cousin he had been close to in their youth, writing this long letter to him - like a voiceover in a film while you see the letter being written on the screen - in essence she hadn't died, she wrote, that she had never forgotten him, that she had written him previously but had never had a reply, like perhaps he'd never gotten them. Or he'd forgotten her. Needless to say, it shook him up. He began to search her out, belatedly as it were. He'd gotten to speak at length to another cousin whose family had been allowed to maintain a distant contact with her following her having been given up for adoption, fostered actually, by her older sister in the wake of their parents' premature deaths. He would also come across a teenage photo of her just before her death in a desk at his mother's, along with this rather sanctimonious memorial to her by her foster father, a Presbyterian minister, saying in effect that he was happy that her struggle for his faith was over, 'praise God'. And interspersed with this Reuben's own recollections of her as a happily precocious, inquisitive child. I think it is a book in him wanting to get out."

"O man, it certainly sounds like it," Stefan uttered. "I had no idea. He never mentioned anything to me about it."

"I think it was just a moment of opportunity," I said quickly enough. "And once the ball got rolling I encouraged it, by prying further. As I said, it resonated with me."

"He's off to the Kinneret for Shabbat. Then he leaves on Yom Reshon, Sunday."

"I know, Stefan," I said. "Don't worry."

It turned out to be pillar base of some kind, cut from marble, once the soil had been carefully dug out all around it, and was larger than originally have thought to have been (though not quite as I'd earlier surmised) - a meter and a half high and squared perfectly, being half a meter thick, with no markings on it that we could see, given where it sat in the shallow niche that had been made by freeing it, about 3 feet from the floor of the trench. "What the fuck!" I could hear all of us, my, myself included, thinking out loud. It was so perfectly "cut," or chiseled more like it. Almost as if it had been made in a mold. It had been wishful thinking to have seen it as the base of a gate's portal, a private home's perhaps. Even then? It appeared to be so "unblemished". It was going to be the genesis of a lot of head-scratching, probably of endless arguments - until many will no doubt think it might have been best Jonna hadn't stumbled across it. But the discovery of it, given its location, was inevitable. I'd wanted to laugh, but thought it best not to under the circumstances discretion the better part of valor and all.

In the wake of all this, Stefan conferred at length with Aharon and Rafi, huddling out of ears' reach of the rest of us peons. The volunteers who'd aided in the digging of it out seemed reluctant to return to their regular squares - as they had nothing exciting to regale to their team mates; one could almost smell the collective disappointment. Until Daniel spoke up to say they all had work to do, seeing as tomorrow was Shabbat (well, he certainly did, what without Jonna there). I continued to photograph "the enigma" as Stefan had begun to refer to it, if a bit caustically. He wanted my shots from that morning, whatever digital ones I had, before I left, in order to send them off to IAA headquarters in Jerusalem as quickly as possible. (While I thought more digging out from it might turn up some further explanation.) So when we returned to Neve Rom for breakfast, I'd stay to develop those from my print camera in the darkroom. In the meantime, I dug out my digital and again shot none too few of "enigma" from various angles, having Reuben place the measuring stick, then holding the reflector shields every which way. I wasn't sure what I was trying to do - and I was certain it was driving Reuben to distraction - other than to while away the time. I suppose I wanted to show Stefan's "enigma" in some way that might trigger however vague an association in the memory of a viewer, certainly some imminent archeologists.

"Patience, Reuben," I said in Hebrew with a certain tongue in cheek chuckle, and he'd laughed suddenly with a half-hidden smile - followed by an audible sigh.

If he wanted to, Reuben could hitch a ride

back to the Tel after breakfast, and I'd drive out once I'd done the prints to get him and my equipment before lunch. Which he agreed to as we were returning to Neve Rom in Rubble. For some reason the air appeared to be a bit clearer than normal (by whatever standard that might be), or perhaps it was this surge of expectation, if not eagerness (really, I asked myself, like some silly teenager), with thoughts of the afternoon with just the two of us on the road. Though I felt it was no less hot than usual here in the upper region of the Jordan Rift at that hour.

"I didn't tell you about this old friend of mine, Lora, doing an astrology chart on Debbie, did I?" he broke the lapse into silence between us as Rubble bumped and grunted in a kind of rhythmic traction over the kibbutz farm road I preferred to take, unless of course I came up behind a "green chop" picker, with a lumbering wagon piled high with freshly cut grass unwieldily hitched to it.

"Oh no, Reuben," I laughed, inadvertently. "That sounds like really filleting the skeleton."

"It was nothing like that," he quickly amended, "I assure you."

"Okay, I didn't mean to scoff, it just caught me off guard. It's just that my perception of astrology is that it's akin to crystal ball gazing. Ignorance is bliss, okay."

"It was mine too, I am still skeptical how neatly it packages things, yet on the other hand the findings, as they were in Debbie's case, did fit the bill, uncannily so."

"So, what were they," I took the risk of asking, knowing he was anxious to tell me (as if by telling me he was fitting together these pieces of a puzzle in his head, for which I had become his sounding board, if not a resounding board, a mental reflector of sorts). "Was it positive, negative or some gray area in between?"

"Overall positive, with questionable gray areas," he came back. "I'll spare you the conjuncts, the squaring, the oppositions, the transiting and all. The equations that intrigue this friend to no end, hers being an analytical mind, but the terminology in and of itself leaves me scratching my head."

"Reuben, stop beating around the bush," I almost cried out, fortunately getting a grip on myself lest I sounded both too eager as well as somewhat exasperated with his mental meandering, his penchant for head-tripping over the inconsequential.

"What my friend saw was a very strong willed young lady," he began quietly as if looking inward into himself, like in order to remember as thoroughly as possibly what this friend, Lora, had summarized for him of her findings. "She could express herself and argue well, and did so with her foster family. She had a very pronounced, modest kind of femininity. A lot of charm and originality. Plus common sense. And an earthy kind of appeal. Sex appeal? I'm not exactly sure if that's that meant - or to whom? Yet, she had a definite temper. With a tendency to rush things. There was a very restrictive male influence in her life (Reverend Marston obviously); and she had a tendency to manipulate or be manipulated by women. (Joy, Mrs. Marston perhaps, these are Lora's assumptions, I might add.) Her adolescence was probably very rough - much domestic discord (money problems, self-esteem, family illness and death of parents?). Therefore it must have been absolutely hell, for the foster family when she went to live with them as well as for Debbie herself. The Reverend was, if anything, understating it. Had she been older she'd have almost certainly been in serious trouble, as Lora saw it. So in that sense, The Reverend was probably right in saying that he gave her 'a faith', or at any rate a port in the storm (which is about how Lora put it). But, by the time of her death she would have been about over that. She would have had a great deal of pride and have been capable of acting out whatever role was expected of her. But she would have devoted a lot of her energies and abilities into trying to break free from the restrictions - ie: with possibly an early graduation, a job, further education - with again the danger of rushing things. There was some indication she was prone to negative peer influence - drug culture having reach suburbia - or was experiencing

some kind of spiritual crisis (if she had internal-
ized it, which Lora doubted but where I was
wont to disagree, having already heard - from his
memoriam - of her battle with Marston to use
Jesus Christ Superstar in the church's youth study
group she led). She was just like me in that respect when I had been an over-enthusiastic
idealist in my teens - only in my case, it was Jack
Kennedy Superstar. Nevertheless, I'd been there,
I really felt I understood her, like we were two
peas in a pod or something. On the day of her
death, to conclude, unpredictable forces were
present in her home life, indicating that she may
have been on drugs or medication. Indicating a
death by violence or some emotional upset.
Lora's take was that she was probably not a very
good driver to begin with, 'as what teenagers
are', to quote Lora (I disagree), and under stress
from several different quarters at the same time.
Which to me is open to question, given the wit-
ness report that she slumped over the wheel
doing something like 20 mph on a suburban
street. Which lent credence to the possibility of
a bursting heart valve."

"Or something." Well, definitely "something", we two. I'd felt it early, this "communica-
tion" that had no name - as had he I'm sure - only
I hadn't needed my mind to get around it like he
apparently had. But in my child's world it was
like in a fairy tale where the handsome prince
"awakens me with a kiss", though in his world

at the time, the very thought of us being, as he put it, "two peas in a pod", was ultra taboo. And with anyone other than my father and mother (free spirits they each in their own way were) he'd have probably courted censorship for his merely allowing me my freedom with him, as it were (that even Joy thought was "cute", though I suspect I was something of a proxy for her own desires, that she'd have died rather than divulge). While I might shudder now, but not without a chuckle, upon recollecting my teen-age enthusiasms, that rock opera in particular, I see now it is something we innately share, not just the longing for the ideal passion that ignites our sensibilities, but an ability to deeply care in our heart of hearts for that which challenges and captures our imaginations, leaving us with this insatiable longing to share. And in our case, being close cousins, it was like we were born siamese twins.

"It is interesting how astrology can be so general yet addresses any number of particulars, given the alignment of sun, moon and planets on a single day. I realize that it is not esoteric any more than it is true science," I managed to say with as straight a face as possible. "I'm not sure I'd want to see what your friend Lora would come up with if she did mine."

"Lora says it has worked for her as good as anything else when it comes to getting a handle on people in personal situations. Like it can be taken for a guide, the rest is upon to you. But how do you see it fitting the Debbie I'm been describing? Even if just superficially?"

As we were rolling into the kibbutz already, I said, "Intermission time, dear Reuben. I've got to grab breakfast on the run and get these prints done to spare our Stefan a peptic ulcer. We'll have loads of time later this afternoon on the road."

And there wouldn't a "three's a crowd" after all. Early on last evening, Siri'd caught up with me before I'd returned to the studio to say that her friend in Tiberias had gone to Eilat and to thank me for the offer nevertheless.

In truth, I had come a long ways, by the time of my death - or rather of Deborah's death in my place. I had done so already by the time Deborah and I met. I'd learned to play my role well - to be a step or two ahead of what was expected of me. Until at times I didn't know where the role and "I" began and ended. (Anne Frank's protagonist's quandary as well, as she depicted the fight within herself, between her opposite halves.) Having submerged myself in it to such a degree until I forgot there was a me. That me that was always lurking just below the surface that every once in a while would pull me up short, set off by some trigger of memory seemingly inconsequential, a mere coincidence was all it would take. But it had been my being at loggerheads with Marston over *Jesus Christ Superstar*, where I had so ardently believed myself right (and he an old hard- on) that had come perilously close to throwing me back to square one. I was saved I suppose by the ongoing "struggle for faith" subterfuge I could quite sincerely pull like the rabbit out of a hat. And I had been under the weather since that early spring with cystitis, like a low grade fever feeling that seemed to unendingly come and go, not without a certain "embarrassment" (I supposed, in that household, I felt I was expected to feel embarrassed for my body's disorder as much as for my bodily functions) accompanying it. It definitely brought back memory of my mother's cries while dying like she did from bladder cancer - and there were lost in transition moments where I'd succumb to paranoia and none too little self-pity. But it was my meeting Deborah that really saved me, her of the infectious personality, my other. Which would open the doors of perception without some mind-altering drug. Suddenly, I was seeing everything from a wholly new perspective. Mind-blowing was hardly the word for it. If Deborah were suddenly alive, I'd gladly relinquish this we of me, I think I'd even be willing to - no I wouldn't go that far, I had things to do.

And right that moment it was to finish developing those prints and select the digitals. Of this object of mounting speculation. Tests wound be run on it once it was physically delivered to Jerusalem. Besides its age, was it indigenous to the site, in that it wasn't a plundered piece brought from afar? Like from Hazor just up the road so to speak, where legend had it there was a grand palace or two from those times, where another archeological team had busily been excavating for some years already, following up the initial one in the 50s led by Yigal Yadin. My photographs, both the prints and the digitals, came out three dimensionally sharp, as I had strived to precisely obtain - and in general I was quite pleased with them. (Though I could hardly expect a box of candy from Naor Dan, praise whomever.) Hazor in its glory years had been like unto a city state, with its own kings, the largest fortified city in the region, trading as far afield as Babylon. It rose to prominence under the Canaanites, was later Assyrian, then Israel's to be razed following Israel's revolt against the Assyrians. Some theory is that it was destroyed from within due to factional strife. But in this part of the world theories abound, much as do splitting hairs over a Talmudic tract. Such as the ancient Israelites originated as a subculture under the Canaanites. But then what is History but the stories we tell. This piece of stone might end up being sub-labeled "Jonna's Dilemma" when all she did had been coming close to breaking her neck, finding it before, say, Daniel did. (And the latest on Jonna's condition, heard during breakfast, was that she was due to be released from the hospital in a few days. But her return to the dig remain doubtful.)

With prints hung up to dry - as well as stacked on frames - they would be ready to handle upon my return; meanwhile, having "edited" the digitals, tweaking some of them to soften what were glaring contrasts in order to create an encompassing whole, where light and shadow worked together rather than as, say, opposing camps - I sent to Stefan. Yom Rishon was early enough for Jerusalem to get the prints.

The heat was rising, but a tad drier - the slightest degree drop in the humidity level was instantly felt, offering a marginal respite - as I revved up Rubble for the return to the site to fetch my equipment and Reuben. The sky, I realized, was so much more blue than usual.

"We'll gas up in Beit She'an," I said as Reuben, who'd stashed a rucksack on the back seat with mine, a Norwegian make for the military or mountain climbing he'd no doubt gotten from Rebekah, climbed in beside me. He wore those sand colored jeans he had worn the evening upon his arrival and yet another light blue canvas shirt with large pockets (but not bulging with notes and stuff, just a thin wallet and probably his passport), with a leather fanny pack fastened around his waist from which he pulled a pair of 1960ish tortoise wayfarers (I almost laughed. He was so contrarily an American in a kind of contradictory way - yet not). And instead of the brogans, that pair of sturdy leather moccasins polished to just short of a shine I remembered too from that first evening. It was like a style he'd patented or something. But, as I've noted elsewhere, it suited - it was so him. And for once in a blue moon he actually appeared relaxed, as if a burden had been arbitrarily whisked off his shoulders, that just below the surface hint of anxiety having taken a breather. Often enough the divide between the writer in person and his protagonist/guide through the labyrinth he'd entitled *(K)hamsin* - that I was continuing to read - seemed paper thin, only in odd moments to be thrown off balance by some dichotomy I could not quite grasp. It was like at once he was that 16-year-old seen through the eyes of a six year old happily gone puppy-love gaga and the ever so familiar stranger he must always have been. (Talk about an enigma,) No matter, I was behind the wheel. (For all that adrenaline kick released quixotically when having fallen in love.) I felt it was good he was there with me again, even if he didn't know it was me - come what may. Because one thing I knew for certain, I was Deborah, after all that may, or would, be said or done.

For the trip I'd gaily jettisoned so to speak my habitual on-the-job garb (including trusty brogans, traded for a sturdy pair of leather sandals) for a sleeveless bodice from which at the waist the attached circle skirt (my favorite feminine wear) flared outward to well below my knees, offering a feeling of lightness for a change, not that I wasn't fleet-footed enough in whatever. It being something I'd put together the winter before, as if anticipating that very afternoon. I liked the colors, being no less conscious than most people, women in particular, of the effect hue coupled with line had on the human libido. And I too was wearing a pair of shades because at that hour of the day hereabouts one doesn't easily drive without them.

"I got into *Jesus Christ Superstar* myself. For a bit." Reuben had been giving me his sardonically humorous take on the scene at the Tel before I'd arrived to pick him and my photo shooting equipment up (it was like everybody had a conspiracy theory on how that stone block happened to be there, that there might even be a curse on it that caused Jonna to fall like she did) when I said this lightly, as if coming from outer space, as if I hadn't been listening though I had, finding it to a degree 'worrisome', the superstition. "Just like Debbie did," I continued. "Well, in my own way. Obviously not at where she was coming from. Mine being such a different milieu. I suspect there was an unconscious teacher in Debbie in that she sought to use it in the church youth group she led, probably to make the message more contemporary, there was seemingly such an earnestness in her overall character - as you said as much about yourself in relation to your attraction at her age to the Kennedy mystique, a New Frontier and all - I've been reading *(K)hamsin*, Stefan loaned me his copy. That was probably the case with all three of us, being oddballs so to speak among our peers. Jesus the rock star in Debbie's and my case held great appeal, certainly a euphoric sex appeal - combined with an altruistic philosophy - to those of us coming along in what is labeled the 'hippy generation', even if she and I were at the distant younger end and still wet behind the ears. And if you feel somewhat sheepish now about digging Kennedy, I suspect Debbie would likewise about *Superstar*, as I certainly do, how we ran overboard with our youthful exuberances, seeing them now as based on shallow premises, if no less sincere. Because we felt something strongly enough to want to share it with others, at all costs. Just because it may have been a shallow surface we felt attracted to, the emotions we invested in these whatever attractions really ran deep. We felt something and we dared to confront our peers as well as those with authority in the cause of it. Does that at all ring a bell with you?

"Exactly, though so many of my youthful passions went the way of my penchant for hunting, God included," he answered. "To a one, they simply evaporated. One day I no longer could get a hard-on, well excited, about certain things.

Stuff like believing there is a God or a Messiah even. Or shooting small animals. I am still told by both staunch Christians and observant Jews alike that I got off on the wrong foot, that I am throwing the baby out with the bath water. So be it, it's all man's imagination made, with the totem pole dry rotten at the core. When only good deeds in the long run count, is what it is all about anyway - learning to live together, in 'communitas'. So, yes, it does make me feel sheepish to remember. I try to look at it humorously though."

"I've been learning to," I said, for a moment hearing Deborah's voice. "Ever since I met someone, eons ago now, who made me realize what it was that I had been seeing all along with eyes wide shut. It's a lifelong tutorial, shedding skins, I think."

At Beit She'an - Rubble with a full tank and a can of motor oil on board to join the extra jug of water, for the radiator, in case - we joined Rte. 90, headed north. Traffic was light, despite the approach of Shabbat, mostly tour buses that roared past us, leaving a plume of burnt diesel in their wake as they scorched rubber to reach their destination before sundown.

"I know I've mentioned that I've been to Tiberias before, just once, for a night and morning only," Reuben offered, offhandedly. "It was in early November. That September/October back in England, I'd been picking hops in Kent to make the money for the trip out. Once in Israel I mainly kipped, as the English put it, with this married couple, Stephen and Deirdre, new immigrants, in Jerusalem. Old friends from London. They had a wedding to attend in Tiberias and they asked me to come along. We traveled by bus. Through the West Bank. A hot and dusty ride through the latter half of a pale sun afternoon, making local stops. Most of the passengers were Arabs, the elderly. I remember this one woman wearing traditional dress, intricately embroidered, holding a couple of caged hens on her lap. I suppose I might have gawked, it was all like out of the movies. The three of us were obviously Israeli, Jewish or whatever, laughingly so, in our western clothes. But no one appeared to take notice, no doubt intentionally so. Even if Deirdre, who had the most beautiful pair of legs, was wearing the shortest of shorts. At the bus station, upon our arrival, she changed into a party dress before we struck out to find the hotel where the wedding was to be held, down on the lake front. I hung out on the periphery of the ceremony, then walked a ways off and sat down on the grass as dusk fell, to where the music and the gaiety in general was at once removed. You know, at once feeling left out while relieved not to have been obliged to participate, to have had to suffer it in my face. I'd lain back counting the stars, thinking of Byron's poem: 'And the sheen on their spears was like the stars on the sea as the blue wave rolls nightly over deep Galilee' - thinking how ironical it was that I was there, of all places, simply lying on the grass. Did his English lordship really known Kinneret's depth or had he simply taken poetic license? I must have slept, because a giggling Stephen and Deirdre awoke me, having brought me pieces of cake wrapped in paper and half a bottle of gone flat champagne to wash it down with.

"Might have been worse. It might have been a bottle of Goldstar," I injected, and we both laughed, a bit ridiculously.

"I awoke the next morning from the rising sun over the lake striking me in the face, and already drying what felt like dew-sodden clothes," he continued, his voice and the rhythm of Rubble's tires on the tarmac coalescing. "With a stiff neck and something of a dull headache. The champagne, I guess. No one had bothered us sleeping out like that, which sort of surprised me. All was quiet back down shore, where the reception party debris on the hotel's terrace hung limp from the dew. Next to me, Steven and Deirdre slept still, her arm thrown across him, her head on his chest. It was like a scene out of a movie, I thought. The sun struck too the distant Golan Heights picturing it in broad relief and I thought of the battle to take them in '67, remembering what had seemed like the unending drone, throughout the pitch black night before, of transport planes flying north. Anyway, watching that sun come up over the lake is something I'll never forget, like the night I saw the moon rise at Ein Fara. It was so magnificently, monstrously huge as it the cleared the rim of the wadi's wall opposite from where I slept near the ledge, at this 4th century monastery literally carved into the cliff - I slept on a wooden bench there, with this beautiful Greek spread beneath me and over me. The next morning when I gushed my admiration of it, Balthazar, the resident monk, a young guy from Austria, gave the spread to me, just like that, though it had been a gift from his bishop in Athens. I still have it. So, yes, I can understand your wanting to come here to try and capture tomorrow morning's sunrise on film. In retrospect, I regret not having a camera that night at Ein Fara, having seen many a moon over a canyon shot but nothing like that. Maybe it's like Rebekah says, some experiences shouldn't be 'recorded' but allowed to live naturally in our subconscious."

"Why were you at Ein Fara?" I felt a pang of something sharply, though I quite agreed with what Rebekah said.

"Stephen again," Reuben chuckled, somewhat abashedly. "Besides the hike, he hoped to find the monk Balthazar still there, whom he'd met some months earlier, on what would become Stephen's many hikes when he and Deirdre had first come on Aliyah, sometimes alone, sometimes with another, this Hebrew U. student named Jill we both had known back in London. Stephen had been concerned about Balthazar at the time. For some reason I forget now. So after his Ulpan Etzion class one afternoon we took a bus from Jerusalem to this village called Anata, where a bunch of little kids threw stones at us (I wanted to throw their stones back at them, not to hit them, but Stephen dissuaded me) as we had to pass through in order to reach the place we could climb down into Wadi Qelt, where the one of us below guided the foot of the one above to a foothold. Once at the bottom and a little ways down the wadi, we came upon this clear crystal water flowing out from beneath a broad shelf, and at Stephen's beckoning I fell flat to my stomach and began to drink. Was that ever good-tasting water. Water elsewhere has never tasted the same since."

There was just a hint of turquoise in the otherwise translucent blue of the afternoon sky that lightened out ever so slightly on the northernmost horizon as we neared Kinneret. With Rubble's windows rolled down, the air now no longer felt like one was holding one's face beneath a restroom hand dryer. I was enjoying the feel of it in my hair, against my skin, the rush of it beneath my top, it being sleeveless as it were, flowing in freely when I stretched out my arm next to the door to grip the top of the steering wheel. A warm caress of sorts, almost weightless, that gave tingles here and there as if my skin was being touched by leaping sound waves, leaving tiny electric sparks in their wake. I was wondering what he was thinking about - yet I should have known. He spoke abruptly, following a lengthy silence. It was as if my Deborah was hardly any competition for his Debbie of yore.

"I would discover in my search for Debbie that her being fostered by a protestant minister had touched off a religious war of sorts, not unlike the kinds that ravaged throughout Europe from the sixteenth to the eighteenth century - you know, the 30 Years War, the War of the Spanish Succession and the like. I'd no idea. That is, the sentiment that fueled them may lie dormant but is far from being dead."

"You're kidding. How so?" I almost laughed. What now, I was thinking?

"Well, Uncle Seth was from a Catholic background, being Polish or Lithuanian, though nothing much was ever made of it to my knowledge. He was a 'lapsed Catholic' in Rev. Marston's words, as if that provided an excuse for his taking Debbie into a Protestant household. Well, into his household. Myself, I never heard of Uncle Seth being overtly 'religious' in any sense, my aunt either whose family from way back when were 'nominal Methodists' (Reverend Marston again). Unlike Kathy and Kerry who had gone to a Catholic grade school as Aunt Reba was

Catholic, though I never knew of her to go to church, not regularly if she did. (My uncle - like Aunt Victoria, his sister - was a Methodist leaning towards a homely fundamentalism in his later years.) I never witnessed any religious fervor during my youth from any of them, other than Uncle Raymond who could be seen quietly reading in his bible. It is possible Debbie and her siblings were christened or something as babies, had holy water or something sprinkled on their heads, as a matter of form. But that was about the extent of their Catholicism, again to my knowledge. If anything, they may have gone en family to a Catholic service, like at Easter, early on. Whatever, it was not talked about, never mentioned. This Catholic connection, I'd subsequently learn, was Aunt Reba's modus operandi for wanting to take in Debbie and Nicholas, as if she ever maintained a Catholic home. (Uncle Raymond was quite content with Rev. Marston being a Presbyterian and all.) But Reba was like that. And she thoroughly enjoyed a cause, a crusade, to get fired up about. Only Joy had a particular disdain for Reba, that had begun way back. As Reba never lost an opportunity to bad mouth Joy. Reba claimed she once caught Joy stealing from her or from Kathy and Kerry. Or had perhaps had strongly suspected Joy had done so. Only Joy had never admitted it, had never confessed, when Reba had run her through an inquisition court of one. Which in itself - Joy not 'confessing' - had been a worse crime than the one she was accused of in the first place. And with Joy 'giving' Debbie to a Protestant 'heretic' of a pastor, Joy was put forever beyond the pale. Reba would hassle both for a number of years, I would hear about, trying to find a way to get Debbie back into the family fold. But what family fold one might ask. Because that was simply the catch word. It wasn't religion, that was in itself the excuse. It was a tribal kind of thing, a matter of honor, pride, intensely sectarian."

"My mother had hinted at this being the case, not to mention Reba's ego, and my talking to Kerry that morning only confirmed it. In that Kerry gave me the name and address of this cohort of Reba's, a Mrs. McIver. I duly wrote her, explaining who I was and why I was 'searching' for Debbie as it were. (This Mrs. McIver I'd learned, my having given Kerry a description of the two stout women in black holding onto Debbie's arms during Aunt Victoria's funeral, was one of those women.) She wrote me back almost immediately, a thick packet of a letter, as if she'd found in me a 'paladin' to take up the mantle of a lost cause. Reverent Marston, in effect, had killed Debbie. By denying her access to her true religion, her being his prisoner, subjected to his brainwashing, at his mercy (in more ways than one, she'd hinted). In response, Debbie had committed suicide rather than submit to the heretic deviation from her true faith. I felt like I'd really opened a can of worms. I replied, with some hesitation, saying I was more interested in learning of the person Debbie had become in those intervening years rather than rehash some personal vendetta of long ago I'd never been a part of to begin with. I had rather slowly worked up steam, let's say, until I came right out and called a spade a spade. Because I, myself, had no argument with Marston in that respect, for fostering her, that it was Joy and certain members of my mother's family who were the initial villains in my eyes (Mrs. McIver - whom I would learn too, had been Debbie's 'godmother' - had no kind words for Joy), and even that couldn't really be held against them in the long run. Marston had made the offer to take Debbie in and it had been accepted. Had he made a cause of it, strong-armed anybody, I had no way of truly knowing. Even if I might have suspected it hadn't been all innocence on his part, that he probably saw Debbie as a lost lamb in need of rescuing (by indoctrinating her into his faith), I have no doubt. (My mother contended he did it for the money he got from the government - until Debbie turned eighteen.) And how much pressure, with sweet talk, he may have laid on Joy, perhaps my Aunt Victoria before she died, is anybody's guess. But to start a harassment campaign against Marston and his family had been neither my design nor desire. I thought that would lay it to rest, but it didn't. I forthwith got back a diatribe of sorts that was both a plea (to punish a grave injustice) and a reprimand (to do my duty towards Debbie's memory if I cared for her like I'd indicated I had). So I angrily now wrote back that there was no justice here to be sought, just revenge. Which I didn't think Debbie would have wanted carried out in her name. What I guess I wanted to say was I was no longer a Christian and couldn't give a shit about what amounted to an arcane religious contention apparently still being fought in some quarters between Catholics and Protestants. After that I heard no more."

I managed not to burst out laughing - though Reuben may have been put more at ease had I done so. He might have laughed with me, until there were tears in both our eyes. Yes, it all seemed like out of a lifetime ago, a bizarre episode that somehow had washed over my juvenile self, being in the eye of the storm. I remember long silences, furtive whispers, the rumble of distant murmurs. All I knew was I was being sent away, expelled from the only world I'd ever known, ripped up like a sapling, roots and all, to be transplanted in a strange and distant soil (within six months, the Marstons would move, he having accepted a pastorship in that city I would come of age in while wrapped in a smothering cocoon.) Not unlike the girl in the Michal Bat Adam movie sent to live in a kibbutz children's dormitory. So consumed by an inner rebellion, an intransigence was more like it, I paid scant attention to whatever was swirling about me. And afterwards, when I made that separate peace in order to bide my time and prepare for my eventual escape, however long it took, I put it all into a rabbit hole or something, buried it in a subconscious realm of sorts and 'lost' the password so to speak. What I do remember is this cloying sensation exuded by Aunt Reba and her chain of friends, in particular that Mrs. McIver. (I didn't like her one bit, just the mention of her name now brought back a sensory memory of the foul talcum powder she used.) It was like they had suddenly begun to own me, that I was a possession of some kind (for some inexplicable reason). Now it all makes sense in Reuben's telling of it. It explains a lot of things that came later. Bloody, fucking hell! What a hoot. Yet there is something desperately sad about it all. A martyr, was that Debbie's legacy? A suicide in the name of religion? The sum total of a life neatly packaged for posterity, for some diehards to get their rocks off over? (A part of me suddenly wanted to pull off the road and puke - but I was saved by a lengthy stretch of guard rails; and as I was forced to drive on the sensation fortunately subsided.)

We'd passed the entrance to Degania Alef a ways back (where his Gordon Museum was located), but I'd been reluctant to mention it lest it interrupt the flow of the latest Debbie related narrative he'd so intensely been expounding.

When we returned later for dinner - at the famed kibbutz restaurant called 1910, after the date of the kibbutz's founding - he'd be able to feel he'd at least been in close proximity to it.

"Here are your palm trees, Deborah! And in abundance!" Reuben burst out suddenly with some enthusiasm, as if he'd just taken notice of the landscape we were traversing. Having turned to me, he'd probably caught my slip of smile unto myself, pleasantly relieved for the change of subject matter that I might immediately respond to with a certain wholehearted-ness. "Some of them look quite old, even ancient."

For long stretches at a time they had flanked the highway now with their tall trunks standing sentinel-like before their exuberant tops burst forth high against the blue sky into those long green sort of plumelike fronds - when they didn't lean wearily amid sword-straight cypress and any number of trees heavy with leaves having encroached upon them. We were fast coming up upon Kinneret.

"No, they are hardly ancient," I countered, in earnest. "The earliest are from the 1930s for that matter. If they haven't been transferred elsewhere - the fate of a tree that can no longer bear fruit - to serve as a decoration, like at Ben-Gurion for example. By the turn of the 20th century the landscape around here was pretty much barren, I've read. Like Mark Twain had earlier described it in his *Innocents Abroad*. It was due to the work of an agricultural training cooperative called the 'Kinneret Yard', along with local kibbutzim, interested in their produce, dates, that these trees are here. It was a guy involved with the founding of 'Kinneret Yard' who was sent abroad to find species that would be compatible to the area who was greatly responsible for their being here. He traveled to Irag, Egypt, Kurdistan and beyond, renting trucks for hauling across deserts and ships to transport by sea. Quite an expedition either way. And those local kibbutzim and co- operatives nourished, repaired them, for replanting. Nothing happens by accident, you see."

"You know, you are like an encyclopedia at times," he chuckled. "In a good way, seriously. Ask you a question and, well, I like it, I appreciate it. I've been more accused of being the same than appreciated, is probably because of my pedantic delivery, where with you it kind of flows naturally, like from an underground spring."

"Oh Reuben, you romanticize me. Remember I'm the Deborah atop that baulk shouting orders before the Devil Dust hit."

"Who can forget."

"Yeah, one of my more profound moments."

We continued to banter in this vein, though it began to trouble me as to where it was leading. Or possibly lead, under faux colors let's say. If it was leading anywhere at all. Because I simply could not "read" him, not really. And I supposed that bugged my ego if anything. Because he gave this outwardly laid-back appearance of just being along for the ride. As he seemingly took in the passing roadside, now densely luxuriant with the local flora, now sparsely so, in between the traffic clogged roundabouts where at one point I had to slow Rubble to a crawl before I was able to shoot through with a gear-grinding roar. All the while alone with his thoughts. It was as if whatever "signals" the two of us had been giving the other those past several days had been bounced off some distant planet, reaching both of us on the rebound like the light of long dead stars. Unless all of this had been a figment of an enflamed imagination on my part, reading into looks and gestures a kind of wishful thinking I knew was morally dubious at the outset. It was probably best that way after all, neither one of us needed to leap into some "existential" quagmire. It had been a silly idea anyway, rather rash at best, more like winging it than even plausibly thought out. (I really hadn't taken him, nor Rebekah, into consideration - which was so unlike me.). So just lean back and enjoy his company as it was, I told myself, with hopes that he enjoyed mine likewise. Because the only thing I could be near certain about was that we did mutually enjoy each other's company, looked forward to it even. Without aforethought I'd play it by ear, as originally conceived and just hoped I could maintain my equilibrium throughout.

Soon enough Kinneret would come into view, in between the pale trunks of drooping eucalyptus and the coarse trunks of date palms, its pastel blue expanse mirroring the now mid-afternoon sky with just that hint of turquoise beneath its surface, like an undercoat subtly showing through. (Straight ahead, in the greater distance one could catch fleeting glances of the minute yet cube like cluster that was Tiberias glittering white in the sunlight.) But before that I would turn off towards the beach I knew was not far behind the thickening roadside greenery. Happy at last to put this panoramic four-laner behind us, upon which Rubble's generally slug-like performance could hardly match that of the ubiquitous modern sedan. Even this antique British roadster, its top down (Reuben had exclaimed it was a 1930s something Alvis for certain), had scooted past us as if in slow motion and then in a kind of whoosh was gone.

"I hope 'the nook' is still there, hasn't been overrun by the commercial camping scene in the couple of years since I was here last," I uttered as much to myself as to Reuben, who'd glanced at me with an abrupt questioning look, as I wheeled hard onto a narrow, paved lane, only to wheel again rather sharply into an even narrower dirt-surface track that wound its way through a scattered thicket of trees past several jam-packed parking places for campers' vehicles (their owners having set up tents close to the shore), until we came to what appeared to be a dead end until right upon it. With another 45 degree turn, Rubble sled bumpily into a squeeze of a break in a high fence topped with barbed wire like something left from some former army compound out of by-gone times and in a minute or so I pulled up in front of a kiosk of sorts (more like a small shack that might have once been a guard house) that for all intent and purposes looked deserted.

"Wait here," I said, as I got out to walk over to an open window, "I'll check things out. But so far it looks like we are in luck."

And we were. Though neither Marty nor Yoni were around, the "check-in" was set up so one could help themselves. One merely signed into a notebook, dropped the money through a slot and picked the next number on the pile (only I reached for the bottom and pulled out the one for my hideaway spot, then wrote them a quick note:

Surprise, I know. Last summer a bust, never got off the reservation, all well in the end though. Am here for the night, to shoot the sun at dawn. You know me, never satisfied. Have a friend with me. We'll be going out for a late dinner. Otherwise, Rubble will be parked incognito, you know. Have to leave early, but maybe a short catchup beforehand?

Shabbat Shalom,
Deborah

"I guess you are wondering where I have dragged you to," I said, as I climbed back into Rubble, clutching our number.

"It has crossed my mind," Reuben smiled.

"I met Yoni and Marty, our momentarily absent hosts, my first year on Tel Ronish where Marty's niece, one of the volunteers that summer, got into a tight spot and I took her under my wing. Marty is English, came out just after the Six Day War. Yoni is from Jerusalem. His army service coincided with the War of Attrition.

"Ugh, that must have been rough."

"Yeah, they met somehow, somewhere during this period, as Marty had stayed on, first on a kibbutz, then as a nurse in Beersheba. When he got out they went back to England, that is Marty did and Yoni followed her. They returned in '73, just before the October War, where Yoni was in the battle to retake 'The Heights'. And here they remain. Yoni writes poetry, Marty manages, owns a small book store in Tel Aviv. I never quite got it clear when they started coming up here summers, or even why originally. I wonder if they even remember, exactly. It was that kind of period for them, I think. But they have no less been doing it for some years, ending up with this place. Obviously, as you can tell, they are pretty laid back about it all. Yet they have it under control no less. The campers who come here, to them, are 'repeat offenders' - like me, sort of. Kind of like an extended family milieu, old friends and new. How they've held out against the big camping conglomerates I often wonder, but so far they do."

As I rattled on, I cautiously maneuvered Rubble towards the spot I'd chosen, 'my spot' when it is no one else's. It was at the far end, where I backed in amid the eucalyptus - the "path" as it were being but hard packed pebble mixed with sand - having passed several vehicles likewise parked en route. One wasn't entirely secluded, of course, what with its airy open spaces between the throng of trees. Yet it did offer the illusion of being semi camouflaged no less, where one could occupy their own small space with the sense of being unto themselves.

"The last beach I camped out at was at Cape Hatteras, on the Outer Banks of North Carolina," Reuben said, as we piled out. "But that was some years ago now. Though there was a concrete slab, we parked back a bit into the dunes, while all around us were these yachts-on-wheels, I called our neighbors' air-conditioned caravans, with generators that ran full blast all night."

"That is why I come here, to not have to deal with what you described. It's against Marty and Yoni's unwritten rules, everyone who comes here appreciates that. One pays a bit extra - quite a bit extra actually. Because it is a luxury nowadays. You might hear some noise from afar, okay, but that's inevitable given how close the commercial places are, like the couple we passed on the way in here."

"How do your friends manage to keep it going?"

"It's a mystery, truly. Everybody wonders. But come give me a hand with the 'scarecrow'."

"Scarecrow?"

"An inflatable tent for one of us or whatever. Me, I prefer to sleep in the back of Rubble. You know, rough and ready Deborah. In any case, we'll leave a battery lamp burning in it when we head out for dinner, least some newcomer can't readily find their location in the dark and think this spot empty. "

"You certainly do think of things. Rebekah is like that. I was wondering about dinner."

"A surprise, dinner. My treat. I think you'll like it."

Was he now sizing me up against Rebekah? Or could it be his suddenly mentioning her name was unconsciously or otherwise his putting up a hastily constructed barrier in front of himself when I spoke of our possible sleeping arrangements? Or was he sending a message to me likewise that I shouldn't expect any moving in on me on his part (if that had been on his mind), not that he wasn't "intrigued" by (or hadn't considered) such a possibility in the offing in some large or small way. I could even stretch it to where his sizing me more with her than against her might render a certain justification should something "happen" after all. Well, I could just ask him straight out if he wanted to fuck me, get it out of the way up front. Both of us being healthy human beasts no less. Together on this hideaway of a beach, alone. Hadn't it been what I had been angling for all along? No matter what I had been telling myself at any given moment. I'd definitely laid the ground work for all possibilities. Had set the stage.

Well, not quite. We had to get this tent pumped out and secured first. The organizer in me taking charge, a talent that wasn't inherently natural but had developed in me over time through necessity. It wasn't exactly a small tent either, though normally I could handle it alone, with some effort. Half igloo in shape, it purported to sleep four comfortably as advertised, complete with four inflatable mattresses to boot.

Hauling it out of the rear end of Rubble, we hiked it out a short ways among the trees and plopped it down on a smooth patch at the foot of a eucalyptus trunk I had unceremoniously decided upon. A skeptical frown had crossed Reuben's face, my guess being that he couldn't figure out how it would stand up without poles and stays.

"You pump," I laughed, handing him a bike pump. "We'll take turns, okay. But you first, while I iron out any wrinkles, if there are any."

Across the lake the hills were gradually turning from sand color to amber, the heat noticeably falling, though the air remained warm under the trees still, yet light, which possibly had as much to do with the lowering humidity as to the optical illusion offered by the broad open vista beyond the beach. And once in a while one felt the hint of a breeze on moist skin. While much to Reuben's surprise the material rose taut, taking on the shape of a raised tent.

"There's a frame of supple tubes that when filled with air stiffen, pushing outward and upward. Though we do have to peg down the four corners lest a real wind blow up. The old fashion way still."

"Let's go stick our toes in the water," I suggested.

"I'm with you there," he said, as he drove down the last peg. "Though I'd like to stick more than my toes in."

"All things remain possible," I laughed. "Come on."

Were I Debbie would I again insist he sit me on his shoulders and carry me out to the beach - or cradle me in his arms even, or I could ride him piggy back for that matter. I'm tall but not that heavy after all. Just long of limb. And, okay, my ass wasn't exactly skinny anymore. The thought made me inwardly chuckle. Little girls can be cruel in their own way. I shook myself. I didn't want to be cruel. To have possibly put him in an awkward situation. (Though shorter than me, if by a hair or two, I knew he was quite strong.) I'm glad I'm Deborah now. For both our sakes. But as Deborah was I any different actually? With whatever it was I was doing with him here with me. Or thought I was doing until I realized nothing was as I thought it should be. As if I hadn't known better at the outset.

Instead, I stuck my arm through his, measuring my lope with a steady gait lest I pull him along with me, as we struck out between the trunks of the trees, the sand beneath our feet thick with pebbles. He seemed to take it as a comradely gesture, as I released him a few yards on, while continuing to walk by his side. In the near distance, the several other campers appeared to have nestled in, none of whom cast a glance our way, much less called out.

"Those palm trunks are really rough looking," Reuben commented as we passed a particularly knobby one. "Or maybe tough is the more accurate description. I suppose they are that way for a reason."

"Isn't everything, " I laughed. "But in the palm's defense, I think it has to do with 'maturing'."

With that, he laughed, before asking. "You've come here quite a bit, I've gathered. Only it's been awhile.

"Yeah, two years ago, with Nell, That's Marty's niece. I'd bring her for Shabbat, One time we stayed through Saturday night, as Marty and Yoni wanted to make a party for her, with a few of their camping crowd. The next morning I had to get both of us up well before dawn in order to get on the road not long after. We reached Tel Ronish not that long after dawn, but don't ask me how. Towards the end of the season, Nell, not being well, helped me out like you have been doing. I enjoyed her company."

"But not since."

"I'd wanted to return," I said somewhat hesitantly. I'd taken a lot of photographs that summer. But I never seemed able to find the time to get away. And, well, Nell had died that winter back in England. It seemed complicated at the time."

"I'm sorry. I guess I shouldn't have kept pressing so."

"Thanks, no, it's okay. But here we are." We had reached the water's edge, as the pebbled beach gave way to a low fringe of outcropping rock augmented with small stones of disparate sizes, long since washed ashore when the wind was up. "Only, I must warn you, at this time of the year the water is quite warm. And watch out for the snakes. They like to crawl around on this outcropping of rocks hereabouts."

"I grew up with water moccasins."

"These are Israeli vipers remember."

It struck me how much like children we are, funny enough, as we pulled off our footwear to stand, if but calf deep, in the warmish clear liquid, slushing about with short kicks then digging our toes into the pebbles and sand. Not unlike stomping about in a mud puddle, only as grownups we normally pass on the stomping bit - in mud puddles at least.

Hands on hips, staring out across the lake, Reuben said, "I'm a salt water person myself. It's in my blood - the pirate ancestors however imaginary, I suppose. I've never cared much for bodies of fresh water. I once sat on the walls at Acco, most of a morning, my feet dangling over the side just looking out at the sea, daydreaming of, among other things, Napoleon's fleet appearing on the horizon while breathing in its air. Completely forgetting the time."

"I do know what you mean, really. I never got to mess about in salt water when a kid, or any water that much, but at my far-north summer retreat place I've really come to appreciate it, to dig it as your characters in *(K)hamsin* would say, But Kinneret here, of psalms and song, is the national reservoir, all that pure snow melt from atop Mt. Harmon, which eventually ends up as salt, in the Dead Sea. There's irony in that, you have to admit. And if one waxes nostalgic enough they risk turning into a pillar of salt. Like somebody's homesick wife you may have heard about."

"Oh Deborah, I do love how your mind works," he said a bit wistfully. "A labyrinth of prisms in the service of this instinctive kind of logic. It's like mine, that way, only faster. I'm certain that you have deduced already that I'm cerebrally a slug."

"Don't forget, Reuben, that I do have the advantage here in that I am, more-or-less, on home turf. Or a home turf, of sorts," I responded just a little coyly, but with earnest conviction. "That possibly colors your perception in some ways. Best to take that into perspective."

Except for that I liked just being with him, I was unable to define what it was that I really liked about the now him (other than the usual cliches - time honored, or time worn, crutches of rationalization.)Like what was the fatal attraction? (I was no longer eight years old.) It was like he was a secret within himself. Is that how he saw me as well. (But I really was a secret within myself --maybe we all are. Selves within ourselves, Babushka dolls all.) Let it go, a tiny voice was whispering into my ear. With some persistence. Enjoy the ride. It's a "mystery". (And mysteries were best solved - if one was ever solved, only posing further questions - by listening to the silence. If they were meant to be solved after all.)

Out over Kinneret a wind was picking up, soon waves would be rolling ashore, leaving behind a light froth as each receded into the one that followed.

"Come on," I said out of nowhere. "We've a bit more arranging to do at the campsite before we head out to dinner. I hate having to rush. And it will be pitch dark when we return."

"Is there a place to wash up, I've been meaning to ask."

"Actually there is. And a rather decent accommodation at that, we won't have to haul up buckets from the lake, if that is what you've been thinking."

"Well, you do like to rough it."

"That's one side of me." I gave him a tongue-in-cheek smile. " But wait until you see where I am taking us to dinner."

I felt like we were chasing the retreating daylight as if to hold back darkness just a little longer - as we lumbered down 90 in the direction from whence we'd come. In this part of the world dusk descends fast in slow motion. With the sky seemingly so clear yet while shadows crawled out over the landscape. In only a few minutes we'd reach the Degania turn off, but it would be dark by then. I thought of saying something, making a comment on this fleeting hiatus separating day from night, the mystery inherent in these transitions we tend to take for granted. Something nonsensical even, to break the silence. Because neither of us had spoken since I'd pointed out the bathhouse he asked about just before we'd turned out from the campsite compound's gate. But I sensed the tension now in his body and didn't. Though he sat back straight, he seemed to lean forward ever so slightly as if in anticipation if not exactly apprehension. Like his was an unswerving gaze into some far distance perhaps never to be arrived at. Or was it simply he no longer knew what to say to me, that he could possibly trust himself to say. Reuben I knew wasn't afraid of making a fool of himself, in that I sensed he was quite courageous. But to make a fool of himself in his relationship involving another? In that, he was forever causing me to reassess him - well to question myself at the very least.

Was it him I wanted, was it me he wanted (if he really "wanted" me at all - Rebekah or no Rebekah - had I stretched my feminine instincts too far in the service of wishful thinking)? And was that what I wanted resolved? Like why were we here in my scheme of things - that had borne fruit so far, in that we were at least here? How sweet or bitter could it be to find out? How hurtful to one or to both of us? If he'd made his move on me back there by the edge of the lake, if I - in spite of all reasoning to the contrary - had simply reached out and slid my hands behind his neck to draw him close......

And just as I was turning these thoughts around in my head, it was Reuben who suddenly broke the silence, as it were, as if he had anguished over how to put it and it suddenly poured out of him. It possibly spared us a serious road mishap, I mused, what with the rising tension wrought by that train of thought.

"In our relationships," he began, "men are crippled by a preconceived fantasy of what it is supposed to be like - all very one-sided of course. Somewhere along the way it is something they set their hearts upon - and just when they think they've found it, have it in hand, the commitment, the ring on the finger, whatever, and it doesn't pan out, they can turn murderous. Often guys who never dreamed they'd hurt another. Thus so many battered girlfriends and wives, if not worse, from almost at the outset. Through no fault in general of the women, whose hopes and visions are normally based on reality, or less illusion to be sure. Like 'I'll let you be in my dream if I can be in yours'. Not so with men who demand that the women be in their predetermined dream or else. Well, something like that."

"And you are speaking from experience, Mr. Headey?" I replied not un-cheerfully, wondering what had brewed this up and why now exactly.

"Yesterday evening at the moadon, I read an article in *The Jerusalem Post* on the rise of violence against women in Israel, both Arab and Jewish women, perpetuated by spouses, boyfriends and often in the case of Arab women, family members, so called 'honor killings' and the like. I guess I was surprised by it, it happens elsewhere but here I hadn't expected. Okay naive me, I know. 'A country like every other country', the Zionist dream. That, regrettably has come true in more ways than one. Like be careful of what you wish for. But it got me thinking beyond the pin-the-tail-on-the-donkey blaming - 'economics', 'The Great Bitch', uppity slaves, etc. - to the root causes. Because it really is a fundamental human problem, must always have been. And, yes, I've seen a few incidences up close, personally, and heard of many more. But more importantly, disturbingly so, are the disappointments I've encountered in just about every serious relationship I've had before Rebekah."

"Why is she different?" I asked, perhaps with a bit of annoyance I hope didn't show. I didn't mean to sound annoyed. But his standing her up, like, in front of me again. Although I told myself to can it, getting paranoid doesn't really fly.

"I think it is I hadn't expected anything initially from our involvement; like I'd had previous involvements where I have viewed the other upfront as a compliment to my ego, in the eyes of my milieu, the fantasy of their playing this role the reason I fell for them, wanted them. In short, I no longer trusted 'love'. With Rebekah my feelings for her grew out of the involvement itself. Perhaps it was for her as well. The two of us kept surprising each other, or rather against all odds we continued finding it surprising together, still do. I think she had more trust in me than I started out having in us. I didn't expect it to last."

"Why against all odds?"

"She was a beautiful woman, naturally sexy. Older than me. A 'foreigner'. Married, both leading separate lives, with no plans for a divorce. Children in college. An artist. The antithesis of my still somewhat straight-laced world, for all of its latter-years bohemian coloring, I'd known up 'til then. Like she'd stepped out of a European movie of the 60s. Or Scandinavian one. Not quite a *Summer with Monika*, you know that early Bergman flic I've mentioned before in a different context, but close. An older Monika, say, who had it together. There was this sense of 'freedom', well, liberation, about her. I simply wanted her physically. Yet we found we had so much in common and continue to do so, uncanny though it is. She'd read an awful lot, both English and American writers. For the sheer enjoyment of it, to satisfy her curiosity, her command of the English language far superior to mine. She was the proofreader for my first novel, encouraging me with her genuinely appreciating the stuff I wrote. More importantly, I think, is that she can laugh at my being ridiculous at times without laughing at me - making me laugh too. She possesses a natural sophistication, with poise and dignity. She's very sure footed, that is, she doesn't knee-jerk react, but thinks whatever through. Saves her emotions for her passions you could say. But most of all, she is kind. I'm forever bewildered by her wanting to be with me, for having chosen me. Besides too wanting to jump into the hay, I suppose, and bewildered by us, I should think so. Something we both share, with humor, as time has passed. We laugh a lot together."

"Sounds like a fairy tale." I couldn't help myself, not without some envy, though it wasn't said as cynically as it might sound.

"A fairy tale for grownups, Rebekah'd call it." he chuckled. I was relieved to see that he hadn't lost his sense of irony, a soft irony of sorts. "Yes, it can look that way. We simply enjoy being together, sharing together, though we each do our own thing separately. It is something a lot of people don't understand, which bothers me sometimes, but not her."

"You must be missing her a lot."

"I'm sorry. I digressed, never finished trying to make my point earlier." He said it like a kind of apology if not quite a plea. "Yes, I do miss her. But I have enjoyed meeting you, Deborah. Please don't doubt that. It's meant a great deal to me. I can't begin to tell you how much. The surprise in finding you here." Then, as if catching himself, "I mean someone such as you here."

"I've never quite trusted love either. Not unlike what that Rev. Marston said about Debbie. Yet in our cases, Debbie's and mine, it probably stemmed from our being orphaned early. Also, there are far too many people in this world who'll say they love you and let you down. They may mean it at the moment, but the moment doesn't last for them." But what I wanted to know was what was someone such as me 'like' - after his painting this photoshopped picture of his beloved that he'd been 'surprised' to find 'here'.

"You know, Rebekah and I have never said 'I love you' to each other. Not in those exact words. It's as if to say it would jinx, certain cheapen, what we have together. We simply show our affection for each other, in however great or small ways, as oppose to making these verbal declarations, be they sentiments."

This last glimmer of daylight was about to "give up the ghost" as we crossed that short span of a bridge over the Jordan's mouth where the river ran westward, disappearing beneath the overhanging foliage that formed the northern boundary of Degania Alef, before it would inexorably turn south. I mentioned this to Reuben who barely got a glimpse before we'd passed it by.

"We can see it better tomorrow morning," I suggested, adding. "We have a table reservation for eight thirty, though this being Friday night, Erev Shabbat, we'll probably have to wait a bit no matter."

"You had to make reservations?" He actually sounded somewhat incredulous and I had to laugh.

"Yes, Rip Van Winkle. Israel has changed."

Several hundred yards on, I veered to the right into a lane abutted by eucalyptus, beyond which was the Degania cemetery, before turning right again to pass briefly through a dense grove of date palms, their heavy trunks resembling so many legs on a herd of pre-historic beasts in Rubble's headlight beams. Before entering into a residential-looking area where I remembered the restaurant being nestled, sorely conscious of Rubble's obstreperous roar between changing gears. I remained somewhat stung by that remark of Reuben's, "I mean someone such as you," though I realized he'd meant it as a form of "apology", yet feeling amiss for what I didn't want to right that moment get into, would rather let unfold (maybe with a little help from that someone such as the me he'd been surprised "to find here"). While too, I found myself suddenly jealous of Rebekah - that I'd never really thought about before, feeling I had everything under control. Because I found myself richly admiring her in a way that puzzled me first and foremost, which was what I found surprising. Here was apparently a woman who did not conform to the rules of the game, yet really did "have it together" like he'd said. Was not one of those whimsically destructive divas celebrated in fiction and film destined to a tragic demise when not a supplicant for redemption - both of which can make one want to puke. No Emma Bovary here; not even my heroine Cathy Earnshaw. (Because Cathy did have it together but lost it.) It was somebody they must have broken the mold for, after she was made.

"'1910'," I offered, "is named after the year of the kibbutz's founding, Degania Alef being the first kibbutz, a significant date in the history of the country. The restaurant is no less distinctive in its culinary offerings. You'll see."

I said this as I turned into what I remembered was the restaurant's parking place only to find it seemingly full. But as I drove further I came upon a spot where I could just about wedge in Rubble - and I did. Among the plethora of sedans and vans (and I mean the variety of models all looking like from the same cookie cutter mold as opposed to actual numbers, in that the parking place itself was relatively small), Rubble stuck out like a sore thumb. Like it belonged more with the covered wagons, definitely a generation ago's farm equipment without a doubt.

"I see what you mean," Reuben uttered. "Maybe we will have to wait. But I am still trying to get my head around the idea that a posh eatery can actually be found on a kibbutz."

"The wait will be worth it."

"I am in your hands, at your mercy," he looked at me with a half-smile, trying to hold back a grin. "As if I haven't been more or less these five days already."

"Could you have wished for better?"

As if I haven't been in your hands, at your mercy, since that moment our eyes met, since that long ago afternoon you picked up an obstinate six-year-old and put me atop your shoulders, dear Reuben - if only you knew. That is what I had wanted to say, to tell him, which made it all the harder that I couldn't (shouldn't, so forget about it).

"You haven't heard me complain, have you?"

"And that is why I am in your debt, in ways you couldn't begin to imagine."

"A woman of mystery, as Stefan remarked." His eyes were laughing now I could tell, even if I had not been able to see his face turned to me, caught in the moment by the tenuous shine from a nearby pole light. "I won't ask more until I hear further. I'll only say that you have never looked more beautiful than you do to me this moment since we met - in that lovely dress you made yourself and behind the wheel of your Rubble, the quintessential Deborah Rosenfeld. But come, aren't you hungry?" His hand had reached for the handle to the door on his side as if to bound out.

Yes, I was hungry, but right that moment more so for him to just plain "take me", physically I needn't have to say, but just about as ravenous as well for that with which to fill a void I could not define, a fissure I knew that couldn't ever be truly filled, not at that late date, and certainly not this way, that could only be sealed with scar tissue. Let's say that the thought was tempting - and no less humorous when contemplating how we might have traversed the gear box in our scramble, forget about scampering over into the back seat piled with our respective rucksacks (at that moment I thought of my father's big old Mercury and that night at the drive-in when I sat on his knees) - but when there is the will. As we climbed out I felt the air lighter, much like earlier, if not more so - that breeze on the lake had remained up. I could almost imagine it ruffling up those humidity-wrought tangles in my hair.

It seemed to have fallen to me, who had mostly initiated whatever interplay occurred between us from day one, now that I thought about it. Okay, he had taken me that summer afternoon in hand by lifting me to his shoulders and carrying me through the tidal rise over the road, but only because I'd dug in my heels and adamantly refused to remove my shoes and walk through it. And that chess game, while it was for some reason long lost in the mists of time why he showed me his set, it had been I who'd insisted he teach me how to play. He hadn't had to do either, really. On the road that afternoon, I was Joy's responsibility, he being but our host, and probably half- bored with us all at that. Although I suppose he felt that since he'd led us into the unforeseen predicament it was naturally incumbent upon him to lead us out. And he didn't approach me like I was being a pain in the ass, as I probably would have deserved, as both Joy and Nicholas were accusing me of being. (Had I done it to get his attention already, clever little me; and had I somehow just known that I would and therefore had been willing to risk my siblings' wrath to do so?) Calmly, he had squatted in front of me - me most likely already feeling that I had overdone it - and had simply said in an even voice, "Don't worry. I'll carry you, okay." I like to think that he recognized something special about me - if not that something within himself had, consciously or not - just as I had begun to feel instinctively, I think, there was something special about him too. So maybe it wasn't that he was "passive," as he could outwardly appear. Like since we'd left Neve Rom. Not in the classical sense. He was in a league of his own, I was beginning to consider. And my sudden irksomeness had more to do with this inward struggle of mine over wanting to force an issue that so far I had yet to genuinely define. Other than I wanted him to fall for me or something, in some kind of way, a special way, as if it were my inherent due. (If only he hadn't painted that rosy picture of Rebekah like he had, of all the times.) Even with just the Debbie in me that I knew he already detected, even if he didn't, couldn't know why. (Maybe it was because I'd felt he'd let me down, way back then, my "hero", when I never heard from him again.) Yeah, no wonder I remained "a mystery", even unto myself. It was like a skin I was attempting to crawl out of that was in need of a final push, kick. With that thought, I pushed open the door on my side.

"Allow me to be the tour guide, if you will." I said, facetiously, taking his arm as we met up. "This way, sir."

Crossing the quadrangle known as "Pioneers Courtyard", having explained to Reuben that it was the original hub of the kibbutz, the glow of lights from under the roof over the restaurant's portals or porch glowed like an inviting beacon, like I remembered it, in the thickish dark, along with the eager chatter of voices and succulent wafts of Mediterranean delicacies. I continued to hold him by the arm, mine tucked into his, in a casual sort of walk, more like close friends than a romantic couple, as we rather leisurely strolled along a broad surface of smooth stones set in irregular patterns that crossed the clipped grass lawn like a floating pier might upon the placid surface of a marina basin. It was probably the close proximity of the lake that brought such an analogy to mind.

"You see this sort of architecture here in the Balkans, but with the climate it's very Californian, although in its particular expression of the vernacular it would be right at home anywhere in the American southwest, but for the date palms," he chuckled almost to himself, as if reminiscing out loud on something that just caught his fancy. "This quad, from what I can make of it, might be the hub of a rural hacienda in New Mexico. I almost expect the Cisco Kid and Pancho riding up at any minute. Sorry, a bit before your time perhaps. The Cisco Kid was an early 50s TV western, before that on radio. They were Robin Hood figures, often on the wrong side of the law helping those who had been taken advantage of by the establishment in one way or another. I could hardly wait to get home from school to catch the next episode. O. Henry actually created the character in a short story in the early part of the century."

"I'm not so young as not to know who O. Henry was," I laughed outright, happy for the diversion. "His stories were still a part of the high school curriculum when I reached my teens. I liked them."

"I diverted as usual, didn't I. That's what can happen when you beat around the bush like I can do while stretching my initial thought too far afield. I just find it ironic, I guess," he continued, "how these remnants of Moorish architecture from Spain reached to the Americas on one hand and to the Ottoman Empire on the other. Of course, the Ottoman Empire did have a more direct link with North Africa. I've seen the photos of earlier Degania, often shot from a distance, singular houses and barns or what have you built of stone, some of these here probably. With the low-pitched terra cotta roofs. But nothing prepared me for this. This right here is to be expected, given its period or origin, but back there from where we just walked, it looks like a modern suburb in the same mold. If it had been daylight I'd probably be really freaking out."

"Wait until you see inside of the restaurant, it's like early Californian, Zorro country, complete with the exposed rafter beams and iron grills at the windows, though more as a decoration, the latter. Southern California meets the Eastern Mediterranean - well, the Levant to be precise. But those southern Italian smells wafting in the air are about to drive me crazy if I don't get to taste them like yesterday."

"In that case, let's say that the south of Europe meets the Levant in a Greek taverna. In Israel, on a kibbutz."

"Where else."

As we strode in onto the porch bathed in the soft luminous shine of a dozen light sources, along a stucco wall and from the overhead rafter beams, I thought I caught the lift of chins of any number of the diners, as if for a split second there was a cessation somewhat of the many conversations that abounded in earnest. Were we that handsome a couple? If not a shade "different". To merit a once-over by so many? Well, Reuben did look "American" (or his style of dress did, though he'd left the fanny pack with his shades in Rubble), while I have more or less always been taken for Israeli, at first sight at least. (Though I may have never done National Service, I knew I looked like I could have.) But these were a generally sophisticated crowd by their appearance. Or maybe the seams in my homemade long skirt had come unraveled? No, of course not. Nor are Israelis in general taken aback upon seeing a couple where the woman is the taller of the two. Such crap to be concerned about all of a sudden. Perhaps it was myself that was coming "unraveled", and that it was starting to show. Whatever, it was best to just take it in stride, I told myself. There was an empty table set for two, on the outer edge by one of the roof posts, a choice spot. Could it be for us already, I really hoped, because I was like about to rub the magic lamp or whatever to ask the genie to make us disappear.

Had I been alone I doubt I'd even noticed

have

235

anyone taking notice, if it hadn't been a figment of my imagination to begin with. But with Reuben, and for all intent and purpose a couple, arm in arm still, I was unduly conscious of how we might look together, the stuff of teenage fantasies long ago put on some top shelf.

"So far so good," he smiled causally at me, pressing my forearm to him. "I like it. Thank you."

It indeed was our table, our good fortune coupled with an intriguing mystery. (Later, in the toilet I would overhear several women speculating among themselves - in a rancorous Hebrew mixed-slang vernacular - about who might have been the celebrity couple rumored that had been due there that evening but who apparently failed to show. "No, it definitely wasn't that tall, lanky creature and the aging pretty boy she has in tow, one of the women proffered. Imagine a bona fide celebrity showing up wearing that sleeveless dress showing off those pale shoulders and sunburnt arms of hers in the middle of the summer, she'd lose her card-carrying membership in whatever. If I'd seen her on TV or in a photograph somewhere I think I'd remember that face, a face that changes character seen at different angles, in different lights, while it remains her own. His though, I think I have seen but I can't remember where. I think that is what it is about with celebrities - they tend to look like somebody we know, only more so. Which is why we are more attracted to them than to some real-life look-alike. No matter, they are 'strangers'. She speaks Hebrew no less, but apparently he doesn't. Okay, she's one of us who has lived much of her life among 'strangers', because she has that self-assurance in that she doesn't give a fuck what just anybody thinks while being able to handle herself well in any situation she might find herself in. But his stand-offishness gives him away, just saying. He's an in-grown toenail. I think they are a charming couple, famous or not. Maybe more so because she is taller than him and it bothers neither of them..... Well, I for one like a taller man. It's easier to pigeonhole taller men... I get the feeling that this guy here would not be that easy to pigeonhole, and for some reason she does appear to be all that more attracted to him precisely on account of it, yet I'm not certain if he at all has a clue .. ". I emerged from my stall simultaneously as did a couple of the women emerged from theirs, whose tongue-swallowing embarrassed looks I met with what I call my cockeyed grin, with just enough mischievous glint in my green eyes to say I didn't give a fuck, that in all I had found their speculative discourse actually quite amusing when not ridiculous. The self I saw in the mirror above the wash basin I turned to wasn't all that bad looking, was quite good look-ing, all things considered, hardly the "lanky creature" I'd just been called, though lithe perhaps, just pleasantly so, not that I'd ever take my appearance for granted such that I could ultimately rely upon it. Quickly I ran both my hands under the hot water tap, then ran my fingers through my thick unruly hair, mussing it up, before heading nonchalantly to the door, leaving a pin-dropping silence behind me. Maybe they were right about one thing - maybe Reuben really didn't have a clue, or that he was an exceptionally good actor. How did Robert Burns put it, about having the gift to see ourselves as others see us - which is what I had been doing with Reuben all along.) A slender young woman in white shirt and black pants, her long dark mane pulled back into a pony tail, had rushed up to us with a curious smile, and after a short welcoming inquiry had ushered us to the very table in question, handing each of us a menu and asking me (in Hebrew) if we wished for a refreshment before hurrying off. "Water, for now," I answered back, in Hebrew, seeing that Reuben had nodded the same. That much Hvrit he doubtlessly remembered.

"This is really a hefty menu, the offerings I mean," Reuben teased. I could tell from the tone of his voice - which meant he was pleased.

"They do half portions, you can have two tastes for one, and we can share if we like."

We bantered back and forth the pros and cons of a potpourri of offerings (Mediterranean, like those earlier smells had promised, to indigenous "Israeli", or "Arab-Israeli" to throw a bone to the politically correct when it is Turkish-Syrian to begin with, so I have read), Reuben soliciting my opinion on the myriad vegetarian and stone oven configurations he naturally assumed my being familiar with each (since I was wont to portray myself as a near-native apart from having eaten here previously). Again I tried not to laugh too much at his tendency to be picky, sometimes almost to the point of splitting hairs.

"It's not exactly kosher here, is it?" he offered offhandedly. "But of course, it's on a leftwing kibbutz. Or used to be one. I suppose more or less still is. Not that I keep glatt kosher, obviously."

"Stefan told me you converted to Judaism. I never came out and asked you about it. Though it crossed my mind."

"Let's just say that I became a naturalized citizen of the tribe. It was sometime after my return to the States in the aftermath of the war. A friend put me on to this orthodox rabbi who was willing to take me on - and shepherd me through the process. Then, once in London, I returned to being the secular Jewish humanist I'd always considered myself being at heart. Holding to the spirit of the law, if not necessarily the letter. Which was the undertone of our new Jewish arts magazine I told you about."

"And the dichotomy didn't wear on your conscience?" I said, with a certain hint of amusement. "Sorry, that's unfair."

"No, because for me it was always about becoming one of the people, 'Ahad Ha Am'. I think
Rabbi Melchor recognized that. Not that I don't
respect the observant, but religion for me is
more a poetic metaphor. God being the creation
of our imagination, all gods. I don't disparage it,
far from it. It is just I prefer to be my own Jew. If I
am to be true to myself and others. It's all about
enabling us to do good anyway. You know, Mitz-
vot, doing good deeds."

"I think I see our server eyeing us from inside the door way, with a pitcher of water in her
hand." Hopefully nipping in the bud a long, and
with me, utterly unnecessary justification. "Do
you think we are ready to order?"

She was quick and pleasingly attentive, very
professional, she with the long tightly-pulled
pony tail and glints of light in a pair of dark impenetrable eyes, helpfully suggestive without
presumption, aided by a hint of humor but most
of all patience with Reuben's and my pulling the
menu apart only to recreate a series of eclectic
choices between the two of us - until, as if on cue,
my bursting into involuntary giggles beneath
the sanguine gaze of our server's nonplussed
smile. All of a sudden she reminded me, in an
utterly weird way of Sushila - sans Sushila's violet blue eyes - and I wondered, slightly chafed, if
Reuben had too noticed. To conclude our order,
in Hebrew I asked for up front or right away a

half bottle of my favorite Portuguese red wine that I was happily surprised they had to offer, before sending her off with that all-purpose cockeyed grin of mine, as if to share with her, in this instance: I know we have been pains in the ass, if hopefully good-naturedly so, for which her forbearance wouldn't be forgotten.

"I hope we didn't piss her off." Reuben uttered. "That menu is too much. I could have ordered bits of just about every dish on it."

"Me too, in case you didn't notice," I said. "No, she's cool."

The flow of light from the porch spread out onto the lawn in the Courtyard next to where we sat - reaching all the way out to between the trunks of a pair of towering date palms standing sentinel-like before their being sucked up into the shoals of darkness where fireflies flickered in the warm, softening air of the night. Minute blinks much like memory flashes from the bottom recesses of our buried psyche, popping up as they can do without rhyme or reason - little imps I termed them; that long ago I learned to just let be (because sooner or later most likely a picture will turn up, if I don't dwell on it, don't try to force the issue). A bit strange a thought to be suddenly having, I mused, before catching myself to return to the present. Sounds of across the tables banter were rising and falling about us, from which I picked up the odd word or phrase while Reuben had that tad anxious look on his face that he was perhaps elsewhere amid these somewhat unaccustomed sights and the incomprehensible if not completely unfamiliar words he heard spoken - that something of a country kid in him still that unexplainably added to his attraction (Or at least to me it did, big time. Another mystery, okay.)

I leaned back in the chair and took a sip of the glass of water I'd just poured. So, who then was the me he actually saw? Or, more precisely, this "someone" he had been so surprised to have found here? And why had it been so important for him? And why couldn't I just take it at face value? That if nothing else a deep and possibly abiding friendship had developed, if in a bit unusual way, a friendship he perhaps needed - or discovered he needed - upon relating his "Debbie story" over those last several mornings - right up to an hour ago - had realized he'd been looking for without knowing it? So why must I make a megillah out of it? Only I couldn't refrain from wondering what in that respect did I possess that possibly Rebecca didn't. Did it harken back to this Debbie thing he couldn't, didn't want to let go of?

"What do you imagine would be A.D. Gordon's take on Degania Alef today, this restaurant, the kibbutz's catering to the tourist industry with its own hotel and all?" I broke into his pensive silence in order to escape my own thoughts spinning their wheels. It was almost as if he had been waiting for me to. To judge by the sudden coming awake look on his face, a certain sharpening of focus in his eyes. Like a match had been struck, I laughed inwardly as I prepared for the answer I fully knew I'd asked for, had really wanted in that he'd reveal more of that self within a self that was at the core of his existence.

"The Tolstoyan idealist in Gordon would be disappointed, thoroughly so." Reuben began hesitantly, as if searching for the words, as was his wont. "He had pinned such great hopes on the Jewish People being redeemed through self-labor. To rebuild the land and be rebuilt by it. Shedding the skin of those negatively viewed occupations Jews had more or less been regulated to in the Diaspora. While the realist in him would weigh things in consideration. Or try to. But when it came down to push and shove, he'd probably say that the people simply didn't work hard enough, that the job was left half done. Or undone. That is, the job to restore the land was given over to the machine, by which time the people had become prisoners of the machine. The generals took over from the poets and idealists. Like it always happens. Thus, like the land, the people have remained but half restored. And blood rather than sweat, had ended up reclaiming the land after all. He had begun to greatly fear this would happen by the time of his rather premature death. By the way where is the Gordon House in relation to where we are here?"

"Maybe a couple hundred yards behind where you are sitting." I nodded my head in that direction as I spoke. "It's by the river in any case."

"The Jordan?"

"Just a ways down from where we crossed the bridge out on the highway. Speaking of which, Stefan's told of a relatively new kibbutz down in the Negev, perhaps not affiliated with any association, that maintains Gordon's philosophy as its guiding principle. Mostly made up of young chaverim, men and women. Many of whom had grown up on a kibbutz. With their national service and some studies already behind them. They work and share communally. Like the kibbutz training farm you describe in *(K)hamsin*, only on a much larger scale. I've thought about checking them out, to do a photo shoot. Much like I did in my *Summer on Kibbutz* way back when. Where I first met Stefan. I think that may have been why he'd gone on at length about them, in hopes I might take the hint, well find it more interesting than only just doing archaeology site photography when in Israel. Not that he wants me to quit doing archaeology sites, especially his, not by a long shot. Just Stefan looking out for me. I could of course simply drive up to the gate and blow the horn. Me in Rubble, yeah. Only I've found that when it comes to such societies it works best to have an introduction from a respected source, can save a lot of unnecessary misunderstanding cropping up. But, alas, I've not yet found, no, not taken, the time to find one. I couldn't blame them for being up front standoffish. Especially now that they have attracted media curiosity, where you are the sensation one day and dropped the next."

"The kibbutz I was on has 'privatized'," he uttered. "How I hate that word. Because they over - borrowed like so many others did, were encouraged to do actually (so I've been told), during those heady years in the wake of The Six Day War, then the October War for certain, Sadat's visit, only to find themselves owned by the banks or whatever when the economy bottomed out (Degania's held out, I think, if just, by the skin of its teeth). As for Gordon, he didn't live to see the 30s, the effects of the Depression coupled with the arrival of Arab Nationalism and the Arab Revolt of '39, followed by World War 2, the Holocaust, the changes it all wrought. Not to mention the underground war with the British leading up to '48, then the fending off of six Arab armies hell bent to wipe out the newly proclaimed state. I've read that Degania was overrun not once but twice by the Syrian army during the '48 war and each time recaptured with the help of the Haganah, though one of those times it was mostly burnt to the ground. In any case, the Syrian advance into the Jordan Valley was thwarted."

"Yeah. If those stone walls over there could talk," I laughed.

"Whisper at least," he replied. "Of the young Dayan having trysts in the hayloft."

"Only the family, I believe, had moved to a moshav before Dayan reached his teens."

On that note our wine arrived. I dispensed with the tasting ritual with a knowing smile, thanking her but saying I would pour. When I had half-filled Reuben's glass I said coyly, "Do you think you can handle Rubble if I flake out? I really like this particular wine."

"I think we have a better chance not ending up in Kinneret with you behind the wheel crocked to the gills than with me cold sober."

At that, he took a sip. I could see that he was pleased with the taste, as he slowly took another as if to savor the taste on his tongue.

"Don't underestimate yourself, Reuben. Or me." I kind of laughed. "Or us together."

The question had certainly been in my mind since the evening we met. I myself had certainly fantasized it from time to time, since my encountering him, but never daring to go too far with it, nothing beyond the preliminary venture. I sought to frame it so as to be the least intrusive possible, but tiptoeing around it like a mouse I realized only went to make it all the more suggestive through subterfuge. No, that wouldn't do - not with Reuben.

Lowering the wine glass from my lips, I looked him directly in the eyes, inwardly holding my breath, and asked, with hopefully just enough of a curious overture to hook him, in as even a voice as I could muster, "Have you ever imagined what might have happened had Debbie lived and the two of you had met up again? When she was an adult - or at least no longer in foster care? I think I may have asked that before, if in a different way."

He hesitated just for a second. It wasn't quite as if my question had caught him like a deer in the proverbial headlight beams. Or with his pants down to be more specific.

"Yes, before she died I used to. The possibility had seemed so real then, so close at hand, within but a year or two. I used to try to imagine under what circumstances and what we might say to each other, that is if she even remembered me still. Well, I think she would have remembered me. By the time of her eighteenth birthday, I would have been twenty-eight. My one great fear though at the time was that she'd become a dyed-in-the-wool indoctrinated Christian due to having been fostered by the Marstons, and would look upon yours truly at best with a jaundiced eye."

"And after she died? Did you ever imagine what she would have been like had you two met up later on in life? Like when she'd have been older, with a greater, well enlarged, perspective on the world. Without necessarily being shocked by the person you'd become? By your having changed or exchanged tribes as you put it?"

"I fear that my imagining what she might have been like was but wishful thinking. Even when I looked at all angles of the personality of the kid I'd known - that single-minded persistence she already had enough of to spare, her intelligence, her insatiable curiosity, an innate stubbornness. And wondering how much of it would have survived into her adulthood, how first of all it would have gone to shape her adulthood in any case, coupled with her life experiences along the way."

"You must have come up with something of a composite picture, no?"

"Well," he hesitated. "I suppose I did, I have, sort of. Yes, of course I did, have done."

"So, who is she?" That blue of his eyes or the heat they gave off I felt boring into me - no, penetrating me - giving me this tingling rush as he looked unblinking into mine. "I mean, what, or who would she have been like? A composite picture? Should you dare to make an educated guess."

I could see that he was struggling; I could feel a tension building up, with suddenly an almost-frown forming above the bridge of his nose.

"You. Yes, like you. exactly like you. More or less."

Fuck me! He seemed to have uttered that

"You" almost inaudibly - I saw the motion of his lips - as if he had known already that it was what I had expected him to say - and knew he needn't have had to say it out loud. Though in retrospect I'd wonder if I hadn't imagined it like that. Well, I'd begged for it, hadn't I. I hadn't let good enough alone. Of course, I hadn't wanted to, I told myself. That was the dynamic of the thing. It had developed into a life of its own.

"I'm flattered, Reuben." I managed to keep as impenetrable a face as I could muster, I think, kicking myself as I spoke. "Even as I am jealous of her."

Our food arrived as if on cue preceded by its savory smells. Like our punctual server had been given a copy of the script beforehand.

As Reuben and I picked through and parceled out between us the various half portions we'd ordered that she placed before us, we did manage to avoid a down and out food fight that really would have given our fellow diners something memorable to talk about - by taking it with a sense of humor, he more so than me at first (Reuben, considerate to a fault, I discovered could be quite competitive), until in unison we simply broke out in laughter, the giggling child in both of us having come to the rescue. His pizza Sicilia, its thick crust topped with ricotta fresca, a rich tomato sauce and artichokes augmented by the innards of a bulging vegetarian gyro - onion, grilled sweet pepper and zucchini - along with my Potato Gnocchi with its asparagus, chestnuts topped by garlic butter and shaved parmesan that I further wedged with arugula, carrots and citrus plus a mix of grains and nuts from my Green salad portion - being our anchors respectively that we even further subdivided according to whatever we fancied a taste of from each other's plates. And, yes, slices of Focaccia from the stone oven accompanied by various dips. After which I wished I could have licked my fingers rather than having to discretely wipe them with the generous napkin across my lap.

Before we properly dug in, I poured more wine into Reuben's glass and with mine in hand proposed in the way of a toast:

"Here's to our sweetest dreams. May we savor them with a grain of salt." And before he could perhaps give me a puzzled frown or the like, added, "Thank you for the truly much appreciated help at the dig site, your unending patience with the idiosyncrasies that go with the territory in my like crazy job, besides weathering extracurricular devil dusts to Jonna's taking a tumble."

I said it sincerely without any note of the humorous sarcasm I know I can be famous for. And from the studious expression that now formed just above the bridge of his nose he apparently accepted it without rancor. Putting down his glass (I suppose I had half expected a return toast) he simply uttered "Thank you", before asking if I had any further news about Jonna (that he had been meaning to ask). I really thought it was on the tip of his tongue to mention - for want of what else to deem it - our "discursions" on Debbie.

"Jonna?" I caught myself. "Only that her injuries were not as serious as they might have been and that she was doing better than had been expected, but as for her returning to the dig, the jury is still out."

He nodded, solemnly. Before proffering:

"Has anyone figured out yet what it was she found? When I got back out there this morning it was under a cover."

"It's too soon to tell."

"But you saw it. We both did. You photographed it."

"Yes, and Stefan writes the report. It is unwise to speculate at this stage. I'll leave that to the researchers at the IAA. Just disregard anything I said before. If it got out that Deborah speculates it's this or that - even if in all innocence I am right or wrong ether way - it could go to undermine Stefan. All I can safely say, and this might be too much, is that it is a large block of marble. In any case, I haven't a clue, not really, that's my official line."

"It sounds awfully clandestine?"

"It is actually," I continued. "But more like tiptoeing here through a political minefield. When you have rank academic egos in-house and the ongoing political situation externally. For those of us associated officially with the dig, with any dig, there is a sort of unwritten procedure to follow. It makes life simpler. Yeah, I know it's weird. In this part of the world that which can be used as misinformation can be used to start a war or something. Just saying. Then I added, with something of a wink and a grin rather than shrug off his rising concern. "Okay, it's silly - but real. It doesn't mean I'm any less curious."

"Okay, question number two. Have you ever been in love?" It was a totally different Reuben all of a sudden, what with the tone of concern rather than that of curiosity in his voice. His eyes were again smiling at me, if with a tinge of apprehension now in them.

"Yes, deeply in love, as a matter of fact," I almost blurted out perhaps too brutally, unintentionally so - both taken back as much by the nature of his question as I blatantly welcomed the change of subject. And taking up my fork in my hand, added, on a hopefully lighter note, "Hey, I thought you too were hungry? We best start tucking it in as the English say, before this food goes cold."

Which we did with a certain amount of belated gusto. That included jabbing our forks into various delicacies on one another's plates when not offering a forkful of something of our own for succulent comment. We did make a conscious attempt to be somewhat discrete about it - though we were about as obvious as playful puppies to those at the nearest tables (that column by us did offer the illusion of at least limited privacy, though we were hardly seated in the shadows) - if the restaurant's patrons in total had noticed all that much, between enjoying their own food, the hustle-and-bustle of the servers and the fervent conversations buzzing about us. Rather than risk my harpooning his tongue, Reuben would take my offered fork to place its contents in his mouth while I recklessly accepted his on my tongue with about as much savoir faire I could muster. As if it was perfectly natural to do so when enjoying succulent dishes together over a narrow table. And of course, a bite of his Pizza Sicilia with a chunk of grilled sweet pepper I'd asked for ended up on my lap - well, on my napkin at least. I think for a brief time we closed out a rising tension - in short, kind of forgetting ourselves. I know I did, making the most of it. There was this thing about Reuben that gave me the freedom to do it. I thought about ordering another half bottle of that wine, then decided against it.

"I, like Debbie, too fell in love, so to speak, when a preteen. Grownups would of course maintain that both of us, myself for certain, were too young by far, would deem it a 'crush' much as we might have on the film or pop music idol of the month - the little that they know or remember from their own childhoods by the time they believe they can sit in judgement." Where I was going with this, I didn't know, as I was making it up almost faster than I could speak. "He was a counselor at one of the summer camps the school arranged for us to attend according to grade and a particular interest. He was of college age, as were all of the counselors, some older than others. With eight or nine of us allotted to each of them. What I first noticed about him was that he was something of an outsider, certainly a loner. While he was congenial to a fault, he never joined in much with his fellow counselors, keeping aloof even from the several good-looking girls among them. These camps, like the school itself, were co-ed. Summerhill meets Rudolf Steiner, if you are familiar with Steiner and A.S. Neill's take on childhood and education, but always keeping in the middle lane like the good liberals they purported to be. One could learn a lot, if one applied one's self. School was my drug of choice, so to speak. I loved studying - which in its own way kept the world at bay, while giving me an anchor, orphan that I was, remember."

"Yeah, I'm sort of familiar with Neill, I read his book long ago. And I know of the Waldorf method, if by proxy." Reuben said. "But you keep calling this guy, this counselor you fancied, 'he'. Did he have a name?"

"I was in love with him, Reuben. Just as Debbie was in love with you. It wasn't grown up love, as if the majority of grownups really know what they think they know what that is. Nor was it sexual love, well not overtly - but that feeling, the thrill it gave, right down through the core of our being, was - even if we had no name to give it. It was a child's fantasy of romance, though romantic it was, in our hearts, in our minds as well. Pure ecstasy. Whatever people's ages they are forever seeking 'signals' like from 'out there', are giving them off too, And upon the odd chance that two people's signals met, it breaks the shell, no matter the age, a connection is made, a spark is given off. It's almost cabalistic. It is cabalistic. His name, you asked. It was Reuben. Now perhaps you can see why I took to your telling Debbie's story like I did. Almost ruthlessly pumping you like I did. In a way it was all too good to be true, right down to your name of all things. I could feel I was Debbie all over again - by proxy of course."

"Were you called Debbie when you were little?"

"No," I chuckled, I think, almost aloud. "I was always Deborah. I was never really 'little', you see."

"Okay," he came back in earnest. "But do you think he felt for you the way I felt for Debbie?"

"I like to imagine he did, whether he realized it at the time or not. Maybe not. Maybe he just wrote me off as a kid. I have no way of knowing. Did Debbie ever really know how much you loved her?"

"I hope she did, I hope she remembered." I could feel his struggle between a desperate wish and gnawing doubt. "The things Kerry said make me think she did. If I had only gone to her that day of Aunt Victoria's funeral. Like I wanted to do. And told her that I would always love her. That I would never forget her. That we would meet again, that we'd find one another."

"She didn't forget, Reuben. Debbie didn't forget. Rest assured of it."

I can't say for certain that my rather extemporaneous retort made a dent of any kind in this inner debate of his, what with his face remaining that mask of sobering thought he so often appeared to project, that I suspected was but a chameleon-like cover for all occasions. Yet, the semblance of a yearning of sorts I thought I saw flare up in his eyes - that he was probably quite unaware of being so exposed - did go to making me feel that I had touched something in him. If not my words per se so much as the sheer intensity of my uttering them had. Because it was the closest I could ever imagine coming to telling him that I had been "his Debbie".

"What do we have here? The never-predictable Devorah taking our writer friend on a local culinary tour," a familiar voice behind me, speaking a taut Hebrew (my translation here humorously clumsy in its literal trajectory) broke into the stretched silence Reuben and I had fallen into (as Reuben, his eyes cast downward at the remains of food on his plate, seemed to take to heart what I said). I slowly turned my head to see the chiseled features of Naor Dan spiffily decked out in a white linen shirt and a fashionably dark pair of designer jeans, obviously on the way out. And before I could decide whether to ignore him or not, he continued, unabashedly, "I've heard of your possible 'find', exciting, yes, and unearthed by that lovely Scandinavian who regrettably hurt herself. What might it be, do you think?"

"All in due time, Naor, my digitals will be on your desk come Yom Reshon. Along with Stefan's report."

To which he nodded thoughtfully and without an "enjoy your meal" sauntered on over to this long nordic blonde - the signature Naor Dan arm-candy - awaiting him half in the shadows on the far end of the porch.

"I reckon Naor has his Shabbat cut out for him," Reuben retorted sardonically.

"A Shabbat is about the length of Naor's staying power," I quipped, before relenting somewhat. "Okay, that's mean of me, I know. Naor's a good archaeologist, with a promising future, but personally he is full of hot air. I've never trusted him."

"You really do play it close to the vest, don't

you?"

"Yes, it is a poker game, Reuben." I spoke more thoughtfully now, in a measured tone of voice. "It is not my job to speculate, just to shoot the pictures. That's why I am good at it. Like I was saying. Best to leave it to others to see what they see in them. Or want to see in them."

"I do see what you mean, really. I guess I've been sort of playing the devil's advocate, I apologize."

"Oh Reuben, no need to apologize, but thank you."

"So I wouldn't be violating the State Secrets Act if I ask you what kind of books do you mostly read, your favorite authors and such. And as you are in the midst of reading *(K)hamsin* it won't count."

Was he teasing for a compliment, if not at least a comment, couched as it was in a ploy. I decided on the rebound to reply in all seriousness. As he'd unintentionally backed himself into a corner - not unlike I suddenly remembered how he'd moved his chess pieces. In any case, I welcomed the change from a subject that threatened to lead down a one-way street.

"But I really do like your style of writing, of being swooped up in those lengthy sentences of yours and carried along for the experience, it's akin to a piece of music or what a piece of music does to a particular listener," I began, both to catch my breath and to think of how to answer his question, without getting bogged down in details, like why I liked this work more or like another less, it being a conversation for another time and place. "I read eclectically for want of a better word - be it fiction or non-fiction. (Which today is so much just another form of fiction - pulp fiction taken to a new level). I can think off-hand of one or two very fine histories, biographies too. And I speak here of contemporary works. But novels are my forte, my bread and butter. I read for the perspective - that of the individual characters as well as the author's. And for the story, of course. Whatever the genre."

"Fine, so do I." He was chuckling I could see. The Debbie in me could still enjoy his teasing that she'd happily found a way to turn to her advantage. "But will you dare divulge the names of an author or two. For the record, if you please."

"Okay, offhand, but remember, I'm a free-lance reader." I was laughing too, more like giggling, having been disingenuous to a fault, and called out for it. "Elizabeth George to Henry James - his novellas, her for a particular recurring character or two in her mysteries, he for *The Wings of the Dove*. Let's see - Lisa Alther's *Kinflicks*, Mario Vargas Llosa, I.B Singer, P.D.James, John Le Carre, Yael Dayan (in particular her *Envy the Frightened*), Yoram Kaniuk, Batyah Gur. Old standbys include Sinclair Lewis' *Main Street*, Fitzgerald's short stories and Carson McCullers' *The Member of the Wedding*. Also, Tennessee Williams' surreal poem-play, *El Camino Real*, Molly Bloom's soliloquy, in *Ulysses*. To name but a few. In the 20th century at least. *Wuthering Heights*, because I identified with Cathy until I didn't." I'd probably gone overboard already, but there was one more that I simply couldn't leave out. "Oh, and *Smilla's Sense of Snow* by Peter Hoeg that I only just read. Like me, Smilla due to an early death was wrenched from her native milieu where she had to create her own rules, reinvent herself, in order to maintain her equilibrium in an uninviting world she was forced to navigate at her peril. No doubt you are beginning to see a pattern forming here?"

Stop apologizing, I almost bit my tongue. Why should I suddenly give a fuck as to what my selective choices here say about me personally or otherwise? It's only a dinner conversation."

"An eclectic mix indeed," he gave me one of his half smiles. "If dissembling at first glance."

"I'm not purposefully muddying the water, Reuben. I rather like juxtapositions, to savor the ironic. Nonlinear writing is what turns me on. I too think nonlinear, like your protagonist obviously does. I just might be able to include *(K)hamsin* to this list, if I manage to live long enough to finish it."

"Touche. Point taken. I won't even dare ask if you have any hobbies."

"One, people watching, Through the lens of my camera."

"Okay, here's an easy one," he laughed. "Nothing to do with the esoteric, if you will, just curious. Do you play chess?"

"As a matter of fact I do." I tried to make it sound as if I were sucking on something sweet. "Do you want a game? I think we can find a set."

"No, I'd only end up being beaten by another Deborah."

"But this time you wouldn't be whipped by a kid, poor boy, some of your otherwise tattered ego would be left intact."

"How sweet of you, how very considerate, Ms. Rosenfeld," he began sarcastically, with his tongue in his cheek, before something akin to a lightbulb, however subtle, flicked on I could see, in those exceedingly transparent blue eyes, causing him to change course in midstream, along with his tone of voice. "Hey, you want to hear something funny. Not funny, sort of ironical, considering. I just this moment remembered it, for some reason. "Kerry told me that Aunt Victoria, at the time, had a Jewish friend named Deborah - the woman had a German Jewish last name that I forget - and this is who she named Debbie after."

If only you knew how ironical, dear Reuben.........Some might even see this as a strange foreboding, if they but knew. Well, at least a sign or something. Like as if the Deborah I became, if purely by happenstance (a happenstance I took advantage of), had been preordained, had been in the stars or what have you. Now that he'd mentioned it, some tenuous recollection came back to me, long buried under the burden of such long ago memories, obviously something my mother must have told me very early on, only I cannot for the life of me conjure up any recollection of this friend to accompany these stories, that if true (though I doubt her being Jewish would have made a dent that the time), I must have heard more than once. But in the here and now it was certainly something to reflect upon, if not to give in to musing about a sense of destiny. The irony inherent is more than enough.

Returning to our table from that quick trip to the toilet, with those aforementioned words from our fellow diners in the adjoining cubicles aflame within me still, I observed upon approach - before he saw me - Reuben's sober, if not actually grave, demeanor that had descended upon his face during my brief absence, like as if a visor of sorts had been shut down over his window to the world. As he sat there in public as if in a kind of solitary confinement - such was the sudden image I had of him. I could see what one of those women meant by saying "he hasn't a clue", she obviously having judged the book by its cover, what with his being able to appear so closed to his immediate surroundings, - which I'd begun belatedly to understand was his way of absorbing whatever was about him - be it sight or sound, the very weight of the air for that matter - of his "taking it all in". Which went to include me first and foremost I reckoned, like where had I been coming from - that besides my picking him for an assistant, devolving as it had into our dialogues on Debbie, then my willy-nilly invitation to come along on this trip, my treating him to tonight's dinner. Me the all-purpose woman of mystery as Stefan had pointedly said of me to him. Perhaps he'd felt flattered by the quite-obvious-to-all attention I had unabashedly bestowed upon him, me a complete stranger (as far as he knew), and it goes without saying he was probably curious to a fault as to my reason for doing so - apart from my often vocal appreciation for the help he rendered that most likely sounded like a self-conscious excuse. He had to be deep down curious as to the why, not to mention the wherefore I was coming from. Like I must really dig him (to use his own '60s lingo), couldn't wait to get him into the sack. Or was it that I was somehow using him, playing him along in a game of sorts as a source of amusement, me this alone, woman-of-the-world type, to satisfy some stereotypical feminine whim (whimsical fancy I might humorously add to that). If it was not just my being confused about my intentions that was holding me back so far, perhaps too the fact that there was Rebecca to consider, whom I knew he had to consider as well (which was about as close to the truth as anything). Or, on my part, if it really did come from some place deeper, thus an attraction hidden beneath the good buddy relationship I had affected with him, perhaps leaving him to wonder all the more about my motivation for all or nothing. (And what if what I might have so far misinterpreted as his playing it cool was merely due to his inability to figure it out, figure me out? While his curiosity may have gotten the best of him: that he knew he too was playing it close to the edge.) And as he had just revealed, I reminded him of Debbie, that I was the personification of who she would have been like had she lived. He had to have thought long and hard on what it was about me that had brought him to draw such a conclusion - and an ever so accurate one at that.

Which meant it very well might have been love at first sight on his part too (if I dare call it that - let's say an allure at first sight, infused with mystery, intrigue, the forbidden too). While he'd tried to deny it, had not wanted to accept it, still didn't. And he certainly wouldn't want me to suspect his feelings, all the while denying them to himself, that he hadn't dared think of in the light of day and had kept hidden deep within himself. He didn't want to betray Rebecca either. Betray their relationship, his feelings for her, what they meant to him, what they'd shared together. If so, he had to be questioning himself as to why he was allowing himself these feelings for me, Deborah - if he was, of course - whom he had only known for a few days, when he knew he could never leave Rebecca. Would he then end up hating me for that which he might be unable to halt? While on the other hand, I did not hate myself for being unable to cease my feelings for him. Be they real or faux, by whatever criteria they might be judged. Given all these contradictions (and counter contradictions), maybe it was I who hadn't a clue?

"You have that look on your face of having heard something very amusing," Reuben slowly broke into a smile (I sensed he was pleased to have me back, what with that general unease seemingly inherent in his demeanor evaporating) as I took my seat. "It has that Rosenfeld hint of the mischievous in it."

"I'll tell you later. I promise. You'll enjoy it." I kind of laughed as I spoke, relieved for the break in my gathering tension his opportune remark had offered. I would take it that some remnant of amusement from that overheard in the toilet lingered still on my outward features as opposed to the seemingly ridiculous debate I had just been having with my better self.

During my absence, Reuben had finished up what was on his plate, while I had a bite or two left. I was chewing on these morsels, which even if gone cold were good to the last crumb, when our server materialized wanting to know if we enjoyed our selections and would we like desert.

"Turkish coffee, or whatever you have closest to it, b'vakasha." Upon offering an appreciation to the chef, in Hvrit - then with a nod to Reuben - I, laughing apologetically, switched in part to English, adding as an afterthought, "With a Turkish delight floating in it, beseder, okay."

The look she gave me was as if to say I was "meshugas", crazy, if not having imbibed too much of that Portuguese grape, before a wide grin spontaneously appeared on her face just as she was about to turn on her heels and, with a swish of her pony tail, take off.

"I do think that you and our waitress are on the same page somehow, strange as it seems," Reuben said as he attempted to suppress a chuckle. "But you never finished telling about your early love, this other Reuben, at some summer encampment."

Sometimes you get more than you hope for, when you least expect it. I had to think fast, if not simply let it come to me in the telling of it. As long as my improvising didn't get the best of me. Or get ahead of me tripping the light fantastic.

"It began on a hike, our thing, or my thing at least. I tripped on a root - no, I wasn't smoking anything, not at that tender age anyhow - and went tumbling down a rocky embankment, backpack and all. I thought I'd broken my ankle, what with the pain and immediate swelling, but it turned out I'd only twisted it, well a bad sprain I guess. But the thing of it was I couldn't walk on it. It was really hurting and I was afraid that I'd sustained a permanent injury of some kind, would never walk again. I guess I was in a panic - quite unlike me really. So he, this Reuben, lifted me in his arms and carried me x number of miles back over what was really a rugged trail, as if he had a choice. Some of my fellow classmates shouted teasing remarks as we set out, one or two sniped that I was feigning it in order to have him all to myself, that it was selfish of me, haha. But he merely laughed, carrying me in his arms (it might have been easier, seeing as I was already tall for my age, to have to toted me piggyback but for the pain his holding me by my ankle would have wrought); he told me not to listen to them, that it was just an age old natural envy thing, nothing personal - like they were going to have to hoof it out carrying their own backpacks (mine he'd lashed to his - so besides me he had the weight of my back pack on him as well). To keep me entertained in order to take my mind off the pain coupled with a nagging fretfulness, he talked to me. (He told me how he'd once broken his leg on a wilderness trip as boy and had to be carried out, how he'd felt ever so embarrassed, had let down his school mates, which had been silly of him he'd realized when older - that helping each other is what people do, and that someday I might be in a position to help someone injured be it physically or otherwise, which I have been: I was thinking of what he'd said only yesterday when we were faced with getting Jonna to the hospital, me driving her in Rubble once we'd gotten her down off the Tel, before we learned that that Magen David helicopter was on its way.) I think I started asking him questions about himself to start with, like what did he study in college and why, whatever desperately came to mind, my Deborah kind of curiosity questions, however childlike remembering them in hindsight, as they literally popped into my head - and he seemed to enjoy answering them, probably took his mind off the extra weight he was lugging, though he never once gave hint of being tired, probably because he didn't want me to feel any worse than I had. Afterwards, I was in a rehabilitation facility for some weeks, where he brought me my homework and stuff, and would tell me humorous stories, even read to me. Confide in me too during the odd moment, asking my advice, if rhetorically. Caught up as we might become in the heat of the moment. I definitely had it bad, as they'd say, I lived for those hour-long visits, almost daily at first. In his company I felt so 'grown up', like I was a 'woman' already - me imagining how a woman might be - when not my vivacious preteen self. Remember, I was tall for my age, with my hair long already and possessing a certain amount of faux sophistication that seemed to come naturally to me, playing it to the hilt. And being an orphan had imbued in me this certain air of independence. It was like I was omnipotent, the glass shoe had fitted. But as summer was almost over, it wasn't long before he had to return to college. Towards the end I sensed a certain stiffness, well a reserve, replacing what had been between us a kind of jocular informality, the propriety inherent in the age difference reasserting itself, like he'd caught himself, thus reverting to the roles we were originally deemed to play, as if the equality we'd shared, had perhaps gotten carried away with, had become subject to circumspection, for want of a better word. I often wondered if he hadn't been spoken to, if not exactly warned, that things had been observed and reported. Perhaps with the best intentions, failing to see our 'relationship' as I myself saw it for better or for worse - had perceived it to have been. But looking back on it, I think it was more like that, for all the fun we'd shared during those hours of his visits, he saw through me for the delightful, interesting kid that I was, just that and nothing more, while he was about to return to a real world, thus his letting me down as easily as he could, without acknowledging the whys and the wherefores."

Our coffee had been brought, with indeed a pink cube of a Turkish delight floating amid the froth - once it had been ceremoniously poured into two demitasses and delicately placed before us. A slight nutty flavor that meshed with cardamon arose in its aroma as we lifted our cups to our lips.

"I think he had a crush on me as well. A kind of crush, that had caught him off guard. Or so I liked to think, to give my ego a boost." I was on a roll, I couldn't shut up, the coffee was doing it, with the first sip it was like a hit going to my brain, I should have known better. "Only I was obviously way too young for him, at that time, needless to say. Like at the other end of the moon. And, like I just said, I think he had become sorely aware of it just before the end. I think he wished we were the same age, or in the same age bracket and that I'd still have a crush on him like I so obviously had had, as I believe you said you'd grown to feel the same with Debbie, remember. Which probably induced this unreachable longing in both of us. If you can imagine I could perceive such stuff already, instinctively if unable quite yet to fully reason out. And like Debbie with you, but unlike Debbie I hadn't dared ask him to wait for me until I'd grown up - but I'd wanted to, perhaps knowing better already, the improbability inherent in the inevitable . Being a few years older than she in my case, I was just a little more hip about things, I guess. On the other hand, it is painful to be in love with the idea of someone, if that is what it is, at any age."

I watched Reuben's face studying mine, or those inquisitive eyes of his rather scrutinizing me, the looser my tongue seemed to get, not in a critical way but out of a kind of concern for that girl I had created, for the guy as well but from a different angle I suspect. How much he saw himself, in whatever way in the story, I couldn't begin to fathom, I was not sure how much I saw of myself in what was essentially a Deborah story after all. A Deborah story to parallel Debbie's story, involving two somewhat dissimilar Reubens. With a slightly older Deborah for good measure. Because first and foremost I was hiding behind myself while at the same time trying to explain myself, quite well aware of the taboo territory I was skirting. Debbie had a family who thought her thing for her older, teenage cousin "cute", the more I must have prattled on about how I was "in love" with him, from what he'd told me about Joy's letters - only Joy probably hadn't told the half of it. (Which now made me want to heartfelt giggle self-consciously.) If it had been the Marstons I'd have been given a polite talking to, have it explained to me how I was "mistaken", that I mustn't allow myself to get so carried away, while Reuben was a "nice boy" who nevertheless must be interested in girls closer to his own age, which was "natural", for I was but a family member he was fond of whom he good-naturedly humored (given my tender age), so I must cease and desist so as not to put him any further on the spot. To ask God in my prayers to guide me here in particular. If

I'd been Deborah's age though as in the story I'd just concocted, I'd no doubt have been hauled off to some guidance counselor if not a child psychologist who would want to know first thing if "Reuben" had acted in any way "untoward" where I was concerned. Like what might he have done otherwise to have inspired and encouraged me, etc., etc. If my parents hadn't died when they did and I had persisted in what most would term a highly romantic "obsession", would my mother have eventually given me a "talking to", her being fond as she was of her nephew as well? I don't think this thing that Reuben and I being "old souls" who'd found each other would have washed either. Though my mother had been of an independent mind in most matters, fiercely so, who didn't give a fig what others thought, however "unconventional" the root of the matter.

"I have loved Debbie dearly, from day one. As I believe I've mentioned previously," Reuben began, after some moments of silent reflection. "But I wasn't so much 'in love' with her in that earlier time, just that I felt close to her like I had never felt close to one before, just in make believe, wishful yearnings. Only she was a child still; that precluded the romantic side of it I longed for with a girl - though if you remember me telling you, at moments I really wished she and I were of the same age with her feelings for me just as strong once a woman already, or at least on the precipice of becoming one. I was a pretty much a loner, inside myself (to where I had retreated years previously) as opposed to being lonely - well, that too, in my youth, okay. While, yes, during later periods following her death I would daydream of the woman I could imagine she'd have possibly become, should we have met again, of our becoming romantically involved like a man and a woman involved, even if we were cousins. In those wet dreams I fashioned, I really was in love with her, yes, very much so. Even after I met Rebekah, happy as I've been with Rebekah. Debbie still draws on me, if she only could have lived. For her own sake most of all, to have known life and love. To have struggled towards and reached her potential." Here he broke off, almost two quickly, as if biting his lip.

"As for your Reuben," he abruptly continued, apparently having decided on a different tack, "I'm certain he wished too that you'd been closer to his age at the time, how could he not have, you being you even then, and more so physically so already as well, though in a few years the age difference wouldn't have been a hindrance. He's probably thought of you many times since, I certainly would have, if you don't mind me saying so. Like Debbie was, you're like bloody something else, Ms. Rosenfeld."

That got me laughing, to which he joined in with me, probably in order to compensate for having said more than he'd intended, to hide a certain embarrassment I detected, that almost caused me to choke on a burst of silent giggles from trying to rein myself in. I hope I hadn't gone as blushing red in the face as he had - which could have been seen as much as exposure to the sun as anything, in both our cases.

"I won't say any more, if you won't," I managed to get out, hoping I wouldn't cap it with a coughing fit (which I didn't), to which he returned a sheepish nod of sorts - not that I thought for one minute he regretted that near come-on compliment that had in the rush of it all ever so earnestly escaped his lips.

"And in the nick of time, no doubt," he said quietly, not without some mirth, "here cometh our Girl Friday. again, uncanny timing.

"When waitressing for any length of time you grow a second sense about a patron. It goes with the territory, and a novice she's definitely not."

With my declining her inquiry if she could get us anything further to eat or to drink, our server very seriously presented me with the check, as I had been speaking for both of us throughout and in Hebrew, only to break into an involuntary smile when she saw my rather bountiful appreciation after all, as I handed her back the bill with my card.

"Plastic to pay on a kibbutz," he chuckled shaking his head. "It's like I've seen everything. Rip Van Winkle? I'm more like the Ancient Mariner. I know, it's silly of me."

"No, in a way it is not. Silly of you, I mean. Something is missing in just the few short years since I first came here, for that summer on kibbutz. Israel is fast entering Cyberspace, has truly embraced the new high tech world. It is a matter of survival too, I know, the way the future is being perceived universally. It's no longer a metaphor for explaining something abstract, it means we are living like in a brave new neighborhood within the bounds of the old. Are living again in 'strange days'. Like in that old song. As if we ever left them, in my lifetime at least. A loss of something to my way of thinking, in essence a denial. Which I am not alone in thinking. But the consensus is that we can't afford to look back."

"We?"

"The Israelis in particular. But, yes, 'we', in that I work here, am a part of here, if only part time, physically. I'm a Jew too, and that is full time wherever I may find myself, as my name certainly attests to, that means I feel a responsibility. I do like it here, warts and all. That should be obvious. Just because I don't talk about the situation like what is happening in Gaza or on the other side of the Green Line, in the West Bank or right here in Israel itself for that matter, doesn't mean that I am unaware of things, or that I look the other way, don't have opinions."

"I know. Me too. I do care - and worry, am sometimes downright afraid. A vortex. The whole scene. It's as if this whole part of the world is caught up in a prolonged 'dust devil'. 'Strange days' is indeed an apt description of where our times have long descended into. I didn't mean to-"

"You're forgiven. But on probation, Mr. Headey. For the next 30 seconds."

I genuinely hate being cutesy clever that in shallow moments I can pull like a rabbit out of a hat in order to extract myself from having fallen into whatever over my head. Or beating around the bush in order to avoid calling a spade a spade. A taking refuge in the esoteric.

With that under wraps, I had to beat myself back to a middle ground and chart afresh the course, as it were, the sometimes sailor in me mixing metaphors as I sought to come about against the residual drag of Portuguese wine, a momentary indirection, and Turkish coffee. It wasn't the first thing that had popped into my head, but it may as well have been, given how I nearly gushed it out.

"I was never really a 'spiritual' seeker. Contrary to anything I may have previously said. Or implied. Not per se anyhow. The *Jesus Christ Superstar* thing notwithstanding. My quest was more on the order of getting people together, well, putting them together for some purpose, altruistic but with a hidden agenda. If just to have them share in something that I could relate to, okay, that I wanted them to relate to as well.

As was Debbie, with her wanting to deconstruct Jesus, much as I guess I did to a certain extent - to find the Jewish Jesus in my case, find the man at least and succeed where Magdalena failed. Or so I greatly suspect had been Debbie's shtick as well, what else, from what you have told me of Marston's portrayal of her. As were you with the Kennedy mystic, admit it. We wanted to be a part of something greater than ourselves, at the same time own it. Teenagers that we were. It is what the three of us have in common, made us what we were, who you and I deep down still are. What did you call it, like two peas in a pod. How about three peas in a pod. And I apologize if that is a repeat. It's just I can't emphasize it enough."

For a moment there I wondered if my coming in for a near crash landing of sorts hadn't aroused the attention of our fellow diners, what with my "bolero" of a spiel reaching its crescendo - or so I'd felt, before catching myself, being somewhat winded, my lips and mouth parched dry. But the diners at the near tables continued to talk and eat, the servers rushing back and forth in dutiful attendance. The world about was seemingly going on in its ordered place. I gave Reuben one of my sheepishly mischievous grins for reassurance, and the look he gave me back told me he got it, no more painting pictures necessary.

I straightened my shoulders, lifting my purse - a firehose and leather pocket - from the table.

"Shall we?" I more or less nodded, with him

pushing his chair back in response. "I'll go see what happened to 'Friday' with my card."

We almost collided in the open doorway. From the tautness of her face around her eyes, though her dark eyes retained their sparkle, I could see that the evening had begun to wear and tear on her, on all of the servers. The crowd of diners had swollen considerably, that I really hadn't paid much attention to, since our arrival; I suspected that most of those sitting in the seats at the bar, who weren't already eating, were waiting for a table. The credit card machine had developed a glitch, naturally, thus her not returning it to me sooner, she hurried apologized as she handed it with the paperwork that required my signature. There was a large convention meeting in Tiberias that week, she'd continued in a near breathless Hebrew, and 1910 had been taking up the spillover. I offered what I hope wasn't taken as a condescending sympathy, thanking her for what had been a wonderful evening for me and my "friend", that it had meant much to us.

"It has been our pleasure. And," she said just as I was about to turn to go catch up with Reuben, "there was this guy here earlier, who many of us know, who said that you are a famous archaeologist photographer?"

"Yes, Naor Dan, I saw him." Grinning, I made like to roll my eyes. "I'm Deborah Rosenfeld and I work with an archaeological team excavating a Tel near Beit She'an, My third year already. I'm the dig's photographer, that keeps me busy enough. I photograph the finds - and where they are found. For the likes of our Naor to sit in his office in Jerusalem to study along with our director's reports. Otherwise, I simply shoot photographs at wherever a job takes me."

I caught up with Reuben, a solitary figure standing in the shadows out by the trunk of one of those towering palms, the one farthest to the side, with a long narrow bench pushed against it, his back to the white glare of the lights on the portals. From even a short distance the restaurant's din sounded all the livelier now that I was away from it, was no longer cocooned within the burble where I'd become mostly inured to it. The heat in the air had grown thinner still. Across the courtyard a bright light or two beneath an arcade broke the dark's weighty omnipresence.

"Thank you for the evening," he said as I joined him. "I've enjoyed it, with you."

I believe he smiled when he said that, if shyly. Before he quickly added, if not quite in the same breath. "What species of tree is this hoary monster?"

He nodded towards the adjoining tree, with a trunk befitting an illustration in a book of Grimm Brothers fairy tales.

"A sycamore, I think, or rather 'ficus sycomorus', but don't quote me. Anyway, they are in the Bible, quite indigenous. The fruit is like unto figs, is extremely sweet. They usually bear about now, but this one looks picked clean already. 1910 offers a variety of deserts. Including the chocolate delicacies made right here on the kibbutz. Perhaps we should have."

"I'm stuffed." he demurred. "Your Turkish with that delight was an inspired idea, the perfect denouement, finis, topping it all off."

He sensed that I had begun to giggle inwardly almost before 'denouement' had escaped his lips. But it had nothing to do with his play of words that he may have taken for light criticism. I slid my arm through his again, hugging it tight to me as we retraced our steps towards the car park.

"I just remembered I promised I'd tell you later why I might have had on my face a 'pleased look' when I returned from the john," I began, picking my words carefully (no, I certainly wasn't going to mention that "aging toy boy she has in tow" bit), in the hope of extracting the humor out of what was truculently nasty, well, spiteful (one could but wonder what one woman in particular had for breakfast - or didn't get enough of last night, deeming me a lanky creature like she did: no matter, I felt vindicated, having had the last word). "There were several women in the other stalls rather vocally wondering where was the celebrity couple rumor had it had booked a table for this evening.

I noticed we'd been given the once-over upon our arrival - so that was why. But, alas, we didn't pass muster. You looked familiar to one of them, if 'American', sorry, so possibly you could have been. But I was dismissed out of hand. I didn't have a St. Tropez tan, besides having the audacity to wear a sleeveless dress with my white upper arms exposed. Two of them were left speechless when I walked out of my stall, gave them an aw shucks grin before wetting my hands and running my fingers through my hair, taking my time traipsing out. I would wonder if they are not back there still, their mouths agape. And to think, I thought we were given the once-over because we were such a handsome couple."

I did strive to make it sound as ridiculously funny as it had more-or-less been, leaning heavily on the irony, in hopes of getting him to laugh with me.

"I'm just glad no one in that case came over and to ask me to autograph their napkin." At which he began to chuckle, he this time hugging my arm close to him, as I began to laugh outright, along with him. "I think you have nice arms, whatever their color. Two-tone, isn't it?"

"Why thank you, kind sir," I managed to get out, wanting to give him a hard tug, and we began to laugh all over again, suddenly two silly kids, as we walked on, our bodies, I felt, so touchingly close. So achingly close.

How much of that which Deborah had shared

with me of her life could have been made up -
much as I had just created the story about the
summer camp, an injury and that college boy
counselor named Reuben that I as Deborah had
fallen in love with, in order to project a parallel
of Debbie and Reuben (for what purpose I had of
yet to think through)? Her trust fund had been
real. Which by the time it had run out I had been
well enough established. It had been a generous
sum, if no fortune - well not by the time it had
paid for that school down through the years -
that I believe I made use of as Deborah herself
might have done - or would have wanted me
to have done. She herself had been ever so real,
in the moments of those hours I had basked in
her presence. For having felt robbed of myself, I
had certainly invented a new persona by being
Deborah (how much had it helped that physically that we had been the spitting image of each
other - remarkable, spooky even, as that was:
had my foster family ever see us together, each
other's "doppelganger", they couldn't have told
us apart), and through it had been able to find
myself, my footing as it were, shedding those
"years of bondage" in the process (where I had
had to more or less please everyone out of the
guilt they'd laid on me - from the Marstons to Joy
for that matter) - in order to hold on and survive
until the opportunity arose for me to make my
move in whatever form it may have taken. Being
able to play another went to set me free, to find

myself - to define myself. Like a pen name often does for a writer. Or a nom de guerre even.

My time with Deborah, those precious few weeks, saw those religious trappings begin to slide away from me - as they were but skin deep apparently to begin with, which did surprise me at first, in moments of sudden realization. And my splitting, my taking off as I did as her, a newly minted Deborah, certainly a work in progress, pretty much made it complete (eventually). My "beliefs", as they were, had been all along more an enthusiasm as opposed to being those of a "true believer". In Reuben's case, garnered more from reading his novel, *(K)hamsin* than anything in particular he'd told me, I think he'd continued a while longer in his quest for a "God" to fail him, his making Aliyah as he'd done being more spiritual a longing than a physical one, a last hurrah for him where inevitably the shit would hit the fan. Yet, he'd survived it, his equilibrium intact. A family trait we both share - tenacity.

"I didn't mean to put you on the spot in my reply about who I might imagine Debbie, had she lived, to be most like." Reuben broke a kind of holding-one's-breath silence some yards further on." It had just come out somehow, like out of the blue."

"I know. I did ask for it, didn't I?"

"It's just I'm not frightened by you somehow as I might have been of Debbie had we ever met again. Maybe not so much frightened as intimidated. She was so brilliant. Well, you too. But you don't make me feel completely a fool, not at all really, as I guess I feared she might have done, without meaning to perhaps. She would have seen that I was not the heightened image she'd had of me, far from it, with feet of clay as they say."

"Has anyone ever made your feel like a fool?"

"No. Those I've known who were more intelligent than me never played that card ever, unlike those who think they are more intelligent than others will often try to do."

"Debbie wouldn't have either. You two would have simply hit it off with a meeting of the minds. Hearts too, maybe. You two would have just hit it off period. Only with the age difference erased. Besides, she'd have been so happy to have found you again, just to know you hadn't forgotten her. Believe me on that too."

The two of us continued to walk, almost touching, he with his head slightly downcast, as I kept hoping he'd say something, to the point that I wanted to nudge with my elbow in his ribs. It was like when he wasn't gushing forth he could be as sealed as a vault, all that whatever buried deep within him stuck in his craw so to speak. Not that he wasn't acutely aware of everything within his sphere, his orbit. I liked him for it while at the same time feeling left out. Which made me inwardly laugh all of a sudden. We really were so fucking much alike, akin, whatever you want to call it. So it was up to me, okay.

"Why did you call Debbie 'Gigi'? Give her that nickname in particular?" I almost asked "Why did you call me 'Gigi'", catching myself just in time.

Early on I had never given it much, if any, thought, it being a cute and catchy name, of some spirited young girl in a movie by that name: it was just his very own special name for me, I being his "Gigi". Until by chance I got to see the old movie well into my teens, vaguely recalling at the time of having heard its impassioned theme song sung by Louis Jourdan. As well as that other song from the film, the somewhat silly *Thank Heaven for Little Girls* sung by the elderly but spry Maurice Chevalier. But not until I would read Colette's novella did I really begin to wonder how it related in his mind to a six-year-old kid, unless he'd only seen the movie - but even then.

"You know, in retrospect," he spoke suddenly, "it has never failed to make me cringe, my calling her 'Gigi', cute as one may say the name sounded. I'd heard the song, *Gigi*, knew it was from a Broadway musical, but hadn't seen the movie, and as for Colette and her novella about a young girl being groomed to be a courtesan falling in love with an older guy, I'd never before heard of either. I simply thought it was just a cute and endearing-sounding name of a

song about a young girl in a movie of that name
that seemed to fit Debbie, her lively mind, her
ebullient personality to a tee. Later, I didn't
want to think about what she might someday
have thought should she too discover the name's
source. But probably to add insult to injury, had
it been known, my brother's best friend had this
spirited palomino called 'Gigi' that liked to run
up behind you and nip your ear. So my calling
Debbie 'Gigi', it just came to me as things do.
Like an inspiration or something. Like she was in
herself an inspiration. And at the time it was as
readily based as much as anything on my association of the name with that horse, the sound of
the name exemplifying the personality of each.
Hey, why are you laughing? Deborah?"

I'd gripped his shoulder to steady myself, I'd
begun to laugh so hard, unable to contain myself,
talk about one's funny bone being tickled. But I
could feel him tensing up. With bewilderment.

"A horse!" I managed to get out. "That's precious. It's brilliant. Don't you see?" "No," he uttered.

"Oh Reuben, forgive me. It's my totally weird
sense of humor. It's the irony of it all. And the
wine and the Turkish coffee. And the lightening
of the air what with that breeze from the lake."

"And just when I was thinking there must
have been something in your Turkish delight
that wasn't in mine."

"It was the sound of the word, simply the

name, Gigi, that caught your imagination, a sheer inspiration on your part, that you intuitively identified with Debbie's persona. While the fifteen year old girl in the story, who falls in love with the man she's being groomed as a courtesan for, who in turn falls in love with her and marries her, and a horse, a golden palomino, being merely the catalyst here. It's so perfect. And if I may say so, so are you. That is, the you I have come to know these past few days."

"But Debbie wouldn't have known that."

"No doubt she'd have figured it out, if she hadn't already. She knew you intuitively as well. Girls, even little girls, have a way of knowing these things."

More and more it felt like I was like talking to him now from behind a glass wall, through an intercom, with my back to him so that he couldn't see that it was me (or suddenly seeing the Debbie in me at last, having already subconsciously suspected that I was or had been her).

"Some years ago, I was a second-string still-life photographer on this film being shot on location, in the American Southwest, about a loner of a man finding his long-estranged much younger wife - whom he had pushed away due to his personal hang-ups. He followed her, well he found her working in a kind of peepshow parlor where the client could see the through a one-way glass partition, a woman who was expected to both visually and verbally address the client's voyeuristic fantasies. On the first visit, the man is unable to speak so he flees, only to return the following day where he begins to tell her a story about a husband who had been propelled by inner demons to destroy this beautiful thing he'd had with this woman, his wife. Slowly, it dawns on her that it is her story too, their story. So, sitting on the floor with her back against the wall under that "window", so that he can't see her face, she tells her heart-wrenching side of it - still not certain but suspecting that it is her long lost husband."

"*Paris, Texas*! I saw that movie, with Harry Dean Stanton and Nastassja Kinsky. Sam Shepard wrote it, or most of it, with Wem Wenders the director and Kit Carson finishing it. Or so I've read."

I nodded and he continued, suddenly excited - well, alert.

"It was not long after seeing it that I had that dream of Debbie writing to me."

Where had I gone wrong, had I lost him (had I ever had him, really had him, way back when even)? Did I want him still? Was all this worth it - apropos of nothing, as it is said. I thought of taking his arm again, only to think better of it. When we get back to the camp site, we'd see. It was beginning to feel like a toothache in the heart, this game I hadn't meant to play, not like this.

As I drove, the visibility along the shore had this thin blueish tint in it, as much as did the ultramarine dome of the night sky above had - or maybe just hint of it in both is a better depiction - with an airy quality that abruptly solidified into a heavy, pitch-black wall on the hinterland side across highway 90 here - much as I remembered it from three years earlier at this time of the year (and about the time of the month too). The moon, already high over the water, was this ghostly galleon of a specter, like Alfred Noyes luminously painted in his poem, *The Highwayman*. All the while, Rubble's headlights resembled two minute laser beams boring their way forward through seemingly impenetrable waves of darkness.

"Byron would have been out of luck tonight looking for stars on the Sea of Galilee. Though there is a bluish hue in those waves out there, like wet ink. But the only sheen is that of the moon itself mirrored on them. It looks like the wind is still up."

I chuckled at Reuben's playful tendency to wax lyrical with a twist at the odd moment. It was at that moment I realized that I had been feeling a kind of eeriness ever since we left 1910 - but a kind of eeriness of the heart rather than the usual kind lodged in the pit of one's stomach. The thought came to me, however, that I might not recognize in time the turn off to the camp site, when not accustomed normally to experience such self-doubts, relying instinctively on an innate sense of self-assuredness that I could handle come what may. Was something trying to tell me that I was in uncharted waters here?

"Is Rubble hard to drive, hard on your body, that is?" Reuben out of nowhere asked a couple of kilometers on. "Because you appear to handle it with such apparent ease, like it is second nature to you. I once drove an old pickup truck on a summer job, the only brake being the hand brake among other things. It was at a summer camp on a lake and I was a prospective counselor."

"If I were to drive from here to Eilat, I'd probably feel it the next day. Fuck yeah." I almost laughed aloud. "Especially if Rubble had only a hand brake. Otherwise, it is no harder than anything else. Rubble gets me there, so far, and that is what counts. It is challenging sometimes, I admit, but fun. And my long arms help."

"From all that ladder climbing, no doubt.

"From sculling mostly, I was once on a sculling team. But up and down ladders twenty times a day is not to be scoffed at."

"I've seen them on the Charles River in Boston, scullers that is. And at Oxford on the Thames".

"The university town I landed in upon my crossing country from the West Coast had a sculling group and one of the first things I did upon arrival was to join it. Being a complete novice at the outset, I simply thought it was an interesting thing to do. Somehow, it appealed to me. Besides being consciously aware of needing to get into shape physically, after this protracted infection that had taken its toll. Talk about having noodle arms. I kept it up religiously through the following spring, until leaving for that summer ulpan. Which I had been really thankful for when it came to handling the kibbutz work assignments. Like shoveling out the Refet after the milking. Especially that. But now I mostly row this little wooden sail boat off that Scandinavian island I told you about, if during the warmer months I can get a couple of weeks between jobs. Sail it too, after a morning's row out around the skerries, taking photographs purely for myself. I'd bought that first camera around the time I joined the sculling crew. They were a good bunch. You could say I cut my teeth on photographing them. The posted results of which went to engender sponsorships for the group in the town. It made me feel good too, being able to give back a little."

"I grew up in boats, as you know, but at age 18 I went off to college, and except for the couple of years here on a kibbutz, I have lived in cities. I miss messing about in boats, but what I miss too is having someone who'd enjoy messing about in boats with me."

"Rebekah?" I asked, wondering where this was going.

"Rebekah enjoys looking at water, painting reflections in water, which she is a master at doing. We've camped out on beaches, like that time on the outer banks. But that's as close as she wants to get to it. When she was a kid this older cousin, also a Jonna, pushed her overboard from a rock to teach her to swim the hard way. She managed to get to the shore and climb out on her own - determined not to show she'd been scared shitless. That did it with her and water. Water over her head especially. As she grew older she'd spend her summers away from the coast with her paternal grandmother on an old farm where the grandmother rented a retirement cottage in this lush, inland valley that had been the grand-mother's family locale since the mists of time. Where she could help with the animals, walk on her hands doing somersaults and jumping bare-foot into steaming cow pies. The latter when she was a pre-teen actually. In any case, she was more in her element on a farm. Or in the countryside at least. Yet, she remains a city girl nevertheless."

"When I was a kid," I chimed in, "I think I'd have enjoyed that as well, the farm animals and the cow pies too, if I'd had had a chance to. Though I became quite good at doing somer-saults one year at summer camp. And I think I can still walk on my hands."

Okay, enough, I stomped myself figuratively speaking on my toes. I was not going to play the competition game, as if I could keep up with Re-bekah in that vein. Though I had to admit that I had led Reuben into it here. Yet with his bringing up Rebekah as much as he had that evening, had I really truly "lost" him, even if I'd never really had him? Or had I given too much slack to the line, allowing him to wiggle free - another supercili-ous scenario. The always dead-certain Deborah, in that which counted most, was not so certain, period. "He is only a man. One like many. Why is he so different?" The haunting lyrics of that An-drew Lloyd Webber song from *Superstar*, full of hunger and regret, reared up to give me some-thing like a belated kick. Perhaps I didn't - or rather, wouldn't - know "how to love him"? And Rebekah did. Why had my six-year-old self been so besotted by his sixteen year old self? And now twenty-five years on I find myself drawn to him still. Like he had in his possession my heart from a couple of lifetimes ago. Or what? Just as what was the Debbie he could see in me? Had lingered in me, had survived in me? From a child of six, of eight or nine when he last saw me, that he'd never been able to get out of his mind? Like those imps or whatever they symbolized that could haunt, bedevil the characters in Issac Bashevis Singer's stories. I felt like hitting him, make him say something, to break the silence.

"I suspect," Reuben began, as if he'd again read my thoughts, his voice slowly rising above the searing roar of Rubble's heavy tires on the tarmac, "I have been forever searching for that other half of me that shared with me my playing house under the back porch summers when eight or nine, a parallel universe where my make-believe girlfriend and I had it all to ourselves, this near perfect harmony, existence. Until I grew too tall to sit up without my head striking the joists. It was just the two of us in my little bubble of a world at once removed from the general unpleasantries of real life as I knew it, certainly my fractious home life. It was acting out a daydream, a wish fulfillment. I grew out of that, the playing house thing, but not the longing for a one and only, to talk to, to share everything with, who would just want to be with me. But such an elemental - I refrain from using the word 'pure' - relationship is probably not humanly possible, shouldn't be, is ultimately narcissistic. And too much of that and like the kinds of guys I was speaking of earlier, you'll miss the real possibility right under your nose. Because besides being able to recognize it, it would require working for, that can't be had on a bed of roses. I cried after reading *Green Mansions* (I was a teenager already), over the death of Rima. It was like everything beautiful was ultimately destroyed by others who could not share such feelings, were jealous and fearful of their existence. In a way I think that must be how I had felt, in some weird way, about Debbie being taken from me, as it were. When I had already more or less deserted her, thinking she'd long outgrown liking me like she had."

"You are beating yourself up again, Reuben. Debbie the child was growing up, and not just physically, she had a lot on her plate by then, and would shortly have even more so to bear. But the depth of her feelings never deserted her. I know that from feelings I held dear at around her age and a little older. Like I've just been telling you. She never gave up her feelings that one day she'd find you again, it was so ingrained in her personality, which among other things helped her to hold out through thick and thin. And from what I have heard tell these past few days, it was more thick than thin. Which brings me to a question I've longed to ask, Your character who was more or less you in *(K)hamsin* went on Aliyah with a girl he met at that farm, who is still with him on June 5th, the day the war starts, did the two of them ever marry?"

"No." I sensed that erupted from him rather abruptly, with him backing off as he continued. "She left him for a guy just back from the army, about six weeks later, moving in with him. My dark moods and growing disenchantment with the direction the country seemed headed for during those halcyon days, with the war just won, when the possibilities for the better or for the worse had seemed endless amid a deafening euphoria. My grousing had been the straw that broke the camel's back. She split."

"I'm sorry," I said. "I didn't mean..." Only, in the next breath, to audaciously ask, "Did you ever marry?"

"Well, in London I came frightfully close, if a rabbi friend had had his way. Only I fell out of love with her by falling so much more in love with another. Only the other one, I felt I had much more in common with, like a shared Jewish sensibility, and to whom I would but belatedly dare to disclose my feelings - she had been halfway out of the door en route to Israel to do graduate studies at Hebrew U. Then I fell in love with another, a friend's cousin, a bedazzling schizophrenic (talk about being a sucker for punishment), before I sort of wore out my welcome in more ways than one in England. And another (I was back in the States by this time), ten years my junior already, a budding writer and a fiercely budding feminist to boot, who indeed taught me a few things, I have to admit, was also en route to college with a four year scholarship no less. The story of my love life until I met Rebekah."

"At least you'd have escaped Debbie's wrath, for not waiting for her, at least not marrying another, had she turned up on your London doorstep once she'd turned eighteen. That is if she'd lived, of course. Summer junkets for high school students to England and Europe, Israel too with stopovers in London, had become de rigueur by then. Don't think she wouldn't have searched you out and have fought like a wildcat, any one of those girls would have been reduced to tatters. Well, definitely tears."

"Oh no," he cried out, facetiously, well almost so. "But isn't it fanciful to think so, to a degree. Fatuous too." I figured it hurt him because he seemed to wince, if inwardly. Yet, he was laughing, and so was I, and the more he laughed, I laughed. I think it was the first time where something I said really made him laugh. It was a good thing we had the road mostly to ourselves, what with Rubble beginning to career all over the place as I sought to catch myself, getting a grip on the wheel. Don't think that the Debbie in me wasn't ready to go for Rebekah's jugular as well.

"You know, sometimes you can be brutally funny, Deborah, even when it is not funny, well not exactly. I'm aware that to most it would seem ludicrous," he said, as he reached out and laid his hand softly upon my shoulder, with his fingers playfully touching the side of my neck almost absentmindedly through my thick hair, sending sliver-like shivers down my spine. Before, as if having second thoughts, withdrawing it.

"It isn't that Rebekah hasn't fulfilled my wildest expectations, she has," Reuben went on, as if maybe to cover his tracks. "More so than I could have ever imagined possible. Or deserve for that matter. If there is such a thing as the other half, a completeness. For better or for worse. I can't believe I'm so lucky. It's just there is this something missing thing; or I think there is something missing, or is it that I want something to be missing, diabolically so, that rears up every so often that I have to push back down in the rabbit hole from whence it springs. Call it a tantalizing imp, whispering in my ear. It can really be bedeviling. It's really stupid, ridiculous, I know. Maybe it is simply I can't take being loved. You are the first person I've ever really mentioned it to. My longing for a sailing companion, superficial as it may sound, to share my love of being on the water, just now triggered it. I guess to you it is still more of my wanting my cake and eating it."

There were those moments when his attraction to me was so palpable that it could not be mistaken for anything else, however deftly he could hide it in plain view with a spat of quasi self-depreciation. But I was not going to take the bait. I was not certain if I should laugh again or be pissed off. I think what I really wanted to do was hit him, awkward as that that would have been while keeping Rubble on the road. I love men, but I didn't always like them. They could make themselves so hard to like, uncannily so. And Reuben's habit of shoving what he took to be his clay feet in my face in order to throw me off the scent had become fucking unconscionable (be it to the Debbie in me or to the living, breathing Deborah). As for what was going on in his mind, I had to admit I had about as much a clue as he must have had in regards to what I was thinking, much as our human animal natures felt to be vibrating off of each other - as if to say they could smell each other's unquestionable close familiarity, if that was all. That limb we had been inching out on, I expected at any minute now to hear a cacophonous splintering.

I decided to keep my eyes glued to the highway lest I roar straight past that turn off that was difficult enough to see in time in broad daylight, where now the long shadows thrown by the tight cordon of date palms only deepened when the moon went behind some rogue cloud. Reuben, meanwhile, had merely drifted into a reverie mode I called it. Where it was as if only his physical presence remained - much like those shells emerging cicadas leave behind on tree trunks.

What would it solve, or resolve, if I fucked him, that is if we fucked, had sex together, whatever? Yes, I wanted to fuck him, as much as I ached for him to fuck me - deep and hard and full of shooting stars and gentle, like the roll of those waves on the lake out there at once splashing ashore when not just rippling the sand with its flows and ebbs in between. I didn't want to be made love to any more than I want to make love. Between us there was no need to make bullshit anything. Our thing for each other, with each other, between each other was in the marrow of our bones, like from day one, in the fiber of our flesh and sinews - in our genes, okay, I'm waxing fucking mystical, I know, when I am otherwise an utterly rational human being, whatever that means. The two of us were made for each other, fashioned for each other (I don't say "meant" for each other - that's a whole other ballgame); we are "just are". He knows it just as I know it. Have known since that moment on that tide covered road when he lifted me to his shoulders, since our eyes had made fleeting contact five nights before when I'd belatedly barged into the meeting upon my return to Neve Rom. Since our stars had made their celestial alignment according to his friend Lora's astrology chart. (Now I have truly gone esoterical.)

I had yet to meet someone I would honestly trust so far as to completely sexually surrender to, which probably says more about me than the partners I've had. Until now, with Reuben. Because looking for that sharing trust is like looking for a needle in a hay stack.

Yet, where would it leave the two of us? Would we be able to just walk away as if nothing had happened? Us, of all people, he and I? When it is what we'd have to do. I'd only hurt him in the end, even if I hurt myself even more so by doing it. Could I be truly seriously involved with another without telling them, him, of Debbie. Being Deborah now might be enough, with most

- but not with Reuben, not with Debbie wedged between the two of us? And making him an accomplice even if he were willing to share that burden that was best left for me to bear alone? No, it was too much to lay on him, on anyone, however game they might be at the outset. For the two of them would have to share a lie, while as Deborah alone only I was only responsible for myself, to myself. But, was it him I wanted after all, I was still asking myself. Wanted at such a price he'd be liable for as well? Or was it something deep down in myself irrevocably lost? From my childhood that I had been torn away from? That my better sense told me was irretrievable. Because even if I came to him as Debbie, if we fucked, I wouldn't be the Debbie in his heart and mind, but Deborah her substitute at best, possessing that whatever that made me remind him so much of her. Any more than he would be the Reuben of my heart and mind of yore. He'd be Reuben, the grown man, the novelist (not to mention being in love with another), and not the teenage object of my pre-pubescent "crush".

"The turnoff, it's right here, I think," Reuben suddenly cried out, calmly yet with a tinge of steel in his voice. That I belatedly recognized too, in the wake of his words, Only I'd been going too fast to make the turn, not in the pitch dark at least. So, as there was no traffic behind me, I simply, if a bit abruptly, braked - leaving Reuben to brace himself with a splayed hand on the dashboard - before backing Rubble up.

"Amazing, you spotted it, when I am the one supposed to be familiar with the territory hereabouts. Thank you."

"Just one of those things. I think it was imprinted, frozen, in my memory because of how you'd suddenly veered off on a dime here earlier," he laughed. "Not that I'm criticizing, mind you."

"No offense taken," I laughed in return, as behind Rubble's headlight beams I pulled into the narrow paved lane, only to immediately wheel right again, with more of Rubble's roaring as I quickly changed gears, onto that even narrower dirt track, relieved that I hadn't drunk as much of that wine as I might have done, to carefully bump along between the scatter of parked vehicles nosed into the thicket's reaches - until we came to its dead end and the sharp left turn put us right up to the closed gate.

Before Reuben could ask, even humorously, like, "what do we do now, scale that fence topped with barbed wire," I said, "I have the padlock key in case its locked due to the terrorist alarm of a couple of days ago, but Marty and Yoni usually just close it at night. Let's go see."

The gate was unlocked, which meant Marty and Yoni were about, thus I had a chance of catching one or both of them come morning. I turned to Reuben's approaching silhouette, what with the glare of Rubble's beams illuminating him from behind. Like an animated shadow being projected upon a well-lit wall, to the crunch of gravel beneath his shoes.

"If you push the gate back," I said, "I'll drive through and wait for you to close it again."

"Why don't you go on. I need to check out the facilities, the 'house of use'," he laughed.

"To give it a Michelin rating, yeah."

"No, Conde Nast."

"Going posh, are we?"

"I'll let you know if I find my way to the campsite. I think I can with the little bit of moonlight out. Otherwise, I'll have to rely on your radio signal vibes or whatever you do give off, trusting I can pick up the frequency."

"I'll trust you can."

Perhaps I should have given him the flashlight I keep in Rubble, only I might have need of it up at the campsite, most likely would have need of it while I went about checking things out. I'd keep an ear open for the sound of his approach, his walking on that coarse gravel should make a modicum of noise. It was comforting to know that Marty and Yoni were there, or somebody was, because I was looking forward to catching them come morning. Kind of like the world was in its ordered place after all. Or my world was, in part at least.

The battery lamp I'd left burning inside of

that tent was like a beacon more or less to back Rubble in by, minute though it was. Rubble's roar in reverse must have been heard all the way across the lake, forget about the campers far and near on this side (I wondered if there were any in residence who might remember it from two years before, like that morning Nell and I had to get back to Tel Ronish at the crack of dawn, I'd only had Rubble for about a year at that time). Yet I managed as usual, with a bit of teeth biting, to edge her just perfectly in between the trees, my perch for the night.

Having checked the perimeters with the flashlight to make sure nothing was amiss, in particular that there was nothing Reuben might trip over should I not hear his approach after all, I sat for a moment in the Land Rover's rear wide-open doorway, with my legs dangling out over the edge. Down through the trees to the beach there were silvery slivers of moonshine in between the silhouettes of those tall, dark trunks, out of which drifted itinerant puffs of that breeze off Kinneret. I almost thought I could hear the roll of the waves coming ashore. I had been thinking of the next morning's photo shoot; my camera case was stuffed beneath one of the elongated side seats behind me, the Leica loaded with fresh film, within easy reach for a grab and run. I was trusting the little alarm beeper on my watch to awake me within minutes of dawn. My plan was to bed down here on the hard floor in the back of Rubble with a pillow or two, though given my length it would be something of a squeeze. On the other hand, there was the tent out there with those inflated mattresses I could see in the lamp-shine through the entrance netting, indeed like an inviting beacon - with Reuben. Something was going to have to give within the hour - but what, and where was it going to go?

It was suddenly a bit of a perturbing thought that Reuben really was ten years my senior, not that I didn't "know" it. Since he'd been so since I was six years old. It was just he could seem so much younger, younger than me even, with that unabashed boyish quality he possessed like a kind of "charm" his personality naturally inhabited. Or was I that besotted six-year-old still? Only I wanted him to love me as Deborah. As I wanted him as the Reuben now. And right that moment I wanted to smell him, to taste him, to feel the weight of his body on mine, to feel him deep inside of me, having penetrated the core of me, with the tangle of legs and arms holding me, mine clutching him tightly as he rode my body inexhaustibly in quest of my heart, that I would lay open for him when he'd least expect it. Only a quick lay was no more what I really wanted with him than he'd want with me if he was going to betray Rebekah, even if just in his conscience. And that was all I had to offer him, considering. In any case, what I didn't want was Debbie squeezed in between us, her having wormed her way in between us, as it were, due to Reuben's and my search for her so to speak, that admittedly I had initiated. Had I felt able to fess up to him at the outset would it have made any difference? Because first and foremost I would have always been Debbie? His Debbie. Debbie whom I had left behind, whose skin I'd shed. And besides making him an accomplice to a crime in the eyes of society, there was that congenital heart defect thing. Thus more wedges created. We were damned from all angles, considering our histories in the interim. As if deep down I hadn't known this from the moment our eyes met. I felt our fates in this respect were about to come to come to a head, and were out of my control, in that four people were involved here - one of whom being our catalyst, now the fly in the ointment.

"Hello! Deborah? You there?" I heard his voice almost simultaneously with the sound of light footsteps coming alongside Rubble. With a hint of uncertainty, not anxiousness, in it. Well, he could have thought I'd taken a walk out to the lakeside. So much for my certainty of my vigilance in any case, my mind having been elsewhere.

"Here," I laughed, "dangling out of Rubble's rear end. So, what's the verdict?"

"Verdict? Oh yeah. Well, not exactly Conde Nast, I suppose," he hesitated, for the comic effect. "But a Michelin for sure. There were no scorpions scurrying about and the water was hot."

"Marty and Yoni will be pleased to know."

The light, bantering mood from moments back at the restaurant had returned and though not forced there was a certain dissembling about it that I suspected he too sensed and likewise chose to ignore. He appeared relaxed, at ease; that light blue canvas shirt he wore hung loose now, had been unbuttoned against his chest. Grabbing his rucksack from the back seat that he swung over one shoulder, he gave the appearance of simply not being in a hurry rather than held back by perhaps indecision on his part. (We had agreed that he got the tent since I'd already made a nest for myself in the back of Rubble.) The air had this feathery feel about it, a peculiar lightness I was wont to attribute to the shine of the moon filtering down through the trees as if one were swimming weightless in between them at the bottom of the sea. (I know, like what had I been smoking.) It wasn't exactly a normal sensation one would expect to experience on an otherwise humid summer night by Kinneret. I suppose I was high on something, though the substance in this case was purely psychological.

"I guess I'll hit the hay then, won't keep you," he said nonchalantly, with a smidgen of a shrug, an attempt at a dispassionate hint of humor, while hesitantly readjusting the rucksack's strap on his shoulder. "As you need to be up early for the sunrise and all."

I followed after him, keeping a step behind. I hadn't planned on doing so, it just happened. I mostly just wanted to reach out and touch him, put my hand on his shoulder, on his rucksack at least, let it rest it there. I guess I simply didn't want to let him go just like that, while having no plan on how to keep him - one without inflicting wounds upon everyone involved, myself included. He had to know I was right behind him, but he showed no acknowledgement of it, maintaining that ambulatory gait of his as usual.

"I guess I can't help but be curious as to why you said yesterday afternoon that you really wanted me to come along with you," he suddenly said, about half the way on, "when my original reason for wanting to come, the Gordon House Museum, would be closed for Shabbat?"

I allowed his words to drift between us and fall away to the side. When he'd approached me on the path as he had, following the afternoon tea, the words had broken from me, without aforethought; perhaps I'd simply been clinging to straws, call it a throw of the dice. And here we were. Just the two of us. We'd come a long way since that moment on that dirt lane the tide had risen over - that he'd yet remembered as vividly as I did, no matter how many lifetimes ago it had been, with no longer the disparity of our ages between us, as if that had mattered to me then, when I'd yearned for his undivided attention forever and a day. Was this how it was to come to an end? And here of all places?

"What I meant by saying so bluntly like I did that I could imagine a grownup Debbie to be just like you," he began, having ignored my not answering his question as he continued to walk, as if he were in a strange way ignoring my very presence as I continued to follow him, "is that I am in awe of you, Deborah. You are one of a kind. And that is quite apart from finding you one of the most physically attractive, I mean there is something so 'alive' about you, it radiates from you like a shimmer. It at once brings you close and adds a distance to you, that 'pinch of mystery' about you Stephan mentioned. You are so much like I remember Debbie was alive, even if just a kid, in the exact same way as you are. I'm not explaining it very well. I don't mean to embarrass you. I'm embarrassing myself actually." He stopped and half turned to me, almost like he wanted to see if I were still there. Meanwhile, my right hand reached for his shoulder, as he continued, "I could love you. Like I would have loved Debbie, if she were here now. That's what I mean to say. It would be so easy to love you, Deborah, to be in love with you. Like it was programmed in the stars or some such nonsense. It's like you really are Debbie, I can't stop feeling it."

"I'm Deborah now. I mean I'm no longer, I'm not Debbie!"

"But you are so much her spitting image, in so many ways. I would want her to be like you."

I moved to squarely face him, to block his path. I wanted to beat my fists against his chest, or given my height punch him in the chest. I wanted to fuck him, for him to just take me. It hurt so bad I thought I'd scream.

"Damn you, Reuben Headey!" I cried. "You are fucking impossible! And it is probably why right this minute I really want to -"

With both my hands upon his shoulders, clutching them, I bent towards him, before he might react, before I came to my senses, one of my hands reaching for the back of his neck, my fingers in his hair, and kissed him, tentatively for the split second our lips first touched, that magic moment when flesh touches flesh all warm and wet, sending off sparkles under my skin, before I fully went for him, cloaked as we were in that ethereal darkness like a transparent depth of water, its almost eerie stillness. I was voluptuously kissing him, impatiently, hungrily so, surprised at my almost savagery, like I could taste him on my tongue, upon his, to the depth of my throat all the way down to the pit of my stomach and beyond. As if I was not going to give him a chance to get off of my hook. My brain had completely shut down, Slowly he'd begun to respond, like a tremor from

deep in the earth, he tasting me as well, it was
as if his body was at last awakening, was crawling out from beneath whatever it was that had
been weighing him down. He was kissing me
now, with an ardor I'd not before dared to imagine, not that I hadn't dreamed of it, had made
myself come fantasizing it. Our bodies squeezed
together now as my arms held him tight to me
while his hands moved ever so alluringly down
my back, at once tantalizing and exasperating
(if only he'd rip my dress away and really touch
me), until he reached my hips, slowly caressing
them and my butt through the soft fabric, the
bottom of my stomach beginning to fall out, just
as he started to slide his hands, thumbs first, up
towards my arm pits. I felt my nipples pressed
to his chest beginning to harden in anticipation
because once he reached my breasts a molten fire
would shoot straight to my groin and I'd be lost,
I'd not be "me" any longer but a "we", indivisible.

That was when he'd broken free of me, or had
begun to, more embracingly so than a shudder-
ing wrench, with his one arm holding me to him
while the palm of the hand of the other pressed
my head to his, cheek to cheek, as if some desperate cry had roared up within him, rending him,
releasing me from his grip, he gently holding me
all of a sudden.

"Reuben?" I sort of whispered. I couldn't find
words to continue. My hands had moved down
to his chest. It was like, where had he gone, right

before my eyes.

"We can't do this, Deborah, I mean I can't," he at last said softly with a heartfelt determination.

"I know," I heard myself say, as if there was another me speaking for me, outside of me. "Neither can I."

"I really could love you." There was a rawness in his voice. "But for Rebecca."

"And I could love you. But that's not quite 'should' is it?"

"It was wrong of me to compare you to Debbie like I did," he spoke aside, softly, before bringing his gaze directly into mine, his eyes unblinking I could see, close as he was to me still. "It was like the genie got out of the bottle. It all started with me questioning you about your name for your wheels, that was the same name as Debbie's Beetle she died in."

"Don't feel guilty, Reuben," I said. I didn't know why I wanted to go to his aid, comfort him, when I might have been flaming pissed, was actually - or 'something' at least - even if I had pushed myself on him, had been doing so, if I were to be honest about myself, from the moment I approached him when the meeting had broken up. Only my heart went out to him, as it always had, even as I was being disingenuous by default. "That in itself wasn't wrong, but from all I have learned of her, I do understand how you could see her in me, wanted to see her in me, which is the her in you as well, don't forget, the her you have imagined as a grownup in me, had she lived. Yes, it is uncanny how both physically and in character, personality, she and I might mesh. (I was Deborah seeing ourselves for the first time, Debbie and me, in the reflection of our mirrored images.) "I wish we'd met, she and I, when she was still alive. I'm certain we'd have become fast friends." But I was far from certain right that moment if the Debbie inside of me, and I, still were friends period, given how her desire for him, beyond reason as it would play in the light of day, burned like a volcano still threatening once more to erupt.

"But what I want to say is," I continued, in as unwavering a tone as I could muster, "even if I were Debbie and we'd fucked, well, become lovers, I wouldn't be the Debbie in your heart and mind any more than you would be the Reuben in my heart and mind. We'd be the people we are now. I would be Deborah, the lone wolf prowling the world looking for the perfect photograph and you'd be the Reuben, the novelist, not the sixteen year old crush who carried her up and down flights of stairs and all around the house and yard. We can never be what we once were, wouldn't want to be. 'Movement is the law of life' some poet I read once wrote. We'd have to start from where we are now, prisoners of the past as we so often are. We'd have to liberate ourselves from ourselves for starters. You from Debbie, you can write about her, me from me (my own Debbie I was wont to say right that moment) or whatever. Anyway, from all I've heard you tell me, you do have Rebecca's love. And deep down she has yours. Enjoy this lifetime, Reuben."

I was likewise being disingenuous, blaming Debbie for what was equally my own desire for him as Deborah, despite my boldfaced lie to him just now, that I was going to have to simply suck it up and get on.

As I started to turn, he said after me, more inquisitive than hinting after a confirmation, "We're okay, yeah?"

"We're okay. We are always okay." I managed a smile.

My burrow in the back of Rubble beckoned where like an animal in the wild I could curl up and lick my wounds - and think of one of those perfect photographs I might capture in my frame come sunrise. Inside of me I was the little kid he'd felt so deeply with, as I with him still to the depth of my being.

6

My eyes felt as they were bleeding water as I stepped out onto the arcade that fronted my studio dark room to find the pole lights that lit the convergence of paths to be already burning brightly. I'd forgotten time (I'd forgotten dinner too); I'd managed to pull several prints, of which one was almost perfect, the best I knew I could ever hope for in spite of my forever wanting just one better.

I suppose I had been hiding out, to be honest, using the desire to print as my cover. I get butterflies in my stomach saying goodbye to people, to someone. I never say "goodbye". I prefer "lehitraot", that is "see you again". Just as long as all that needs to be said is said. Deborah, that morning she took off dressed as me, with my wallet and car key in hand, had called back, "Catch you later, Deb," as she'd pulled the door shut behind her.

Curled up in a fetal position, I'd awakened from what must have been a torturous dream to my watch's beeps, in a sweat panic, as I couldn't recognize where I was - until I did, with a jarring pain in shoulder and hip, despite pillows, from sleeping on Rubble's less than comfortable metal floor. At which my brain went immediately into action (I'd exchanged the dress for my "work" clothes upon my return to Rubble the evening before, pulling on my brogans too so as to be able to leap out to the ground like on automatic pilot if need be.) I'd pulled from my picnic basket I'd brought bread pre-spread with nutella, a hardboiled egg and a clump of sticky dates, all of which I managed to wolf down with warm bottled water and slurps of cold black coffee, before licking my fingers as I penciled a note for Reuben to help himself to the breakfast stuff when he awoke. I had less than ten minutes to sunrise, I'd splash my face by the lake to get the sleep out of my eyes and hope I wouldn't pollute the drinking water any further than Rishon LeZion.

It had all come off according to the script (at least something had on this trip), from the soft rosy glow lightening the eastern sky just as the sun peeked above the rim of the furthest range of hills, like a minute fiery ball of a peeping periscope, before ballooning out all white-hot, molten-like, scorch-blackening a sudden rush of in-flowing clouds, until the sky resembled an inter-galactic Götterdammerung as if painted by some Hieronymus Bosch. Then whiff it was gone, but not before I'd gotten off several burst shots with my digital and a number of studied exposures on the manual M3.

I'd felt extraordinarily pleased, giving myself a humongous yawning stretch to work out the kinks, and had cheerily lit out to go find Marty and Yoni. Though when slipping past Reuben's tent my heart had wanted to burst all over again. (As my note had remained tucked into Rubble's rear door I took it to mean he'd yet to awake.) Then upon making good use of those "Michelin rated" facilities, and drying my locks with an old towel I had grabbed from Rubble's back seat, I'd surprised Marty at her kitchen stove while hearing chopping sounds coming from out back of their "shack" that I took to be Yoni hard at it.

Nell wasn't mentioned right off, for which I'd been relieved, this being our first time together since her death; the cumin-flavored hot coffee did hit the spot, and hearing our voices all talking at once, Yoni'd come in looking his rugged sun-burnt-to-leather skin himself, if a few more gray streaks in less hair than I'd remembered. While Marty'd looked as lovely, and was as generous of her person, as ever. I would spend the good part of an hour with them, reviving old memories, promising there would be future ones, preferring to delve into the politics of the Israeli art and literary scene as opposed to that of the National Conundrum, where the humor was both hardy and heartfelt. Before I'd had to beg off, pleading Reuben as my excuse, my needing to get him back to Neve Rom and prepare for his departure in the morning. (And, "yes" it was, to Marty's Momma-Bear inquiry that, alas, given another lifetime Reuben would make me the happiest gal in the world, just like Yoni had made her thus in this one. Hyperbole my first line of defense, for all the element of truth that belied it.)

Marty had commented at first sight of me on how perfectly radiantly healthy I looked despite my rumpled clothes, the habitual trousers and tee shirt, in which I might have just sweated out a fever. And my hair undoubtedly had to have been a tousled fright.

And not to leave anything undone, the two of them were waiting nonchalantly by the check-in kiosk as we drove up to the now open gate (obviously Rubble's roar had alerted them from the moment I'd turned the key in the ignition, before I'd gotten the choke pushed in). Both having wanted to wish Reuben good luck with the Tel Aviv publisher - Marty especially, because she hoped to have a Hebrew addition of *(K)hamsin* to sell in her bookstore - and needless to say check out this "mystery" of a man made all the more so by my hedging, unavoidably self-conscious, explanation for his being with me. (Yoni, apparently, had heard of Reuben's novel in passing from a fellow poet.)

Though the weight of it bore like a ton of bricks on both Reuben's and my mind, there had been no mention of the previous evening's fiasco: there were moments when I felt he wanted to mention it. Otherwise, the journey back to Neve Rom was an exercise in sobering quietude but for the odd inconsequential remark. I remembered a line in a James Agee screen play, "the sick quiet that follows violence". A violence of the heart is still violence. I probably should have grabbed a nap upon reaching the kibbutz, but I threw myself into the work instead. I couldn't wait to see what I had captured of that sunrise.

How long he had been standing out there, not more than a couple of minutes or my eyes would have spied him instinctively, being the photographer I am, the moment I'd stepped out. Before I'd squeezed them shut, sucking in the smell of the grass blades wet with the falling dew. He must have come to a standstill upon spotting me, as if suddenly uncertain as to whether or not to approach, no doubt feeling he'd be momentarily caught in the act the second I looked up - as he had been.

I gave him a slight wave, from the hip more or less. Not that I was trying to be cute: relatively cool. Just a hand signal of sorts. Dispassionate but not discouraging. An acknowledgement no less. I had thought of going to find him, only the printing had been long and arduous, with a definite drag on my concentration from the start. Suddenly I was feeling exceedingly vulnerable. There had been so much left unsaid between us. He was still "my Reuben" as I was "his Debbie" (even if as far as he could ever know only as her Deborah proxy, which would have to do). And that is the way it would always be, had to be. Even if we were to never see one another, hear from one another, again. But for this one last time.

He moved out from under the path light's glare and began to slowly, though not quite hesitantly, cross the expanse of lawn between us, and I sort of strolled out to meet him, my feet feeling more like lead than flesh and bone. What was I going to say to him - all of my rehearsals, as they used to say in filmmaking, had been left on the cutting room floor. What I really felt was gutted. And I was still in those sweat-gummy clothes from early morning. (While he wore the same rags he'd had on yesterday; he looked as fresh as usual like he'd just changed into them.) All I needed to complement the picture was a jacked up Rubble with the hood raised and a tire off.

"You've been working. I didn't see you at dinner," he said after several moments of silence. It felt like the two of us were stark naked standing there before each other, I certainly felt that I was.

"I forgot the time."

"Were the sunrise shots okay? I mean did you get what you wanted, hoped for?"

"It's never quite. I got about as good as I could get, barring perfection. This time." I uttered it almost as an apology, wondering what was I apologizing for. "I guess you're packed?"

"Just about."

"I'm going to miss my ladder man."

"And I am going to miss my sounding board."

"You have been so much more to me than just a ladder man, Reuben."

"A sounding board hardly scratches the surface, Deborah, of what you came to mean to me."

"Whatever Debbie recognized in you, I do too. Like whatever you saw in her, you likewise see in me. I want to be her for you, your Debbie. If you wish."

"If I can be your Reuben."

"You already are, my Reuben." I started to laugh, if gently, to break the tension. "Don't you see, you idiot."

"I don't know what more to say," he was suddenly grinning, sort of sheepishly. "Well, I suppose I do, but best not to. It's the butterflies. I just don't want to say goodbye."

"Then don't. We don't have to say things to each other. We'll instead simply say 'lehitraot'. And wherever you'll be out there in the world, I'll be wishing for you the very best and wherever I may be you'll be wishing for me the very best. We won't ever be separate again, not in spirit."

"Debbie," he began. "I mean, Deb-"

"Debbie is fine."

"Lehitraot," he smiled now, if through what I saw was a tear or two welling up in his eyes, as he quickly turned to go.

"Lehitraot, Reuben."

7

Had I really imagined that somewhere between slumber and sleep he'd entered my room and quietly slipped into bed with me. I thought I could smell him - that particular smell of him that I remembered from days of yore. It had the makings of a dream, of course, that didn't go anywhere - or rather faded into obscurity (as much as I could remember of it upon awakening when I had it hit me that I would be driving out to the Tel alone that morning, in less than a half hour hence). I could not deny the ache for him I felt to the marrow of my being, but I could keep it at bay. What he felt for me, he'd have a better chance of burying it, I suppose, and getting on. Because, deep down, he'd always have Debbie close at heart, the Debbie in his mind, if but Deborah in his dreams. And Rebekah. Or maybe this double edge of harshness on my part had to do with I too having wanted to have my cake and eat it. A Rebecca of York giving up Ivanhoe to Rowena wasn't really me.

Green fields and an avocado plantation swiftly gave way to a crusty slope of sorts before it leveled off while the last stars in the sky but one gave way to the breaking of day, as Rubble bumped and thudded over this rut-ribbed tractor path I enjoyed taking out to Tel Ronish. I enjoyed how it sort of set me on edge in that it prepared me for the work ahead lest I let my guard down, that is my critical facilities. And it did so that morning in particular. Because here I was in Rubble, only a different Rubble and I a different Deborah - though my heart too could go at any minute, even if I hadn't felt any pain apart from its being just broken perhaps. Meaning I had to live whatever life I had on the edge of the nerve. I'd made my Faustian pact. A good bargain. Indeed, a fruitful one. Without regret. Out of which I have caused no injury, if but possibly to myself. And simply will have to live with that, be it as it may.

Why couldn't we've just leaped into the sack, fuck the consequences? Like in those lush romance novels kept hidden in my book bag and traded with a couple of girlfriends back in middle school. But it wouldn't have worked that way in real life, would it. I never managed to steal a pic of him on the sly either. I suspect it had seemed so superficial whenever I might have had a chance at it, when it was the real thing I wanted, a photograph being but a paltry substitute at best (although I remember saying to him that an entire universe exists in a person's face). He had not mentioned Joy and Nickolas in his "reminiscing" and I hadn't asked. Where I had come from was a great part of who I am, as much as it is not. Of the Deborah I am now.

What had he said that Kerry had said of Debbie? "She talked with her eyes, without guile." Or she'd talked with her eyes at least. That she had 'searching eyes'. I remember that photograph of me, the one I'd sent to him. a small color pic, probably from school, the 2nd grade, in which I'm wearing a light colored rather attractive if simple dress which has a black band around the neck and my hair is bunched up atop my head like a miniature Gordian Knot of sorts (a painstaking configuration of my mother's gone awry) with unravelling strands willfully falling loose from it giving me incongruously something of ragamuffin appearance. With my head slightly cocked aside I am looking squarely into the camera with all the natural self- assurance in the world of one twice my age, or older, with a grin on my lips and a glint of mischievous laughter, in a pair of slightly set apart green eyes, like Reuben had put it. I dare to say it exudes an openness, on an equal level with the viewer, well a directness for sure, that says everything and maybe nothing.

Cameras in a sling bag across my shoulder, the equipment I'd need for the morning's shoot under both arms (my special ladder atop Rubble - I'd go down to fetch if needed), I climbed to the summit of Tel Ronish - "a giant of a low-cut tree stump for Lilliputians" as Reuben'd called this mound that was our workplace, his first morning. I was otherwise imagining that those calories garnered at 1910 Friday night were being sloughed off with each footstep trudged forward - and upward. Gaining the summit, I took a deep breath of a drought of fresh air that wouldn't be with us for long, while momentarily gazing into the distances far and near. The landscape below me was lighting up, as if it had been a supine creature aroused and was slowly coming to life like an animated cartoon, all beneath a crystalline sky. Like the air, I knew it would last for an hour or less, that sky, minutes most likely. Dropping my load, I shot a few frames of the length and breadth of the excavation site, lying beneath its patchwork of tarpaulin covers, illuminated as I had never quite seen it before.

There would be digging behind and beneath where that block of marble was unearthed, a minutely studious operation led by Joel, accompanied by Aharon and Rafi, with the intention of leaving nothing overlooked. (Stefan's orders apparently, as he was about to cart the stone to Jerusalem, with Reuben riding with him.) For which I'd be on hand - that is, camera in hand - to capture the action. Jonna, I'd gotten word, would not be rejoining us - that is joining me - that week, perhaps the week after. Which would leave me no time, nor inclination for that matter, to think back to Rosh Rishon one week ago, when Reuben had traveled out here with me and the beginning of our "dialogue" on Debbie, had commenced, where everything had seemed miraculously possible.

But best not to dwell on it for too long a time - the what could have been, should have been - as the season at the site still stretched infinitely before us. And after a certain hour on any given day the sun gave no quarter.